THE DUKE'S
TEMPTATION

RAVEN MCALLAN

The Duke's Temptation
ISBN # 978-1-78686-333-1
©Copyright Raven McAllan 2017
Cover Art by Posh Gosh ©Copyright October 2017
Interior text design by Claire Siemaszkiewicz
Totally Bound Publishing

THE DUKE'S TEMPTATION

Dedication

To everyone who encouraged me to write this
story.

To Ann, my fantastic editor, Emmy, who created
such a great cover; and to all at Totally Bound for
their support.

And of course to my lovely husband, Paul, who
makes sure the coffee (and wine) is handy.

Chapter One

Whenever had a knife twirled so fast it became a vicious, glittering blur of metal?

Never.

Gibb Alford, the Duke of Menteith, had expected to be bored. Or on guard against any female who had somehow wangled her way into the spectacular. Or, although he devoutly hoped it wouldn't be so, both. Not that any woman should be there, but he was by now much too cynical to expect what should be so to actually be thus.

What he also hadn't envisaged was this unfamiliar tug of arousal directed toward the main act of the night. Who *was* a female, although he presumed an invited one. One who stirred his senses in a manner he'd almost forgotten.

Gibb didn't do arousal. Not now. Or, he amended, he hadn't. He stood on the terrace, amidst his peers but alone, a glass of the finest French brandy in his hand. In silence he watched the Chinese firecrackers and flaring sconces set around the lawn vie with the moon and stars for brightness, and willed his body to behave. Not for the first time he wondered what he was doing there. Why wasn't he at home on his beloved Scottish estate? At times being a conscientious peer was annoying to say the least.

Someone bumped into him and apologized as Gibb scowled. He didn't want his concentration spoiled, or his brandy spilled by an idiot like Algernon Follet.

As Follet swayed, Gibb held his goblet out of the way. Good brandy was not to be wasted. Gibb watched his fellow spectator stumble away, miss the fishpond by inches and lurch round a statue, before he ignored the man and instead turned his attention back to what was happening on the lawn. Only to tug at his suddenly too tight cravat because of what he once again saw in front of him.

In the middle of the perfect, manicured, luscious grass, a wooden platform had been erected in front of a large, plain white, thick canvas screen. Before it, the curvaceous raven-haired beauty who had attracted him minutes earlier stood with her arms outstretched, her crimson lips wide and an invitation to every man in the vicinity to stop, stare and give her their undivided attention. Dressed in something made of two-tone material, the like of which he'd never seen before, with hidden slits up each side, she presented a picture of contradictions. Gibb was sure she made each and every one of the audience imagine what the gown might or might not conceal.

The illusion of material not really there was very clever, Gibb mused. The flesh-colored silk that swung loose from her shoulders matched her skin, so he couldn't see where skin finished and material began. The bodice fit snug around her generous breasts in such a way he had to wonder just how it stayed in place. Her lustrous hair swung loose over her shoulders in a riot of curls and sparkling jewels hung from her ears and around one ankle, just above one of a pair of sandals that from a distance appeared flimsy and delicate. In her left hand she held a wicked-looking knife — a stiletto, he noticed — now still and unmoving. Even so, it shone in the twinkling lights that surrounded her.

The last firecracker sizzled and died, and with just the flickering torches to light her, the woman bowed to the assembled men. "I need," she said with a husky, seductive French accent, "a man."

The howls and catcalls would have overwhelmed anyone without a strong determination. She waited, arms folded and with an amused look on her face, until there was once more silence. Then she raised one eyebrow. Even at the distance he was, Gibb realized the woman was toying with them. Teasing them about something they thought would happen and she knew would not.

To his annoyance, his body tightened even more. He did not want this reaction to an unknown woman. Hell, he didn't want it with regards to anyone known to him either. Gibb Alford wanted no one to disturb his well-ordered life. The life where his mind never let him shy away from the sole thing that tore into him. His wife was dead and he was to blame. He was never going to be put in a similar position again.

Never.

The lady fixed her gaze on one of the men near to the front and beckoned to him in what some might call a seductive manner. Gibb chose to interpret it in a different way. Her body language showed nothing of seduction, except for that curled finger. Was it a come-hither gesture? He thought not. However, it worked.

Young Lord Denby Crowe bowed in an extravagant manner and swaggered toward her.

God, Gibb mused, he felt old and jaded. Why could they not see the act for what it was? Entertainment, not innuendo. Why *was* he here? Because it was better than sitting alone in an empty house and wondering why it had all gone wrong. Here were no scheming mamas or desperate debs who saw him as a challenge or a poor wounded widower who needed a new wife. To his horror, not long before, a brazen and giggling chit had even accosted him outside the card room at one of the few soirees he'd felt compelled to attend and suggested he looked at her daughter.

No, no and no.

With an inward shudder of distaste at the memory, Gibb returned his attention to the vista in front of him and the very different woman in their midst.

"Take off your coat, my lord," the woman said with a slow and throaty drawl to her... Her what? Victim? "Pass it to one of your colleagues so it does not get in the way."

Crowe did so, smirked at his friends and stood with one leg bent in a suggestive manner before he put his hands to his cravat.

She shook her head. "Oh no, m'sieur, I would not do that. That is a good guard in case my aim is wrong."

Lord Crowe stiffened and half turned. "Aim?" he croaked. "What aim?"

"Scared?" she taunted Crowe.

Am I the only one to see the derision in her eyes, Gibb wondered? To realize she held them, if not in contempt, damn near it.

"Are you worried that perhaps women do not have as good an eye as men?" the woman asked with a lilt of humor in her voice. "Or indeed that we are better?"

Denby flushed. "Not a bit," he said tersely. "You're a mere woman."

"You think that means I will not hit where I intend?" She quirked one eyebrow and mocked him. "Oh dear. I suspect only time will tell." The knife in her hand soared into the air, whirling almost lazily as it did so. It appeared as if she would cut her palm as she caught it.

Gibb gulped as she put her hand out and caught the stiletto without even looking. The insolence, the certainty she had nothing to worry about hit him like a cannon shot. A woman in command of her senses. Not someone to rely on a man, or demand attention. However, she *had* secured his. All of it. He couldn't remember the last time anything had done that, let alone a woman.

Not even his wife.

From behind Gibb someone shouted out, "Women can't aim and hit to save themselves with anything. Aim for his bollocks and hit his brain."

She laughed and gave a gamine grin that to his surprise went straight to Gibb's groin.

"As I am the exception to your absurd rule, that is exactly what would happen, for we all know where a man's brain is located." The amusement that followed was good-natured and she curtsied. "Let us begin. Sir, I hope you can assure me you will stay as I direct?"

Denby scowled and pointed his finger toward her. "What are you, anyway?"

Gibb had wondered when Denby was going to get around to asking that.

"Ah, that is a question many have asked," she said in that husky throaty voice Gibb had noticed earlier, then laughed. "Wait and you'll find out," she advised him as she once more twirled the knife in her hands. Even from where he stood, Gibb could accept and admire her mastery of the weapon.

So it seemed could Denby Crowe, who was getting paler by the second. Gibb had an amused idea that the man might vomit or run. He hoped he didn't as the spectacle unfolding on the lawn looked as if it was definitely going to be the highlight of the evening, if not his whole sojourn in the capital.

"My name is La Belle Evangeline," the woman said in a slow and husky undertone. "Stand with your back to the screen, and then be careful you make no abrupt movement."

All of a sudden Gibb understood what she was all about. Her stiletto was not for security or effect, it was part of her act. A knife-thrower. He'd seen one, once many years before, although then it had been a man holding the knife. Now it seemed there was a woman about to do the tricks and at one of his fellow members of the ton, not at a partner.

It could be interesting.

It was.

Gibb had no idea if it was the way she caressed the knife like a lover, or how she was in control of what happened that sent his body into an unexpected and uncomfortable state of arousal. Whichever, he wasn't amused by his visceral reaction. He didn't need it, didn't want it and as sure as hell had no intention of acting on it. Danger for danger's sake should not be and would not be in his present, or his future. If it were up to him, he would never be privy to emotions that arose from such a thing.

Or from anything else.

With that resolution firmly in his mind he willed his body into rest—he was not entirely successful—leaned back on a marble pillar and prepared to be entertained.

Denby Crowe stared wide-eyed and stood as rigid as the statuary dotted around the grounds. Gibb watched, entranced as La Belle Evangeline, with a grin he decided was best described as wicked, leaned toward the man.

"Do not worry," she purred in a voice that curled around Gibb like hot chocolate. "I rarely miss." She paused and contemplated the knife she held. Picked up another and spun it between her fingers. The blades seemed ten times longer than before and forty times as dangerous as they shone and glinted in the flickering lights. "And if I do it will be a very sudden death." She waited for the beat of three as the crowd erupted into nervous laughter. "Not, alas, the little death, but one of greatness and finality. So I suggest, my lord, you do not deviate from my desires."

Within seconds, knives were thrown toward Crowe from every direction. When the sultry knife-thrower told him to spread his legs and not to flinch, Gibb wouldn't have been surprised to see him run. She was more than most men could control, and most would not attempt to.

He could. He wouldn't.

To Denby's credit he didn't move—although it was more likely a result of sheer terror than bravery—and Gibb joined in with the applause as the last knife stuck, quivering, into the screen behind Crowe, a mere three or so inches from his bollocks.

Evangeline kissed her volunteer's cheek and held his hand so they could bow together.

The audience cheered once more, resumed their chatter and began to wander back indoors, no doubt to replenish their glasses. Gibb had no intention of drinking anything else. He considered his duty done and therefore as soon as he could find his host he'd make his farewells and head home.

He watched with interest as, once Evangeline and Crowe disengaged, she slapped the man's hand away from her breast. Whatever she hissed at him, and he was certain hissed was the correct word, Crowe wasn't fazed and once more tried to touch her. The knife she held up appeared as if by magic and, amused, Gibb saw Crowe hold his hands in the air and walk away with a brisk step. It seemed La Belle Evangeline knew how to look after herself. Strange, Gibb mused, that his own erection didn't diminish at the thought of her with a readily available knife. Was he unhinged or was it just the novel experience of desiring someone without wanting to? Complicated thoughts for so late at night. Whatever, it was all immaterial. He refused to let his uncomfortable arousal take charge. He would not be at the mercy of his vagarious body.

Gibb turned back toward the house and hunted for his host. Enough was enough. Time now to go home and ponder why his body had chosen to react to La Belle Evangeline and no one else since —

Stop it now. It is over and you do as you wish. And he did not wish for emotions to hold sway. Never again would he allow that, whatever they were. It led to anguish, tortured thoughts of 'what if' and 'if only' and people hurt. He hadn't been able — or cared enough — to curb his wife's wild side, and she'd died because of it. Because of him.

Never again would he put himself in the position of being responsible for someone else's happiness and wellbeing.

* * * *

Within minutes Gibb once more emerged onto the terrace, but this time he continued walking and headed toward the gardens and a gate at the bottom. His own property was a few minutes away on foot, via the mews and a nearby square. Rather than cross the lawn in full sight of the house and perhaps be accosted and delayed, he avoided the shorn-to-within-an-inch-of-its-life greensward and headed toward the shrubbery that skirted the boundary wall. That way no one could detain him.

As he thought back over those who had sought him out during the few days he'd been in London, Gibb decided the sooner he returned to Scotland the better. At least there the calls on his time were husbandry ones and the women who demanded his attention were not interested in amatory things. The minister's wife about the church flowers, the schoolmistress over the need to ensure the children of his workers attended their lessons on a regular basis and his best friend's wife over neglected invitations to dine. With, she underscored, no ulterior motives except the pleasure of his company. Ladies, married or single, who thought to have any interest in him other than his mind would soon quake under his uncompromising attitude.

Gibb took no prisoners.

But then, he trusted Beck and his French wife, Veronique.

Gibb made a mental note to respond straight away the next time they extended an invitation and at least attend a few of those dinners. He had no excuse except apathy and a lack of the necessity to stir himself to be polite and a good neighbor. The ride over to their comfortable house was less than half an hour from where he lived and Veronique had emphasized there was a bed with his name on it if he wished it. And yet he had never availed himself of their hospitality since…

Since…

Really, it was a wonder his friends hadn't given up on him.

His mind on things he needed to do before he could begin his travels once more, it was several seconds before he realized something had disturbed his musing. He was halfway down the impressive garden when noises to one side of him made him stop mid-stride and listen with care. Someone squealed briefly, as if whoever uttered the alarm was cut off. Then he heard someone else speak in a harsh, deep voice. A man to a woman? The sole woman about had been Evangeline, the knife-thrower. Was Crowe harassing her again?

Gibb struck off at a tangent through the shrubbery along a narrow grass track. If his memory served him right from the few times he'd been in the grounds over the years, it ended in a soil-covered clearing.

Just before he reached the area, the moon came out from behind a cloud and he was able to take in the scene in front of him.

It *was* Evangeline, now dressed in a neat, conventional walking dress and jacket, her bonnet on her back, held in place by ribbons around her neck, and a large carpet bag on the ground beside her. However, it was not she who needed rescuing. As he slowed and without a sound stood behind a convenient bush, the man grabbed her and pulled her hair so her head tilted backward.

"Who the hell are you to show me up in front of my peers?" The words shot out of him in staccato bursts. "A French whore. Ha. You should beg for my attention." The man put one hand on her breast and laughed. "Can't stop me now, eh?"

"Let go of me, you *couchon*." She spat out the insult with enough venom to make any sane man take note and back off. Not so her assailant. He attacked once more and she lifted her leg and kicked him and caught him—fair and square—between the thighs in his most vulnerable area.

"Ooft wha..." The man swore as he bent his legs, straightened and wheezed. "You little bi—"

Gibb now saw her attacker was indeed Lord Crowe. Crowe wheezed and got no further. One minute he stood upright and menacing, the next he seemed to fly through the air to end up on his back in the dirt several yards away.

Gibb blinked as Evangeline moved swift and sure to put one boot-clad foot on Crowe's chest and point a knife at his gonads. She was fast.

"You know, m'sieur?" she said almost conversationally. "In my country sweetbreads are a delicacy much appreciated. I would enjoy trying them." She licked her lips in such a suggestive way Gibb's body became taut with tension. "After..." Her voice trailed off and the knife moved an inch or so closer to Crowe's skin.

Gibb winced and his hands moved involuntarily to cover himself. His stomach lurched. She seemed a mite too knowing of just what made a male cringe.

"That part of an alleged English aristocrat would fetch an excellent price and set me up for life," Evangeline said in the calm and precise way she had spoken in before. "I almost wish you would do something else so I have an excuse to go ahead and cut your bollocks off before I attack your sweetbreads."

Crowe blanched and covered his groin with both hands, in much the same way Gibb himself had.

"You?" Crowe sneered. "You wouldn't, you'd never get away with it. My word against a French whore's? No contest."

Gibb decided it was time to make his presence known, and strolled into the clearing. "Oh I think there would be, Crowe," he drawled, every inch a duke. "After all, whose word would they take? Yours or mine? Think about it, a lord or a duke? I assure you I'd tell the truth. All of it."

"What?" Both Crowe's and Evangeline's heads whipped round at the sound of his voice. Crowe looked discomforted, Evangeline amused.

"You'd back her? A…" Crowe's voice faltered as the knife shone while Evangeline twisted it between her hands. Crowe swallowed convulsively. "A woman," he croaked at last.

"Oh, yes." Gibb smiled and was amused to see it made Crowe appear even more worried. He didn't think his smile so alarming. "I am a gentleman. Now, if the lady is willing to let you get up unscathed, I suggest you run away as fast as your spindly little legs will let you and forget everything about this encounter. Every little thing," he said with deliberate menace in his voice. "Banish it from your mind as if it never happened. For I warn you, if I hear anything detrimental about the lady, I will be the one to offer your sweetbreads to the French, not her. And remember, even though I may not be in London very often, I still hear things."

He stood back and nodded to Evangeline. "It is up to you. If you prefer to extract revenge, be my guest. I'll turn my back. Or hold him down, whichever you prefer."

She gave Gibb a swift, gamine grin before she looked down at Crowe. "Such a difficult decision," she mused in a flat voice, devoid of any emotion. It was enough to send shivers up Gibb's spine and he was the innocent party. No wonder Crowe lost what little color he had left and swallowed several times.

"Is he worthy of my knife or my leniency, I wonder?" She tilted her head to one side and put her index finger on her lips in a parody of someone in deep thought. "After all, I have other ways of making him suffer."

Her foot danced lower until Gibb decided it was mere inches away from Crowe's staff. It appeared evident that Crowe decided her question might not be mere rhetoric and stayed still and silent.

They all remained like that in a frozen tableau for several seconds, then Evangeline laughed in a harsh tone, so unlike the pleasant notes Gibb had enjoyed before.

"I must learn to curb those impulses," she said, her voice once more that attractive husky voice Gibb had noted earlier. "So sad, but I have been told on more than one occasion to control my violent tendencies." With a regretful sigh, she lifted her knife to point it away from her victim, before she stood upright. "I have decided he is not worthy of my attention. He may go." She sounded as imperious as a queen issuing the edict of 'off with his head'.

Gibb nudged Crowe with his toe. "You heard the lady. I'd make a run for it if I were you, before she or I change our minds." He took a step backward, put his hands around Evangeline's waist and held her fast. She glared at him over her shoulder but didn't speak. The heat from her body seared his fingers, even through her plain, ordinary dress, and a tantalizing caress of something arousing swept over him once more. He did his best to ignore it. Unwanted and unfounded, he told his traitorous body. Not the companion, the place or the time. Plus it never would be, unless this was a lady who would agree to a no-strings, no-emotions coupling. Somehow, having seen her fiery temper, he didn't think that was a likely scenario. She stiffened then relaxed in his grip before she gave a curt nod.

"As he says."

Without expression, Gibb watched as Crowe scrambled to his feet and staggered away back toward the house. He wondered idly what excuse Crowe would give for his dishevelled appearance and shuffling gait.

It was neither his problem nor his priority, Gibb decided. The stunning woman in front of him was.

"At the risk of attracting your ire, which in all sincerity I hope I will not, may I escort you away from this den of idiots?" He held out his arm and waited.

To his amazement and delight, she giggled. "Better idiots than iniquity I think, but here it is difficult to separate the two. Even so, I do believe you may."

Evangeline wondered if all her wits had deserted her. Was this a case of out of the frying pan and into the fire? Her instinct told her no, her common sense told her to be careful because it could be. She took a swift sideways glance at the tall, dark-haired, smoky-eyed male next to her, noticed the play of muscles under his tight-fitting exquisite gray evening jacket and shivered. He was not someone to be toyed with. She made sure her stiletto was reachable with ease.

Now she saw him more clearly, Evangeline was certain she remembered seeing this man watch her demonstration. He had stood out of her immediate eye line and looked somewhat uninterested. As if he had been there under protest. The sort of person she liked to pick on, even if the best outcome she achieved was to shake them up a little. If he had been closer to the front she would have beckoned him forward, not the idiot she'd ended up being saddled with. Now she was thankful she hadn't been able to give in to that whim, because he would have turned her into forcemeat. Evangeline decided she needed her wits about her. He was a powerful stranger, albeit one who had come to her aid, and she still had no idea who he was. Her mind made up, she would ensure her knife remained in her hand, ready to use if required.

The man next to her glanced down at her weapon and chuckled.

"I promise not to make any sudden moves. I also swear I am not interested in your body. I desire to see you safely away from here and imbeciles such as Crowe. Some people think the courage they gain when alcohol-fueled is enough to deem irresponsible acts acceptable."

"Thank you." Evangeline looked him up and down. He seemed sane, rational and normal, but then who didn't? "I appreciate your restraint." She took a deep breath. She had to ask. "May I be so bold as to inquire who you are?"

He hit his forehead with one palm. "Grief, yes, I forget we haven't been introduced." He bowed very formally. By someone else it could have been a mockery. From him it was not so. Her toes curled into her sandals. "Gibb Alford, at your service. Otherwise known as the Duke of Menteith. I prefer to be called Gibb by my friends."

Oh my. Evangeline had heard of him of course. No one who spent any time around the upper echelons of society, even on the very fringes, could fail to do so. The mad duke, the misogynist duke, the tortured duke and, from those of a romantic bent, the duke with no heart. The one thing she hadn't heard about was why he was so named. "I haven't seen you around," she said as he unlatched a door in the wall and stood back to let her precede him through the gap. "Are you new to town?"

Evangeline picked up her carpetbag, stepped into the mews beyond the garden and wondered how he would respond. Open and with nothing to hide, or with the bare minimum of information? After all, what was she to him? An entertainer he'd chosen to help out of a situation she could have handled, did handle, but on a whim, chose to let him intervene in? It was so unlike her that for one brief moment she wondered why she had behaved in that manner. To enable the young idiot who'd thought she was easy game to save face? Perhaps, but also, if she were honest, it had been to safeguard her livelihood. Knife-throwing might not be her lifelong goal or ambition but at that moment it was what kept her fed, clothed and with a roof over her head.

Until... She shied away from trying to answer that.

"New?" the duke mused and regained her attention. "I wouldn't say so. However, it's rare that I come to the capital unless ducal duty calls. This visit is because I wanted to speak on the Poor Laws. They need updating." He frowned. "Otherwise I shun it — London — and the machinations of the ton wherever and whenever possible."

She could understand that. More and more Evangeline wished there was some other alternative to her present lifestyle. But she would be no man's mistress, or worse, and unless it promised her a better life than she had now, no man's wife. So far that hadn't materialized. Plus she had an agenda, and until she completed her self-imposed task nothing else mattered. Knife-throwing gave her a living. The success of her itinerary would give her a life.

Or so she hoped.

"And you?" the duke—Gibb—asked her. "What about you? Why are you here?"

"As the entertainment, my lord," she said in a lighthearted manner. "What else? La Belle Evangeline, knife-thrower extraordinaire. No more, no less. Although some of your peers tend to interpret that as *their* entertainment and have to be disabused of the idea."

"Hence the knife?" He sounded amused rather than worried. "Do you carry many about your body?"

Was his attitude a good or a bad thing? The last thing she needed was a duke getting too close to her and asking questions she could not—or would not—answer.

"Enough, my lord. You have it correct. And I know how to use them in more ways than throwing them around a body, toward a screen, without hitting anyone." She spoke in a tone that most would accept as 'ask no more'. Not him, though.

"By hitting someone intentionally, in the place you decide befits the crime?" he asked drily. "Remind me never to annoy you." He grinned and her heart missed a beat. He was charm personified.

In this mood, if she hadn't seen him otherwise, she would have said all those reports of his brusque and antisocial attitude were exaggerated.

"Oh, I will. So, that, plus filleting a fish and how do you say, gralloching a deer. I am," she paused, wondered if it was too much of a potential innuendo and said it anyway, "versatile, my lord."

"Gibb," he said firmly. "Nothing else. And I'm impressed. Where did you learn such skills, and such English?"

"In France, my lord. Where else?" *That was ambiguous enough, was it not*? "My *maman* was insistent I spoke your tongue well enough to understand and be understood. No one knew what might have to be done to safeguard a life."

He nodded. "Your *maman* was a wise woman. The revolution plus the long-lasting problems with Napoleon were bad times, and my name is 'Gibb'." He waited and she firmed her lips. He essayed a faint smile. "She did a good job—your *maman*. And Gibb."

Evangeline shook her head. Why was he so insistent? "That is not seemly."

He stopped walking and turned her to stand in front of him before he took hold of her chin and tipped her face upward to look at him. This close, the dark amber flecks in his eyes showed in the moonlight. Tiny strands of gray glittered in his hair as a gentle breeze ruffled it.

He was, Evangeline thought, the epitome of a gentleman.

"Call it a ducal decree. Can we not be friends?" The intensity of his gaze was at odds with his body language, which showed indifference. A strange conundrum.

"Friends? Perhaps. Who knows? They are not something I have a lot to do with at the moment." Although if it were possible she would welcome it.

He smiled so briefly she wondered if she imagined it.

"Nor me," he said as a strange shadow flickered over his expression, so fleeting that if she hadn't been watching as close as she was she would have missed it.

"So tell me," he asked, "are you truly French?"

"What?" The abrupt change of direction flummoxed her for a second. "French? Of course I am."

"But you speak my language as if it were your own, albeit with a charming accent, and know words such as gralloch? Most would say disembowel, if they said anything at all," Gibb said easily, in a tone that belied the piercing look in his eyes. "Unusual."

"I am not most people," Evangeline pointed out, her heart thumping and her pulse much too fast for comfort. She prayed he didn't push and ask more. It was impossible to explain why her *maman* had insisted she learned to speak English, and mentioned that the Scots were different. Not unless Evangeline also shared the secret she had recently uncovered. It would be even harder to explain how she had discovered the reason for her *maman's* reticence, and thus undertaken to come to Britain. "If you truly wish to escort me home we need to head in that direction." She pointed across the square they had reached. It would no doubt be easier than trying to dissuade him.

"Bruton Street?" he said, surprised, as they crossed the square and skirted the gardens, which were locked at dusk every night. "You are also a modiste?"

Did it have to follow that because she lived in a street famed for the designers of exquisite clothes for ladies to wear, she had to be of that ilk? "Not at all, I live above Madame Coeur."

"Who?" He now sounded more interested than paying lip service to their conversation.

Damn.

"Eloise," Evangeline said briefly. "She is the modiste."

"Ah. I do believe I have heard of her," his lordship said in a wry tone. "Many of my peers have, ah, ladies who would like to be dressed by her."

That she understood. Eloise was very exclusive and dressed those she wished, not those she did not. "You should know the name, for she is the one person by whom people cannot demand to be dressed, however much money they have," Evangeline said matter-of-factly. "Exclusivity is her byword, and she chooses her clientele with great care."

"And is she French also?"

What was it with him and her nationality? "As French as I am." Actually, she thought as they turned the corner into Bruton Street and saw her front door a few yards ahead, Eloise was, she had long decided, more French than she.

Evangeline made her farewells thankfully. He had been kind enough to intervene on her behalf. Now she hoped he would be kind enough to leave her alone.

Chapter Two

Gibb let himself into his London home — Alford House, an elegant four-story stone mansion set in its own not inconsiderable gardens, on one side of a leafy square — and shut the door behind him with a quiet click. He threw his keys and hat onto a console table placed handily not two feet from the door and propped his cane in a nearby umbrella stand. His cape he draped over the newel post, and made a mental apology to his major-domo for his untidiness and his housekeeper for the drips now collecting on the shining tiles. The rainstorm had been short, sharp and unexpected. He had been halfway home when it had begun and been soaked within minutes. It hadn't seemed worth trying to get a hackney cab and he'd splashed on, for the rain to stop as suddenly as it had started.

At least the capital looked clean after the storm.

As usual, his staff had done as he'd requested and retired rather than wait up for his return. The shutters were closed and a lamp left on low to illuminate the room. Nevertheless, Gibb was sure that if he rang the bell in his study, his major-domo would appear within seconds, perfectly dressed and ready to satisfy Gibb's every whim. Likewise his valet in the bedroom, the chef in the dining room and the housekeeper anywhere and everywhere. Probably even the scullery maid and the boot boy were primed and waiting, all ready to do his bidding. Anything to make him happy.

For too long he had been aware of how they cared about him.

The looks they gave him—worry, sorrow, compassion, even at times impatience—were sometimes overwhelming. At least from them he didn't get the well-meaning but unwanted advice any dowager who got close to him seemed to think it was their duty to offer.

Remarry, beget a son, rejoin the ton. Spend more time in town. Make a convenient marriage where the lady understood the score. He had tried that once and look where that had left him.

Snap out of it. It is the way of our world.

No, no and no.

Tonight, though, he had what he wanted. Solitude. Gibb rang no bell and made his way into his study, where a fire still gave out enough of a glow for him to see to light a lamp. A carafe and a covered plate waited on the desk. He ignored the food, poured a whisky from his own estates in Scotland and slumped in a large leather chair to ponder the events of the evening.

Gibb sipped the amber liquid and savored its smoky taste as for the first time in ages he considered his surroundings. They held none of his stamp or personality. The furniture had been chosen for function, not aesthetic appeal. Boring and bland, one friend had called it, like Gibb's life. Just as Gibb wanted.

The same friend had warned him that although Gibb might think his life would put women off trying to catch his attention, it did the very opposite. *'Now they all want to be the one to bring you and the house back to life,'* Beck had told him with a laugh. Gibb shuddered. Personally, he did not think it a laughing matter.

Never again.

So why did a picture of a whirling knife, a vivacious woman and long limbs spring to mind?

Gibb undid the three ivory buttons on his waistcoat and stretched out his long legs in front of the embers. Damn Denby Crowe. Damn his host for inviting either of them.

And if he was to continue on those lines, damn himself for attending the spectacular.

La Belle Evangeline had seemed well equipped to look after herself. So, why oh why did he now discover he had a conscience over more than his late wife's death? It did not sit comfortably on him. Gibb was aware that others thought him a tortured figure, one with agony and tragedy in his life, and gossiped about him as such. The number of women who offered to 'help' him showed that. Why couldn't they understand he had no intention of remarrying or getting involved with anyone who wanted anything from him, especially emotion?

He had no emotion to give.

It didn't bother him. Gibb lived his life as he wished, unencumbered by sentiment, happy not to have to pretend something he didn't feel. He had never prescribed to that state of mind and had no intention of starting now. Any sexual encounter was purely to relieve the ache in his body, and understood on both sides to be just that and nothing more. The moment a woman he was involved with thought otherwise, their liaison was over. He had long vowed that never again would he be liable for the happiness of another person.

Even if he didn't care, it was too much of a responsibility.

Now, out of the blue, this young Frenchwoman had pushed her way to the forefront of his mind and his body responded as it had never done before. Oh, he'd felt desire, but not this emotional tug. This unwilling – and unwanted – need to discover more about someone, and to be glad, almost eager, to spend time with them.

None of that was needed, was it? Gibb closed his mind to carnal thoughts and concentrated on the other things about Evangeline. Or tried to. For once his traitorous body didn't respond to his demand and instead remained tense and alert.

She lived above Eloise. Curious. He had of course heard of the famous modiste. Who had not? But why was this woman living there? There must be twenty or more years between them. If she hadn't said her mother was dead he could have thought perhaps… But no, the intonations in her voice when she spoke of her parent with one sort of love and Eloise with another told him that they were not the same person.

However, his curiosity was piqued. For he had thought each building in Bruton Street a self-contained house with no subdivisions. Did it mean she and Eloise were friends or even relations? What did it matter? Gibb had the uncomfortable feeling he was becoming much too interested in the woman. Was his own life so tedious that he now had to ponder about someone else's?

Probably.

He sank his chin into his cravat, heedless of the extra creases he created in his perfectly tied neckpiece, and steepled his hands together, the half-empty whisky glass cradled between them. The cravat would go to be washed now anyway, and he didn't expect visitors at that time of the night—or morning. Deep in thought, Gibb remembered something Beck—the one friend who could speak to him so—had told him in no uncertain terms on more than one occasion. *'One day you'll come out of your self-imposed isolation. Pray God it won't be too late.'*

He'd scoffed at Beck, who, along with Veronique, was in Gibb's opinion much too optimistic about the world and its occupants. Now, though, he wondered.

A log shifted in the grate and a few sparks danced above it to fall back and dim the room once more. Gibb ignored it. He had no inclination to add more fuel or to brighten his surroundings. He perused one gleaming Hessian and thought of pretty sandals and glittery chains.

Evangeline. La Belle Evangeline.

Was this the time Beck had warned him about? It couldn't be. But Gibb had to admit to himself that his interest had been stirred. Woken up and was demanding to be assuaged. Would he allow that?

No, he thought defiant and definite. He was fine. He didn't need any complication in his life. With that question sorted and discarded, Gibb tossed back the rest of his whisky with scant regard for taste or scent, doused the lamp and made his way upstairs to his lonely bed.

* * * *

"Gibb, I need you." The voice was petulant and demanding. The mouth downturned, the expression sharp and unpleasant. "You should be here, now. Why are you not? It is not fair. I will do it. I will."

"Hester, it is not reasonable, or sensible." Why couldn't she understand? Why did she always ask for more than he could give? "You know that. Enough now."

She stamped her foot. "It is not. I want more." Her voice rose with a wildness he dreaded. "Why don't you stay here more often? You know how I am. Why is it all about you? Why do you never pay attention to my wants and needs? Why?"

Why, always why. She knew. She insisted it was her desire. She agreed… "Hester, you know what I said," he replied, weary of her questions and demands. Why did she keep bringing the subject up? "We talked about it, discussed everything. You said you understood and accepted it."

"I changed my mind," she said tempestuously. "You are cruel to suggest it. Listen to me, Gibb. You are cruel. It is not enough. You never listen, you ignore all – "

"Enough," he said in what he hoped was a firm voice. "You agreed to my requests, you said you understood, that it was what you wanted." He slapped his hand down hard and there was a rattle and the sound of broken glass. "You cannot and will not chance that."

"I can… I will show you. I'm going to do it. Watch me, you know I can. I…"

The scream echoed around his mind like a banshee. The jolt went from his fingertips to his jaw. Gibb opened his eyes, remnants of the dream still hitting him as he rolled onto his back and groaned out loud. The bedside cabinet was on its side as was the pretty glass that had stood on it. Not far away, the crystal lamp that had been placed beside it was a myriad of tiny shards that stood out in the half-light that filtered into the room around the shutters.

The water carafe had fared better and lay on its rim on the bright, thick carpet, which sparkled with diamond droplets of the liquid that had been in the glass. That receptacle now nestled up against the wall like a lover. Gibb stared at his hand, where one tiny drop of red gleamed.

Blood. Blood on his hands again.

'All your fault, all your…' He put his hand over his face as if it would blot Hester out. Why now after all this time? It had been an age since he had experienced the dream, and he didn't want it to start again. Gibb despaired of how many times he had woken up, his heart pounding, his skin clammy, her screams bombarding him as he shouted "Noooo" at the top of his voice.

No more, please God, not again. As he'd supposed, the sheets were damp from his perspiration, one pillow was on the floor and the other halfway down the bed. Gibb licked the droplet of blood absently, noted it came from an almost invisible nick, and stretched his arms high above his head. Tired, he looked at the clock on the mantel, just able to see the dial and discern the time. Five-thirty. Had he had such a few hours' sleep? He felt as if he had been in bed for days, and although his body was weary, sadly, his mind was not.

He flung back the covers, knowing there was not a chance of him resting further. Once he was awake, he never went back to sleep. A brisk and probably unacceptable gallop along the Row was needed. Later he'd go to Parliament and make his speech, and hope his vote would make life better for the poor of the country. Until then his time was his own.

Gibb swung his legs over the edge of the bed and looked around him with narrowed eyes. His room.

His bed. Plain brown cover over ordinary linen sheets. Wardrobe, no carvings or furbelows. Bedside table similar. One chair, one side table, plain brown velvet curtains.

As he'd suspected. Boring. Nothing of his personality here either. Even the dish in which he placed his pin every night was plain, basic porcelain. The bland room, where no woman had ventured, almost as sparse as a monk's cell, now seemed to mock him. All of a sudden the thought of sleeping here year after year was horrific. Lord, his life was tedious, not just boring and bland. And he had no one to blame except...

Myself, no one else.

He did his best to look at his abode through critical eyes. Should he decorate? Who for? He was alone by choice and intended to keep it that way. The room was serviceable and there was nothing wrong with boring and bland. Why change it for no reason except on a whim? He did not 'do' whims.

Whatever Beck and Veronique thought, he did have a purpose in life. His role as a peer, and his estates. No more was needed. He had an heir in his second cousin, so the peerage was secure. Donald was a sound man who would treat the estates in the best possible way, and do all that was required.

Even so, something indefinable niggled Gibb. There had to be more to life than this?

He had no answer to that.

And what was he going to do about his unwanted attraction to Evangeline? Nothing, he told himself fiercely. *Just...nothing. Ignore it and it will go away.* So why did he have the uncomfortable suspicion he was deluding himself?

If the boot boy and the scullery maid were surprised to see him up so early, impeccably dressed for riding, cravat tied in a deceptive and simple style, polished boots, shaved and with immaculate hair, they did their best not to show it. Gibb munched a wedge of bread and cheese and washed it down with a mug of ale while he leaned on the edge of the kitchen table, before he swallowed and grinned as they entered the room, blinked, stopped dead in their tracks and tried to act as if it was nothing out of the ordinary to see him thus.

The scullery maid bumped into the boot boy and gulped as she essayed a hasty curtsey. "My lord, can us do anything?" she squeaked, her face red.

"Don't tell the chef I rummaged," Gibb said, dry as dust. "I'm off for a ride, and before you ask, I do not need a groom to saddle up for me. I've been doing it long enough to perform the act with my eyes closed."

The scullery maid, young, nervous and new to the household, gaped at him. The boots, who had been in Gibb's employ for several years both in town and in the country, laughed. "I knows that, m'lord, when Mr. Grimond lets you."

Gibb smiled. "There you have it, Timms, and I will freely admit I miss my time with the cattle when I'm here. If I'm not careful I'll become slothful and get out of shape."

Timms shook his head. "Nah. That's as likely as me becoming king, m'lord. You've got too much self-discipline to go down that route." He spoke with the familiarity of an old retainer.

"Thank you for that. I'll be back in an hour or so and will breakfast then." Gibb tore another piece of bread from the loaf he'd positioned on the table and waved it in the air. "Pass my apologies for the mess I've left of the kitchen and chef's loaf, please. Oh and tell him it was, as ever, delicious."

He left the room and smothered a chuckle at the scullery maid's awed, "Cor, blimey."

* * * *

Evangeline whistled through her teeth happily but as soft as possible as she walked her horse along the quiet and deserted streets toward the park. Riding was the one pleasure she allowed herself, albeit before most of the capital was up and awake. Once she had shown she was proficient, could saddle and bridle her horse without help and mount alone, the stable she dealt with was happy to let her ride before anyone was about to aid her. No doubt she paid through the teeth for it, but it was worth it. Her chosen mount had enough spirit to enable Evangeline to enjoy her ride, and not so much that horse and rider felt constrained by the limitations of riding in the capital.

To Evangeline these few hours were precious and she didn't begrudge the time away from her self-imposed task. That, she knew, could take months if not years, and she was prepared for it to be a long and arduous venture. At least she had her extravaganza bookings to help her discover more about the ton and its members. For after all, the number of French émigrés in Britain numbered thousands and most were not willing to divulge their past.

Who could blame them? Even Eloise, respected by all in the ton, kept a lot of her past to herself. Napoleon might be behind bars, but he had escaped before and his supporters would, she thought, need very little encouragement to go back to those dangerous days of the Terror. It had been a dark time for many. She had, as a child, in the main been safe. Everyone knew her *maman's* late husband had been a miller.

But her father?

The words 'late husband' still jolted Evangeline. For even though she had never known the man who died when she was a babe in arms, she had thought he was her father. Until she had been told something different.

Deathbed confessions, Evangeline mused as she reached the park gates and turned through them. They always had a sting in the tail. This one had been directed at her, and once her *maman* had been correctly buried, she'd begun to follow her request.

'To save him, I had to let him go.' Poor *maman*. No wonder that on several occasions Evangeline had spied her weeping softly as she held a tiny, leather-bound book of sonnets. The book she had begged to take to her grave with her. *'It is all I have of him. My unfortunate Anton.'*

Anton who? Evangeline had no idea, or even if he was an aristo who lost his life, or a commoner like her. Until recently, the one clue to his identity had been buried with her *maman*. Then, as she had wondered what to do next, she'd discovered a tiny scrap of paper with her name inscribed in her mother's elegant script.

Evangeline. England. Eloise. My Anton.

And the address in Bruton Street. No more.

Hence Evangeline now lived in London, safe and happy under Eloise's aegis, and was about to ride some of her fidgets away. It was that or go mad, wondering what she was supposed to do next. Eloise was unable to help. She knew even less than Evangeline.

Therefore the sole 'next' Evangeline was sure about was that on the tenth of the month she was to appear at a party, and that she needed to practice a new trick. She rather liked the idea of juggling five knives before she threw them at a revolving target. She had almost perfected it.

A large gray horse with a tall male figure mounted on it appeared from the direction of the riding track. Evangeline squinted, but as the sun was now high enough to make him appear a mere silhouette, she had no idea if it was an aristocrat or a commoner like herself. Nevertheless she felt cheated. In general, at this time of the morning she had the track to herself. Evangeline fumbled up her sleeve and made sure she had the comforting feel of her stiletto in place.

Damn the obnoxious man of the night before. What was he called, Crooke, Crowe or Crawe or some such thing? Until then she hadn't experienced the necessity to look over her shoulder and second-guess everything or every person she met. She should have taken heed of the itch that had told her he was perhaps not the man to use. But his whole attitude had made her desire to curb him a little. As it appeared obvious he was a member of the ton and therefore it was possible, if not probable he would attend another of her performances, perhaps she should remember that vitriol, and use him as a revolving target? And cut him? Just a little? By accident of course.

Perhaps not, for how would that end? Best to ignore him and everything about him and hope he had been intimidated enough to do the same with regards to her.

The gray horse and rider hadn't moved. Were they waiting for her?

Why?

For goodness' sake, it's someone else riding, no more, no less. Evangeline chided herself as she moved steadily forward. Maybe she didn't have to wonder about quite everyone, she mused as she debated whether to keep to her chosen route and ride down Rotten Row or to give up, angle down a side path and go back to the stables. After all, the Duke of Menteith wasn't one she needed to worry about, was he? He'd been a true gentleman who appeared interested in her safety, but not in her otherwise. Not all the ton was like Crewe, Crowe, Crawe, whatever he was called. In fact it would do her good to remember he was in the minority.

Perfect. She had no time or energy to spare for relationships. So why did she wish, just a little, the duke had appeared somewhat more interested in her?

Contrariness, thy name is Evangeline.

Ahead of her, the gray horse and its rider moved, thence to halt at the end of the trotting track, and now she could recognize who sat so still.

It was him. The Duke of Menteith. Waiting for her?

A thrill of something indefinable spread through her. Why was he here? How would he know she was out at this time? There was just one thing to do. Evangeline urged her mount toward him, aware that her heart beat faster and her pulse was somewhat erratic.

Why was it this man who made her react like she did? What was it about him that drew her to him with a desire to understand more? Because he seemed to be taciturn, or someone who preferred solitude? Both, she rather thought as she remembered how aloof he had seemed during the early part of the previous evening.

Oh, he'd come to her aid later, and even chatted as he had escorted her home, but he'd given little away. Now here he was, a few yards away from her. Her mouth was dry as she got within hailing distance.

"Well met, my lord. Accident or design?" Evangeline made sure her tone was light and amused. It would never do for him to think it mattered one way or another. He didn't seem the sort to want… She cast her mind around for the word she needed, as her English deserted her for a moment. To want involvement, she finally decided in triumph.

Gibb raised one elegant eyebrow and answered her question with one of his own. "Do you often ride at this time? Alone? Is that sensible?"

It was her turn to raise the eyebrow, plus ignore the swift rush of heat that flooded her body. "Why ever not? Until last night I had experienced no trouble, of any kind, ever since I arrived in your country." *Time to change the subject.* "Do you often ride at this time, my lord? Alone? Is that sensible?"

He glowered and she laughed. "Footpads, you know, like shiny, sparkling things," she said. "Like your cravat pin or fob. I imagine even your signet could be broken down and the jewel extracted. And let's face it, it is easy for a knife to cut through a finger if one knows how." She spoiled her solemn intonation with a grin.

"We're in London," he said in a tone halfway between a snarl and a growl. "Where are the footpads? This is Hyde Park, not the stews of the East End."

Evangeline smiled. "Correct." He still seemed to be struggling with his temper. Perhaps it was time to defuse it if she was able. "To be serious, my lord, I'm as safe if not safer than you. I have my stiletto handy, I wear no jewels, the people I see each morning I ride are the same. The milkmaids, the street sweepers, one lone pie seller, the watch on his way home. Two urchins after any job possible. They know me, I now know them." She didn't add the toffs and dandies whom she avoided. She knew how best to make sure they were not aware of her. Sometimes people didn't see what was under their noses and she intended it to remain that way.

Gibb scowled. "I do not agree. You should be chaperoned," he said stubborn as ever. "This is London."

Heaven help her from imperious, dictatorial men. "It doesn't matter whether you agree or not," Evangeline said with a patience she was about to lose. "Or whether this is London, Paris, Brussels or…or…Timbuktu. I am in charge of my own destiny. I have been for long enough."

He grunted. "So you say, but how do I know that?"

She might have realized it would come to this. It was a pity one could not stomp one's feet while on a horse. Instead, Evangeline gritted her teeth, smiled sweetly and beckoned to him. As if he had no say in the matter—and maybe he didn't—he leaned toward her.

Evangeline cut one side of his reins and lifted the knife to his cravat.

"Like this."

"You think so?" His swift reaction took her unawares. He moved and before she had a chance to understand his intention, a sharp, searing pain hit her wrist and went up her arms. Her knife flew out of her hands and dropped to the ground, quivering as the point dug into the soil. Evangeline's mouth fell open as she found herself off her saddle and across Gibb's horse's back before she had time to assimilate what had happened.

"Now tell me you do not need a chaperone," Gibb said in a grim voice. "See how easy that was? You dropped your guard, and do not say it was because it was me who was able to do so. You, my dear, were too complacent." He twisted her around with ease to sit sideways. His horse snorted but didn't move.

Evangeline bit back her impulsive and rude retort and nipped her lip instead. He was correct. *Sloppy, shoddy and stupid*, she berated herself.

"True," she said. "And believe me, that is not a mistake I ever intend to repeat. Forewarned is forearmed. Now, will you be so kind as to get my stiletto for me? It is easier for you to dismount rather than me."

"You won't need to. Be forewarned," he said and hit one fist into his other palm to emphasize the point. "If you ride, I will ride with you."

It was the last thing she'd expected him to say.

"You will?" she said in a puzzled voice. "Why?"

"I have no idea," Gibb said in a tone that rang with honesty. "I had no intention of seeing you again. I do not do involvement."

"Who said I wanted you to?" Evangeline replied, her mind racing. "Be involved *or* see you again." This man fascinated and repelled her at the same time. His aloofness, the sense that something was wrong and how he hid the real Gibb Alford from everyone, even his peers, made her want to discover his inner feelings. His way of dissecting her made her want to run. "Nevertheless, I am happy as I am," she reiterated.

He nodded and dismounted before he helped her to the ground. She shook out her riding habit and glanced around for her stiletto. Gibb bent down, picked up the weapon and handed it to her. "If you say so. I beg to differ. Here."

Evangeline tucked the deadly thing back into place up her sleeve as she admired his physique from under her lashes. Her night vision hadn't lied. He was indeed a fine figure of a man. Well built, with no fat that she could discern, plenty of muscles that rippled under his elegant clothing and a formidable demeanor. Enough to silence any opposition to his ideas or directives. If she had wanted someone to protect her, he was the perfect person.

If. Goodness, what a dither. I am thinking like a silly young thing with no two thoughts in her mind.

"Now." With what appeared little or no effort, he lifted her onto her horse. "Stay there." He gave her a brief glance and swung back onto his horse, which fidgeted. "Please," he added with a faint smile as he gathered the sliced rein with a competence she envied and adjusted his grip to its length. "Nevis wishes to run. Shall you and…" He looked at her mount.

"Honey," Evangeline supplied. "From Mr. Chudley's stables. I have no horse of my own, sadly. However, Honey is what her name suggests. A honey-sweet animal with no vices and a soft mouth." The horse whickered as if in agreement and Gibb smiled.

"Then perhaps you would care to join us in a quick gallop before anyone is around to tell us not to? Are you capable of that? I mean no disrespect," he added as she opened her mouth to ask why he had such a poor opinion of her riding skills. "But it would be remiss of me not to inquire, as I have never seen you ride."

"I'm willing and able." Evangeline toned down her response. The man was infuriating, that was for certain, but she did not have it in her nature to nurture a grudge and he did seem to be genuine in his alarm on her behalf. That was a phenomenon she was no longer used to. "So, yes, let us."

Gibb nodded and turned his horse so they faced the beginning of the dirt track. "After you."

Evangeline grinned, bit back the whoop she would have liked to utter and let Honey have her head. Within seconds Gibb was at her side, holding back Nevis to match Honey's shorter stride. They both rode fast and furious, and without doubt not within the realms of polite riding in the park, as their horses' hooves kicked up mud and leaves and left a trail of dust behind them.

By the time they pulled up at the far end of the track, Evangeline was hot, sweaty and happy. Her hat had slid off her head and bounced up and down on her back with every movement she and Honey had made. Most of her hair had come loose from its coronet of plaits, and tendrils teased her cheeks and curled around her shoulders. She was the happiest she had been since her beloved *maman* had passed away. Warning bells rang in her head.

Remember who he is, and remember what you have to do. She would. Of course she couldn't forget that, but for now, Evangeline decided, she would seize the moment and enjoy these precious few minutes and forget who they both were.

"That was such fun, and—" She glanced over his shoulder to where several horsemen appeared to be ready to start their rides. "Not a moment too soon." She nodded in the direction of those distant figures.

Gibb turned in his saddle. "Sadly, no return run then, and I refuse to canter sedately like a dowager. Shall we go back thataway instead?" He pointed to a little-used path. "We can skirt the fringes then, and leave where we need to." He hesitated, as if unsure how to proceed. "I would like to escort you." His words sounded as if he'd had no idea he was about to say them. "Ah, as an acquaintance, you understand."

Evangeline nodded. Truth be told, she was loath to leave him so soon. There was something about the man who intrigued her more with every passing moment. She made a note to quiz Eloise when she returned from her ride and find out what her friend knew about one Gibb Alford, the Duke of Menteith.

"Of course, my lord…as an acquaintance, I accept." She grinned and watched a line of red run from under his cravat and suffuse his face. "I have few of them," she added rapidly, somewhat angry with herself for her attitude. "A person whom I want to know in that way — such as you — will be most welcome."

"There are many you'd prefer not to have?" he asked shrewdly as they walked their horses toward the far corner of the park. "Crowe being one of them?"

"Crowe, that was his name. I thought it Crewe or Crawe, and had decided it was very apt." Evangeline grimaced. "Nasty vicious things, both of them."

Gibb laughed. "True, but he will bother you no more."

She looked up at him, startled. "What have you done?"

He shrugged. "I did nothing, but I know his attitude toward you will not have gone unremarked even before his actions in the garden. He is not liked by all and it takes little for someone such as him to be ignored and passed over for events." He paused as they skirted three bushes and a lone dog. "It will be ignominious for him to realize that. Sadly, he is not the sort to accept defeat in a graceful way and may decide to take his banishment out on you. I hope you will let me know if any such thing happens."

"Let him try," Evangeline said, confident she would cope. "He will not succeed. I have more spine than to let such a one intimidate me." She didn't promise anything. Becoming reliant on someone was not in her nature.

"No, he will not succeed, I can agree and promise you that, because I will not give him the chance," Gibb replied harshly. His tone surprised her. He sounded almost as if it mattered. "I cannot and will not stand to one side and watch a man treat a woman so poorly." He ran his finger around the edge of his cravat and seemed startled at his response. "I er…" He lapsed into silence. "Your promise?"

"My lord? What is it to you?" she had to ask. After all, they hardly knew each other. "I find it impossible to allow myself to be beholden to you. I need to look after myself."

Gibb pulled his horse to a stop where they were shielded from the main area of the park by a dense stand of trees. Evangeline followed suit and waited to hear what he said next.

"I want," he said slowly, "something I vowed I would never want or do. To make it my business to get to know you better, and I have to tell you, it goes against the grain of everything I have promised myself." His voice was hollow, his face pale, and his expression brought tears to Evangeline's eyes. Not since the Terrors in France had she seen such anguish in a person.

"How do you mean?" It made no sense to her.

He shrugged. "That when my wife died I vowed never again would I be responsible for someone else's wellbeing and happiness."

He was a widower? Evangeline looked at his blank expression and understood not to query his statement. Not then. "My condolences, my…Gibb."

"Thank you. Evangeline, you," he added with a smile, "intrigue me and I have a feeling you need a friend."

"As you do?" she asked shrewdly.

"As I do." He opened his eyes wide. Golden specks showed in the smoky irises and for one moment lightened his somber countenance and took ten years from his age. "Much to my amazement, as I do." His lashes flickered and blocked his expression. When he raised them he was once more the rather private, unemotional man he portrayed to the world.

"Then of course, friend," Evangeline said with a lilt to her voice. "I can't curtsey on a horse, please consider it essayed in my mind. Pleased to meet you."

He threw back his head and laughed. "I foresee a lot of interesting happenings in our future…friend."

Chapter Three

To have feelings after such a long time was a nuisance. Gibb pondered over his massive change of heart as he dressed for his visit to the House of Lords later that day. His decision that he would like her as a friend had come almost as a surprise, but he experienced a rush of relief that he had made the resolution and acted on it. Someone to talk to and spend undemanding time with would be more than welcome. Gibb knew that although his acquaintances numbered many, his true friends could be counted on one hand.

He had escorted Evangeline back to the stables, where, to his relief, a young footman waited for her return, then made arrangements to meet her at the same place and time the following day. That would allow them to decide how their friendship should proceed. Meanwhile he would carry on as normal.

Satisfied he looked neat and tidy—he was long past emulating the pink of the ton set who put themselves forward as arbiters of fashion—Gibb left his home and made his way to the Palace of Westminster. The law he wanted to make his speech about, the Poor Law, was one that needed a lot of work. Gibb himself ran his estates in an exemplary manner. His workers were housed in dwellings that were sturdy, did not leak and were not overrun with vermin. They earned enough to keep their families adequately fed and clothed and their children at school. It was a well-known fact amongst the people who lived and worked the duke's estates that he believed in education for all. That way, he said, everyone benefited.

Although shirkers and the work-shy were given short shrift, those too old or infirm to pay their way weren't forgotten or left to fend for themselves. Gibb's almshouses were a credit to him. He wished everyone realized what was needed to maintain and grow the country's wealth and prosperity. It was a sad fact that many didn't or were not prepared to expend energy or money to achieve what was needed. It grieved Gibb to see so many of his peers oblivious—or deliberately blind—to the suffering of so many of their fellow countrymen. However, he was honest enough to accept he couldn't change everything, just do what he could.

Several hours later, and with, he hoped, his speech as well received as he could have expected, he joined the mass exodus from the Houses of Parliament with no fixed destination in mind.

* * * *

"A good night, last evening, what?" George Doncaster asked him as they chatted in the courtyard. Now official business was over most of the peers who had attended were on their way to business of a less official nature.

"As you say," Gibb agreed as he nodded to several people who passed by and was clapped on the shoulder by one.

"Excellent speech, Alford. You have the gift of the gab."

Gibb smiled his thanks. If his speech helped the correct laws to be passed that was all that mattered.

"He's right, Gibb. You were just what some of these old dodders needed. Waking up. Just like last night."

"Something
 different," Gibb replied in a level voice as he wondered where the conversation was going.

Doncaster nodded sagely. "True enough, and also just what was needed. Ah, apart from that idiot Crowe afterward. I hear you gave him what for. Silly man. He has a pea for a brain."

Gibb inclined his head in agreement as they made their way without haste through a bunch of peers gathered in the hallway. "The lady needed little help from me."

"Caught him unawares, did she? He never pays attention to things." Doncaster pronounced his observations sagely. "It'll be his comeuppance one day. You know, at Watier's the other night he never even noticed he'd discarded two jacks." He shook his head. "The stupidity of some people."

"As you say, but best not to dwell on them or Crowe and his shortcomings too loudly, eh?" It might not be a good idea to let it be known Crowe had been worsted with ease by a female. He would be mortified enough without adding to his humiliation, and Gibb wanted no comeback to befall Evangeline.

"Good point. The man's a sore loser. So, I wondered, no Beck, eh?" Doncaster changed the subject and rattled on. He appeared oblivious to the way Gibb paid attention with half his mind. "Still up north?"

"Veronique is due to be confined within weeks," Gibb said, glad to talk about something else. "He didn't want to travel and leave her and she didn't want to endure the travel. Hence, as you say, no Beck."

They reached the door and Gibb made his farewells to his colleague, laughed off the man's entreaties to join him and a close band of cronies for supper and cards at a select gambling house that admitted only a chosen few and made his way toward a hackney stance. To hail a carriage and driver was easier than asking his coachman to hang around until he was ready to be driven to wherever he chose to go. As the House didn't sit until four p.m., evening sessions could go on and on if no successful outcome could be achieved.

It would have been easy to join his friends and acquaintances. He knew his attendance would not be queried, and indeed he would be welcomed in the gambling house with open arms. Nevertheless it held no interest for him. He and the lady owner, one Miss Elizabeth Burn, had once upon a time been more than good friends. They had parted amicably, but it felt wrong to just walk in without giving her prior notice. Not that he thought she would mind, especially if he ended up the loser, but even so, he didn't feel it was something he wished to do.

As he walked down the street, Gibb realized the nearest hackney stance would be busy with peers who wanted to be taken on to their next port of call, plus people who had enjoyed the river and were now ready to make their way home. Hailing a cab would be nigh on impossible, so Shanks' pony seemed the most likely conveyance. It was lucky he enjoyed walking, although he would prefer it to be over a grouse moor, not across the capital.

Gibb had his swordstick, the area of town was well-lit and he had no worries for his safety. He turned away from the water and headed toward Whitehall. He hadn't walked for more than ten minutes when the rumble of wheels from behind him assailed his ears. He stopped, turned and watched as a hackney drew to a halt, the horse placid and incurious. The coachman jerked his finger at the vehicle.

"Told me ter stop, guv."

A newly familiar head poked through the window aperture. Evangeline looked at him and smiled. "May I suggest we share this hackney carriage, my lord? Judging by the throngs back there, all vying to gain admittance to the next one to come along empty, you will have a long walk before you find someone able to take you up. I have spare capacity as you can see, and unless you are going in a different direction to me I see no reason why not to share."

Gibb inclined his head and swung open the door. "Nor I. Bruton Street?"

"Why yes, unless you wish to be dropped off somewhere on the way?"

"Bruton Street still," he told the jarvey as he stepped inside and closed the door behind him. Gibb sat on the squab opposite Evangeline and tapped on the roof with his swordstick. The vehicle lurched over the cobbles before it regained a steady rhythm and he was able to get a clear look at his companion. "You have been working?"

"At a ladies' soiree," Evangeline said as she settled back in her seat. "Very select. The hostess was bemoaning the fact that all the eligible men seemed to be busy this week so she arranged a little entertainment for those poor debs who could not go on the hunt. My words, not hers. I do believe your name was mentioned, amongst some others."

Gibb groaned. "I wish the harpies would get it out of their mind that I am on the lookout for a bride. I have had one and I do not intend to have another." He stretched his legs out in front of him and did his best to ignore the swift but admiring glance Evangeline gave him. He was neat and tidy but no Adonis. "I like my life as it is."

"They don't see it that way," Evangeline continued with a grin that was evident in her voice as well as in the dim lantern light. "I overheard one lady telling a young girl, who I believe was her daughter, that it was her duty to bring the Duke of Menteith back into the fold."

Argh. Gibb sat upright and leaned forward before he swore under his breath. "Never, no and if, if," he stressed, "I ever did have to remarry it would not be to a simpering miss who was twenty-plus years younger than me and with no sensible thoughts between her ears. Good lord, I didn't want that at twenty, why on earth would I at forty?" *Madness. Pure unadulterated madness.* "Who was it?" he demanded. "Then I can make sure I steer clear."

Evangeline patted his hand. "I don't know. The girl was what I believe is known as an incomparable. Blonde ringlets, blue eyes, exceptional figure and a simper that defies description."

Gibb scanned his mind. "Thick ankles, no dress sense and a laugh that would strip the bark from a tree?"

She inclined her head. "That's the one. She was in dark sludge green with enough flounces to decorate every window in a good-sized house."

"Good lord, Felicity Lumley." Gibb shook his head. "Grief, I'm almost a contemporary of her father. She's just eighteen, silly as they come, and this is her first season. What are they thinking of?"

"Your money?" Evangeline said in a dry manner. "Waiting to be spent."

He laughed bitterly. "More than likely. Thank you for the warning. I did wonder at the sudden flurry of invitations from certain ladies, but as I am friends with their husbands or sons, I was somewhat slow on the uptake. It is rare that I'm in London, and when I am I concentrate on Parliamentary business. This is taking longer than usual, hence, I suppose, the unwanted and unwarranted interest. No wonder several men have warned me off any event where the invitation is over gilded. The sooner I get away from the madness the better."

"You intend to return north soon?" Evangeline asked in what seemed a careful and cultivated tone. One designed not to convey her emotions on the subject.

Gibb hesitated. "I had, but now I'm not so sure. I think it will be in both our best interests if I linger a while, and not hurry away. My estates are in good hands for a few weeks more, and I'm being adept at dodging the doting and eager mamas and their offspring. Harpies show their hands too easily for me not to be able to avoid them."

She bit her lip. "Please," she said earnestly, "don't stay on my account."

He tapped her nose with his index finger and she wrinkled it. "That tickles."

"Good. And remember, it is on my account that I choose to stop in the capital. I too desire a friend."

How could she forget? And how to answer without sounding needy, she had no idea. If there was one thing Evangeline was certain about, it was that dependence on him by her was the last thing Gibb wanted. She contemplated the toes of her half-boots as they peeped out from under her deep-blue velvet skirts, then looked at his carefully expressionless face.

"Then, friend, are you coming in for a glass of wine, or carrying on with your journey?" The hackney had reached the corner of Bruton Street and the driver waited patiently to know what to do next.

Gibb looked at her with a pensive expression. "What would you prefer?"

She shrugged. "It is all of a one to me. We talk now and ride unencumbered with questions tomorrow, or we talk tomorrow and miss out on some of the freedom of our ride. The choice is yours."

He nodded and opened the door to assist her out. "Coachman, this will do." He fished for a coin from his pocket and handed it over before Evangeline took his hand and let him help her down the steps.

The coachman nodded his thanks at the largess Gibb had given him and urged his horse on. Gibb waited until the equipage turned the corner of Berkeley Square and gave his attention once more to his companion. "How do we get in?"

"Down here." Evangeline whisked him along a narrow alley where, she realized, he would be hard-pressed not to brush the dusty sides with his shoulders and the roof with his hat, and stopped in front of a green-painted door. It couldn't be helped. "Through here. This way is easiest. Mind your head, I swear it was built for halflings."

She shot him a swift glance over her shoulder and watched as Gibb did as she bade him.

"Why use it then?" he asked as he reached her side.

"During the day I can share the front door with Eloise, but at this time of night I prefer not to disturb the night watchman."

He looked back along the dark passageway and tutted. "I think I'd prefer that you do, instead of coming down here in the early hours. Anyone could be waiting."

"Where?" She looked at him quizzically. "There are no bends, a very low roof, nowhere to hide, not even some loose brickwork. It is as safe as can be."

Gibb grimaced. "Behind the gate? I refuse to feel foolish because I am concerned about your welfare," he declared firmly. "Crowe is not happy, and I will not want him to think you are easy prey. Anyone could be waiting here for you. Easy prey," he said again. "Even you must be able to acknowledge that."

He was like a dog with a favorite bone. Had she not been told he thought of no one except in the abstract? Therefore this undoubted worry for her was unnecessary, not at all welcome, but strange and comforting.

"I do not think it could happen," she said, earnest as ever. "If anyone unknown comes down here by themselves the dogs will bark, I promise you. And if we are to be logical and think things through, I'm not easy prey, not anymore. It will soon be all over the ton that you are consorting with me, however hard we try to hide it. And that, given your reputation, will make me untouchable. So perhaps you'd better decide if it is what you want, my lord."

"Gibb," he said. It was obvious he had no intention of being swayed by her protestations. "It is my name and I would be pleased to hear you use it."

"Gibb." How easily it rolled off her tongue. "I do not want to turn your life upside down for no reason," she said.

"It will not be without reason," he said. "I can promise you that."

Evangeline sighed. So, he intended to be as intransigent as he could? "Then come inside and we will have a glass of wine and discuss our situation."

* * * *

"And to my surprise, we did," she told Eloise and stood with as much patience as she could muster as her friend pinned a new costume onto her. As usual when they were together they spoke in their mother tongue. It was one way, they had concurred, of keeping it alive to them. "He drank one glass of wine, we decided as by this time it was past three in the morning to forgo our ride a few hours later and meet at Richmond this evening instead, when most people are getting ready for dinner. His lordship offered to pick me up. I declined, and as tonight I have a rare night off, with nothing specific to do, I will take a hackney to the designated place and enjoy his company. Once that was decided, he bowed and left." To her disquiet, he hadn't even attempted to kiss her hand. He'd just looked up at her from under impossibly long lashes and smiled. '*I will show you I keep my promises, Evangeline. Until later.*'

"He is a deep man," she said now. "Worried, with demons and a very finely developed sense of honor. I wish he wasn't so…so closed up."

"It is said he blames himself for his wife's death, you know," Eloise said, her words muffled by a mouthful of pins. "That is considered to be why he is unwilling to remarry."

"He blames himself?" That didn't square with the man she was beginning to know. "Why on earth would he do that?"

Eloise put the end of a tape measure between her lips, measured a few inches off with her fingers and nodded. "Snowf sed."

"I think I understood that. But why?"

Eloise spat the tape out and fixed three pins carefully into her pincushion. "As to that I am not sure. She was, I believe, excessively demanding, and he would not kowtow to her. Over what, when, how and why no one will say. All I know is she drowned when his yacht capsized off the coast of Devon, and he wasn't with her."

No wonder he wanted no responsibilities for anyone else. That he had reiterated more than once they were to be friends, no more. Evangeline stayed silent until she was again dressed in her own clothes and took her leave of Eloise. She must not forget her own agenda while worrying about Gibb Alford. The facts—and gossip—Eloise had imparted told her both a lot and not very much. However, there was other information she needed and had to hunt out. This afternoon a visit to an elderly French woman who had resided in London since before the Terror was on the cards. What Lady Lisette Tonge née Marin didn't know about those who'd fled to Britain during those dark days was not worth knowing.

Evangeline dressed with care. Lady Tonge might have agreed to see her all those months ago, but she was still a lady and Evangeline was what? Apart from the daughter of a miller's wife. That was the one thing that she could say with certainty. Everything else was conjecture. Nevertheless, Evangeline would give no one among the ton any cause for saying she was not dressed as a lady, for any reason whatsoever.

* * * *

Lady Tonge lived a quiet, life — or so she insisted — a five-minute hackney away from Bruton Street. Her English husband had died years earlier — 'No stamina,' she'd said with a twinkle in her eye. "Now a Frenchman would still be thriving. If he'd escaped the Terror, like many did."

Alas, also many had not. Evangeline often wondered if her papa been one of those. Had she passed him in the street, unknown and unnoticed? Or was he a commoner, one who had stood and cheered as heads rolled? Did she really want to find out?

Evangeline had asked herself that question on more than one occasion, and always arrived at the same answer. Yes, she did.

Lisette Tonge welcomed her in French and bade her sit down and drink a glass of cognac. It was of the finest quality and all Lady Tonge ever said was she welcomed the friends who looked after her.

"You know, child, you have the look of someone I used to know. For the life of me I do not remember who, or even if it was here or at home." She sipped her drink and regarded Evangeline over the top of her goblet. "No matter, it will come to me one day. The penalties of old age. I remember hearing about the Terror and how we all felt, but can't remember what happened last week. Except my fool of a daughter decided to tell her even more of a fool daughter to set her cap at Gibb Alford. Stupid, both of them."

Evangeline nodded. "So I believe," she said.

"If he were interested," Lady Tonge continued, "which I know for a fact he isn't, he'd make mincemeat of both of them. Now where was I? Ah yes, just who do you remind me of. That tilt of the head, your hair and those eyes. I am definite that you have the look of someone I know."

Evangeline's heart missed a beat. "Black hair and blue eyes are commonplace, I expect."

Lady Tonge looked at her with shrewd, faded blue eyes and a wicked twinkle. "Not so much here. I will have to think about it. Now, perhaps you could read some of Béranger's poetry to me? I miss the lyrical way our language flows in such things."

"Of course, I miss it." Evangeline nodded and smiled. Her words were not true, for she had never been an aficionado, but for Lady Tonge she would suffer. If it established her as one of Lady Tonge's protégées, who was she to argue? Even if the poetry was not to her taste. She cleared her throat and began. "*Les…*"

* * * *

She escaped just in time to rush home, drink a large glass of water and wonder what on earth Lady Tonge and her elderly companion Mademoiselle Pannier saw in Béranger's work, wash, change and hail a hackney.

Her hair she had tied back in a knot and she'd used a copious amount of pins to secure it. Even if they were to do no more than walk and perhaps have a light repast in the inn nearby, she didn't want to let Gibb down by looking less than her best.

However, she daren't spend any longer or she would be late, and the last thing she wanted to appear was unpunctual.

With a secret smile Evangeline pinched her cheeks and pursed her lips several times to bring color into them—she eschewed rouge when she wasn't working, it made such a mess of her skin. She did her best to make do with what Mother Nature had bestowed upon her and her own sense of style. Her light-blue gown and navy pelisse suited her and were smart without appearing too dressy, and she had to hope Gibb thought her attire suitable for the occasion. If not? It would be a pity, but she'd dressed as she thought appropriate for a stroll and perhaps a meal, and could do no more.

The roads were busy, and the hackney made slow progress until the outskirts of the city were reached. More than once she glanced at a church clock and groaned at the time. However, as traffic decreased, the vehicle's pace increased and she began to think she might indeed arrive within minutes of the allotted time. Relieved beyond measure, Evangeline sat back in her seat and relaxed.

The outskirts of Richmond were not far ahead when the hackney slowed and pulled to one side to let a curricle drawn by two perfectly matched chestnuts overtake them with the distance between the vehicles judged to perfection. Whoever drove the curricle was a whip indeed. How nice to be able to arrive somewhere in such style.

You had the chance. Evangeline picked at a loose thread on her reticule until she realized what she was doing and dropped it like a hot potato onto the seat beside her. Nerves. Why? This was what she wanted.

Wasn't it?

The carriage juddered to a halt before she answered her own question and she picked up the much-maligned reticule and shook her skirts, ready to descend. The door opened and Gibb looked in.

"Perfect timing, my dear. I've paid the coachman so we can walk and talk to our hearts' content. He will wait for you if you require it, or..." He left the rest of his question hanging in the air.

There was no doubt the decision was up to her.

Evangeline counted to three and took a deep breath. "Then let him go and we have no specific time when we have to return," she said, outwardly composed and inwardly quaking. "If that is suitable to you?"

Had she just done something rather stupid?

Gibb listened to her words with a light heart and a sense of amazement. He had hinted, but, he admitted, hedged around asking her outright to move things forward. Therefore, if he were to be honest, he was not expecting a positive outcome. Indeed, he still wondered if he had heard aright. "Are you sure? Oh, I am," he added in haste, as she looked alarmed. "I do not do or say things I don't mean."

She grinned, a gamine, easy smile. "Nor I."

The relief was disproportionate to what she had agreed to. Yet again a phenomenon unknown to him. It seemed his life was changing, and Gibb wasn't sure if it was for better or not.

"Then that is fine." He hoped. "I've paid the coachman anyway so he will not miss out on a fare. One moment, my dear, if you will." He walked to the box, spoke briefly to the jarvey and returned to take Evangeline's hand and tuck it into the crook of his arm.

With a flourish of the whip, the hackney moved away, the noise of the horse's hooves and the vehicle's wheels fading as it disappeared over the brow of a hill.

"Now we can walk," Gibb said with satisfaction. He looked at Evangeline from tip to toe and liked what he saw. As long as one didn't look at her eyes, he decided, a perfect lady stood in front of him. They gave away the fact she was no meek and mild miss. They sparkled and teased. It was oh so easy to grin at her with a carefree attitude that he had not experienced for many a long month. "Is your footwear up to it?"

"Oh yes." Evangeline chuckled and waggled a half-boot-clad foot at him. "I chose to dress for a stroll and hoped whatever else happened my attire would suffice."

He looked her up and down, amused to see faint color wash over her face as she realized the doubler meaning of her statement. To save her blushes he chose not to expand on it. "Perfect. Not only you, my dear, but it is a perfect evening, and I have bespoke a light supper at the inn before we return to town. Is that to your liking, or am I being forward?"

He didn't want to sound sure of her response. It was one thing to hope she would agree, but another to assume it.

"Perfect," she said huskily and cleared her throat. "Such an overused word but what else fits? Absolutely perfect. Lead on."

It was, Gibb decided, a moment out of time. When the universe decided everything should be aligned and work in their favor. Not something he ever thought he would relish, but relish it he did.

The paths they strolled along were clean, dry and deserted and the birds in full song. They talked of inconsequential matters—Lady Frederick's toque, Miss Winton's propensity for wearing puce—along with more knotty problems like the Prince Regent, Napoleon and who was about to become betrothed and not too happy about it. Gibb had a dry wit and he was pleased to see Evangeline appreciated it. She had a good ear for mimicry and made him laugh out loud on more than one occasion.

"You even lose your accent when you do that," he said when she had told him in Lady Jersey's voice that he *'Should come to Almack's more, my dear Gibb, it is not good for you to avoid it.'*

"Ha, the other way more like," he replied to her sally. "The place gives me shivers. So, how do you mimic in such a way?"

"Because I am at that moment not me, you understand," Evangeline said seriously. "I," she said in a perfect imitation of his gravel-rich tones, "am someone else."

He rolled his eyes. "Good god, I'll need to be careful. Or I could put you behind a screen to put the fear of God into matchmaking mamas when they start plotting."

"Oh, I like that. Along the lines of, Lady D, do not think of it. I am watching and waiting. Your plotting will be your downfall." She spoke in sepulchral tones. "I am the one who knows."

Gibb laughed. "You have it right. What else do you know?"

Her stomach rumbled and she put her hand over her midriff. "That I seem to be hungry. How embarrassing."

"Not at all. Come, we'll head back to eat." Gibb turned around and pointed up a slope. "That path is best."

* * * *

The food, when they returned to the inn less than an hour later, was just what was needed, delicious and varied, and the wine the best quality. If every time they met could be like this there would be nothing to complain about, and life would be perfect. Of course, he knew it wouldn't be. Life always had a way of giving itself the last laugh and kicking you in the ribs. For now, though, Gibb decided he'd take what he had been given and enjoy it.

With that thought uppermost in his mind, in perfect harmony, they started the drive back to town.

"Brr." Evangeline tucked the rug he had given her around her knees. "After such a beautiful day it's a shock to need this."

The sun had begun to drop and a chill breeze had set up and tossed the grasses and branches around in the air. He was glad he'd had the forethought to include the rug when he had set out. As he had never taken a female up with him before, a rug was not something he tended to carry.

Evangeline stroked the rug. "This is Scottish, no?"

Gibb gave his attention to his horses as he navigated a somewhat tight corner. "Woven on one of my estates. I spend most of my time on one or another of them."

"You never did say where they were or if you get to them often."

He didn't like the tightness in his throat. Was this the beginning of the need for attention? *No, she is being polite. Making conversation.*

"I didn't mention where they are situated, did I?" he said and strove for an indifferent tone. "Is it important?"

She glanced at him in the half-light and shook her head. "Not at all. I had thought perhaps it is the sort of thing a friend would know, but it is immaterial. I do not need to know," she said in such a polite and prosaic tone, Gibb was ashamed of himself. Before he could try to explain, Evangeline spoke again. "Me? I was born in France, my parents are dead, and I chose to come to England for a better single," she emphasized the word, "life. I live above a friend, so I am very lucky. Plus with you, I now have another friend." Albeit one who divulges nothing, her tone intimated. "Two friends are not to be sneezed at."

Gibb struggled to decide how to respond. "Lord, I'm not very good at opening up, am I?"

"Why should you be?" she said. "We are all who we are and no two people are the same. Think how boring life would be if it were so."

"Perhaps. It's hard for me to be me. So many people are watching and waiting for me to..." He shrugged, embarrassed to show how much he hated all the attention. "To do, I know not. But it is a strange and unpleasant experience not to feel I have any privacy." He hesitated as he understood how much he was about to admit. "You are my friend, and I have treated you shamefully. No, don't argue, it is true."

Evangeline shut her mouth in haste and he smiled.

"I am being as honest as I can. I have several — estates, not friends. Those true friends I can count on the fingers of one hand, and before you ask yes, it suits me." He didn't look at her in case he were to see pity in her expression. He was not to be pitied. His life was as he wanted. Wasn't it? So why did he suddenly feel lacking? "As for homes? My principal one is in Scotland where in general I spend most of my time." His voice gave nothing away. "I have a smaller one in Devon bequeathed to me by my godfather, where..." He cleared his throat, still undecided if it needed to be said. He realized it did. It was speak or alienate someone who accepted him as he was. "Where my late wife preferred to live when not in town. She found Scotland too bleak, too far away from the hub of the ton. Not that Devon is close, but the climate is, she said, preferable." He didn't mention the rest of Hester's demands. "To me, Scotland is heaven on earth."

"Ah, as to that, I've never been, so I couldn't say," Evangeline said in a voice that was devoid of pity — thank goodness. "Nor to Devon, as it happens, although I have heard it is very pretty."

Pity he could not and would not take. Her matter-of-fact tone reassured him. Evangeline would never have that attitude toward him. He began to relax.

"Although," she went on in that same tone, "the pictures I have seen of Scotland are very picturesque and romantic."

Gibb nodded. "So they say, but it is also stark and awe-inspiring. The mountains tower over one, but also..." He hesitated, worried he would sound ridiculous.

"Also?" she prompted.

"Embrace you," he said at last. "Hold you, and guard you and yours."

"It sounds wonderful," Evangeline said. She sounded oh so wistful. "Like *Les Alpes*."

"Just so." He encouraged the horses on. Dusk was setting in and he wanted to be within the suburbs before it got any darker. There was no need to court trouble and part of the route had been in the not-so-distant past notorious for footpads. It still seemed to attract wrongdoers.

The thought of Scotland reminded him of how during the summer dusk and dawn were a few hours apart, with long, light evenings the norm, and in winter the exact opposite. One more thing Hester had hated. "Beautiful, certainly, wild and rugged and desolate at times," he added. "My estate in Scotland."

"Where isn't?" Evangeline asked prosaic as ever and with no hint of homesickness or wistfulness apparent anymore. "You should see parts of France."

Gibb smiled. "I have, and not always in the best of circumstances either." He had no intention of enlightening her about his foray onto the continent. Some things were best not spoken about, even if they could not be forgotten.

Chapter Four

Whoever said history never repeated itself was wrong. Several days later Evangeline sighed, checked her stiletto was within her reach and dropped her carpetbag on the ground beside her. Trust her to decide to leave by the garden gate and once more be accosted by Lord Crowe.

Stupide. Idiot. When will I learn? However, she hadn't even known he was there. This event had seemed much too mundane for the likes of him, and on not spying him in her audience she had relaxed.

Foolish.

"My lord, desist this ridiculous behavior," she said. "I am no one's mistress nor ever will I be. You are wasting your time and getting very close to losing part of your body." She stared at him and expected him to back down. She had worsted him last time and who in their right mind would risk such a thing again?

He scowled at her sullenly. "You think not?" His eyes flicked to someone behind her and before she had a chance to react Evangeline found her arms pinned to her sides and her feet several inches off the ground.

Hot, smelly, beery breath surrounded her and she did her best not to gag. Someone's sweaty hands over her breasts made her cringe. Nevertheless, she stared at Crowe stonily. He was one person she would never give the satisfaction of seeing she was apprehensive.

"Not so cocky now, are you?" he sneered as he moved one hand to stroke her neck, and slid his fingers to probe beneath her pelisse. "No protector around to help out."

Evangeline did her best to keep her expression blank and held back her revulsion by sheer will. Crowe had more sense than she had given him credit for. She hadn't thought he would resort to such tactics and she'd walked, unheeding, into his trap. It served her right for not listening to what she'd been told about him. She could hear Gibb's voice echoing in her head. *'He's more than a bully. He is uncouth, uncaring and dangerous. He holds a grudge so beware.'*

Crowe seemed to be waiting for an answer, or maybe a plea for…for what? Lenience? She didn't deign to answer him. Never would she show fear, especially to someone like Denby Crowe. Her mind raced as she feverishly tried to think how she could salvage the situation. Nothing sprang to mind.

"What are you going to do, eh, now you can't get to that knife up your sleeve?" Crowe asked, mocking her. "No help at hand. What next?"

A frisson of fear slithered down her spine, and she silently berated herself once more. Why, oh why hadn't she expected this and been vigilant? Apart from Gibb, Eloise had told her that Denby Crowe had a reputation for underhandedness and was not one to take a slight or put-down lightly. She also had warned Evangeline to be on her guard, but Evangeline hadn't thought he would attend such a low-key gathering as the one she had just performed at. Tea, buns and not enough sandwiches. Inferior musicians, wittering, twittering debs and a mere handful of gentlemen.

How wrong could she have been? Now it seemed complacency was to be her downfall. Evangeline wriggled and tried to hit something—anything—with her legs. Preferably whoever held her tight in his grip.

"Give up, you'll 'urt yursul." The voice was rough and uncultured. She didn't know enough about British accents to decipher from where it originated. Not that it mattered, the brute was there at that moment and not elsewhere. Knowing his origins wouldn't help her get out of the predicament. She swore pithily in French. The fact neither man commented showed they had no idea just what she had called them. It was no doubt just as well. Doubting their ancestry in such a way was guaranteed not to win her any favors.

Crowe laughed. "Oh, she doesn't like it, what a pity. I wager she won't like anything else either."

"*Couchon.*" Evangeline spat on his immaculate Hessians. "I will carve your gonads out slowly and painfully."

His eyes narrowed and his face tightened into a cruel mask. "You won't get the chance. Joe here will see to that."

Joe—she presumed it was he who held her—sniggered. "Argh, be good to sort this one out."

A movement behind Crowe caught Evangeline's eye. She blinked and was rewarded by a slight shake of a very familiar head. She bit her lip and looked at the ground.

"Ha, so you are worried, eh? As you should be." Crowe tugged hard on her hair and made her lift her gaze to his. His features contorted and he laughed harshly. "You, my dear, made me a laughing stock."

"I doubt it," she said in the most indifferent voice she could manage. "You did that yourself." In truth, before he'd accosted her in the garden that night, she'd thought he had conducted himself in as proper a manner as could be expected after the way Gibb had showed him up. But that had not been bandied about, so why then was he in this state of ire? She didn't believe for one moment Gibb had spread the story about how she had worsted him.

"You think so? You are wrong," he said in a furious voice. "Others heard how you behaved and decided I was not enough of a man to show you what is what. They will not think that anymore."

"You think not?" the newcomer said as he moved forward without a sound, grabbed hold of Crowe's arm and pushed it up his back. Crowe squealed and Evangeline watched with interest and yes, she admitted, glee, as Gibb twisted that little bit harder and Crowe moaned.

"I wonder?" Gibb said in a contemplative voice. "How small this will make you in the eyes of the ton? After all, you needed hired help to accomplish anything. You." He stared toward Evangeline and her captor, but spoke to the man. "Unhand the lady and get going. If I ever see or hear of you again, you'll swing." The moon came out from behind a cloud just in time for Evangeline to see the man blanch as he dropped his arms from her and pushed her to one side.

Sadly for him, not fast enough to distance himself before she managed a swift kick to his knees. He went down like a felled tree.

"Argh, what the…"

Gibb laughed and aimed a shove at the man's rear. "Best be thankful it wasn't your crown jewels and go now before we decide that wasn't enough punishment."

Evangeline watched the man crawl a few yards, scramble to his feet and limp out of the garden and into the mews beyond. "He never paid me," he shouted from the safety of the mews.

"Nor would he," Gibb replied as he stood unmoving, Crowe's arm still held fast. "Do you want to kick Crowe anywhere?" he asked Evangeline in a conversational voice, as her assailant's footsteps faded into the distance. "I'm happy to hold him whilst you do so, and then break his arm."

Crowe made a noise between a gurgle and a moan. "You can't do that," he wheezed. "I'm a lord."

"And I'm a duke," Gibb replied in a bored tone.

Evangeline stifled a giggle.

"What is your problem?" Gibb added. "Not *au fait* with the hierarchy, Crowe? Tut tut."

The moon hid behind a cloud. Now all Evangeline could see were shadowy outlines. Gibb, Crowe, shrubbery and the garden wall. The house she'd staged her show outside was hidden behind a screen of trees. No voices penetrated this far, and in the silence the rustle of an animal in the bushes vied with the harsh breathing of Crowe to see which was loudest.

"I asked you a question," Gibb said with menace. "I suggest you answer without delay."

"You're hurting me." There was no cockiness evident now, just the sound of a man worried about his future. It gave Evangeline a fillip that she should be ashamed of, but she thought, unrepentantly, she wasn't. He deserved all he got.

"And you hurt the lady," Gibb replied. His tone was harsh enough to make Crowe blanch. "So your future hangs in her hands."

How would she respond? Gibb held on to his temper by a thread. Of all the stupid, irresponsible things to do, walking through a deserted garden, by herself, after the recent altercation with Denby Crowe, topped the list. It had been pure chance one of his peers had heard Crowe bragging about the fact he'd best the knife-thrower and make her wish she'd never tried to belittle Denby Crowe, and reported it to Gibb. Forewarned, Gibb was able to be where he was, and thwart Crowe.

She might not be so lucky next time, and knowing what he did of Crowe, unless the man was forcibly halted now, and the fear of dire retribution put into him, there *would* be a next time. Gibb shook with temper—and worry. It was lucky Crowe mistook it for anger at his behavior and also shook.

So much for holding himself apart, Gibb thought ruefully. Lord above, what had she reduced him to? The woman was chipping away at his defenses faster than a cavalry charge. It was disquieting to say the least.

"I meant no harm," Crowe said. The words tumbled out as he strove to redeem himself. "I just wanted to frighten her. You know, shake her up for trying to make a fool of me."

"Rubbish, you liar. Apart from anything else, you achieved fool status all on your own." Gibb didn't try to temper his disgust. "If I hadn't come upon you, you would have done more than worry her. I do not like men who terrorize women." Gibb didn't have to fabricate contempt. "They are not men but feeble imitations. So." He looked at Evangeline, who was once more neat and tidy. "What do we do?"

She shrugged. "He is a mouse, and I wonder if he…is he worth worrying about? I'm sure a word in the right place will let everyone know what he is. Or if you prefer, just break his arm. I'm happy to hold him in place whilst you do so."

Gibb bit his lip and kept his face impassive. He had no doubt she meant it. Crowe's breathing was loud and uneven, his eyes wild, and his color went from white to choleric to ashen in the space of seconds. Lord, he hoped the man was not about to expire from fear. That had not been his intention. He just wanted to make sure Crowe never pulled such a stunt again. With anyone, let alone Evangeline. He pushed Crowe's arm higher, just for a second, and held Crowe up as his knees buckled under him.

"What shall I do?" he mused and watched Evangeline turn away. Presumably so Crowe wouldn't see her expression of unholy glee. Gibb was hard-pressed not to laugh out loud.

He let go of Denby Crowe and the man dropped to the ground, moaning under his breath. "I'm hurt."

"No you are not, but if you don't go away now, and make a mental note never to do anything against any woman again, you'll know what hurt is," Gibb advised him. "I hope I don't see you around the capital for the rest of the season." That would be the cruelest thing he could inflict on the man. Crowe was an avid pursuer of the activities of the ton in the capital. He was not one who excelled on the hunting field, or who was competent at shooting or fishing and therefore eschewed house parties because of that. The capital was his hunting ground. Rustication would be more of a punishment than imprisonment. Especially as Gibb knew the man's home was not overlarge and that in general his parents and three of his sisters lived there.

Crowe shook his head. "Not that."

"Yes that," Gibb replied. "Or I might find myself accidentally telling people, in strictest confidence of course, just what has just occurred. Your choice."

"There is no choice," Crowe replied sullenly. "But I'm promised to Lawson and his card party tomorrow."

"Not anymore you're not. Remember this, there are always choices, unpalatable as some of them may seem. You decided which you preferred, so now go with good grace and spend some time with your family. I dare say by next season, if I have reason to return to the capital, even I will, if not have forgotten this, be prepared to let it lie."

He stood back and stared at the other man. "After, of course, you have apologized to mademoiselle here."

"Oh, I say, no need —" Crowe broke off as Gibb raised one eyebrow and folded his arms.

"You were saying?"

"Ah." Crowe ran his fingers under the edge of his cravat "I apologize for any hurt you may have suffered," he said in a stiff and unhappy voice.

Gibb coughed.

"Very well, and for my behavior, which I assure you will not be repeated," Crowe said petulantly. "Toward anyone," he added in a rush.

"Better." Gibb doubted it was sincere, but better. "And now get out of my sight and remember, even if I'm not in the capital, I know people who are. Be warned you will be watched."

Crowe nodded and turned on his heel. Gibb was oh so tempted to give him a helping kick up the backside to speed him on his way. Instead he spoke to Evangeline in a loud voice. "My godfather is part of the judiciary. I will make sure he keeps a weather eye out for any transgressions."

Evangeline let her breath out in one long hiss and shook her skirts. "That *couchon* ripped my skirts." She inspected a long, jagged rip a few inches above the hem. "I hope Eloise can mend it, for I am fond of this gown. *Zut*, I should have pricked him just a little bit. As for Crowe, the *cabot*, do you believe him?"

Gibb shrugged. When her anger was icy, her Gallic roots showed. "A cur? That's mild for you, my dear. Believe him? For now, whilst he thinks there is a chance of retribution, yes. Toward you? I am certain of it. Toward others? I'll do my best to curb his impulses in that direction. I have enough people I can call on to keep him in check. Plus a few months in the county will subdue him, especially as he will have to take his mother and sisters with him and suffer the nagging they will give him. Lady Crowe is a holy terror and his sisters take after her." *And yet again I'll be bothered with other people's emotions.* Perhaps he could foist the job onto his secretary? He didn't want the weight of responsibility on his shoulders. He knew what that could do to a person.

"Almost I pity him," Evangeline said as Gibb picked up her carpetbag and offered her his arm. She took it and they began to walk toward the gate Crowe had exited through not long before. "Almost. But he deserves to suffer. I was lucky." She grinned, all gamine and cheeky. "And you were here. But I do hope he'll be happy to stick to acceptable boundaries of behavior. Before he goes." She paused to let Gibb unlatch the gate. "And of course when he returns."

"If not, I'll find out and he'll wish he had." Gibb ushered her through the opening and shut it behind them. He would not tell her not to rely on him. She'd find that out soon enough. "Do you have a carriage or shall we walk around to the front and have them call for mine?"

Evangeline nibbled her lip as they strolled toward the end of the mews. A lamplighter walked by on the main road and glanced at them as he checked his lamps. Closer by, a black cat ran from one wall and jumped up another. A yowl and a squeal showed he'd caught his supper.

A black cat spelled luck? Who for? Not the hapless dinner, that was for sure.

"Food," Evangeline said with a laugh. "I need food. Can I tempt you?"

Oh yes. That thought hit him like a hammer and almost brought him to a standstill. He was in deep and drowning. Gibb waited for the familiar panic to hit him. It didn't. That shocked him to silence once more.

"With?" he asked cautiously when he decided he could talk in a normal voice.

"Oh, nothing you can't come to terms with," Evangeline said cheerfully. "Far be it for me to upset your well-ordered life. I thought some supper. I have cheese, fruits, chicken. Ordinary food, I admit, but also a rather superior wine, and some whisky."

Her matter-of-fact acceptance of his limitations stung. Why was he so contrary? Was that not what he wanted? Gibb was no longer so sure. "Supper sounds good," he said at last.

"Excellent." Evangeline gave a little skip. "I'll send my hackney away."

How strange, he wanted the same as she.

"I'll do it. Then let's find my carriage."

* * * *

Have I done the right thing? Evangeline wondered as she sat back in his very comfortable carriage for the drive across town. Luckily few people had been around as they'd climbed aboard, but no doubt someone would have seen and would be eager to spread gossip and innuendo. Would it be detrimental to her employment? Would it affect Gibb and his preferred way of life?

Time would tell, and if it did affect either of them in a negative manner it would be up to each of them to address it in the way they thought best. Could she do it? Evangeline had no idea, but one thing she was determined about. She would try to find out what she had come to England to discover and she would do her best to keep Gibb in her life. Somehow she was sure they both needed each other. With that thought fixed in her mind, she wriggled into a comfortable position and glanced at the profile of the man next to her.

"You are very quiet. Are you regretting your impulses now? I promise not to keep you to any promise you've made. You can drop me in Bruton Street and forget about me."

"What?" Gibb took his attention away from the road and stared at her. "That will be unlikely. Damn this light, I need to see you properly. Let's wait until we arrive at your home and then we can talk without interruption. But believe me, you have no need to hold me to anything. I will do that myself."

Evangeline couldn't help herself. She giggled. "How sad, to have to hold yourself."

"You... Oh lord, I set myself up for that, didn't I?" he said wryly. "I will rephrase it. I stand by all I said. No one will bother you again. No one, that is, except me. As a friend, like we decided."

"That will do." She hesitated, but it had to be said. "I wonder, will our friendship open the floodgates for young ladies to force themselves into your orbit?"

"I neither know nor care," Gibb said. "It no longer bothers me. They can try, but I'm old enough and wise enough not to let them succeed."

"Then that, my Lord Alford, is all I need. And as your friend I should say that I'm sure I saw Basford as we got into the coach and he is not only one of the Regent's cronies, albeit an unknown one, he is also the biggest gossip I know."

"Basford and Prinny?" The astonishment in his voice was evident. "You know this how?"

"I don't think I should divulge my —" Even in the gloaming she could see the hard look in his eyes. "My landlady passes on the titbits she thinks it is in my best interest to know. That is one of them."

Gibb laughed long and loud. It sounded rusty, as if a real laugh had for years evaded him. "Let's hope she doesn't see fit to pass on anything about us to anyone then."

"She won't," Evangeline said. "I resent that you think she might. Trust me, your grace. Trust my friends."

"We're back to 'your grace-ing' again, are we?"

"You seem not to think of me in the way I can be comfortable calling you by your given name. Listen to me. The sole reason she told me that was because of my profession. He is a gossipmonger bar none, and sometimes a little economical with the truth. I do not need too many stories about me circulating the ton. I need to make a living, not lose one."

"I promise you, you will not lose anything because of him, me, or the ton."

It was easy for him to say, but, in all seriousness, how could he stop it? Nevertheless, Evangeline nodded her thanks. What else could she do? She was not one to hold a grudge and had long accepted this was difficult for him. If he had decided to be her champion she would accept it, for as long as he felt able to be so. "What do you know about Lady Linford?" she asked, changing the subject. "I am to perform a limited part of my act at a ladies' tea she is holding. The request came from her husband, who said his wife was excited to see at first-hand and in her own home what was entrancing the gentlemen of the ton. So far any ladies' engagement has been for younger ladies, not those of a more…" She paused, not sure how to phrase what she needed to say.

"Mature age? Old harridans?" Gibb suggested. "Gossipmongers, dowagers and leaders of the ton?"

"Just as you say."

He understood perfectly.

"Anyone would think I was a performing animal or something." She rolled her eyes and made a funny face to ensure Gibb accepted she was not really complaining. "Jump though a burning hoop and roar."

He inclined his head in understanding. "Jeanne Linford is sound, even if she tries to set me up with a wife. George is also," he said in a bored tone. "You could do worse."

"And you sound disinterested," she snapped. Lord she was contrary. Why all of a sudden did his tone and diction annoy her? He'd warned her on more than one occasion what he was like.

But he isn't, not really. He'd been less and less distant as the time they spent together increased. She had thought they were beyond this indifferent response. She wasn't sure she could cope with his abrupt changes in mood. It was hard enough keeping herself friendly but not overly so as it was. If she also had to watch every word she said, it would be nigh on impossible to stay level-headed, and keep the distance he preferred between them. Something which had to be made clear.

"Fair enough, my lord. May I say if you continue to blow hot and cold you can blow so in a different direction. I do not need to have to second-guess you at every turn." The coach drew up in Bruton Street and she flung open the door without waiting for Gibb or the coachman to aid her. "Come with me or stay here, it matters not." The steps were lowered in a hurry and she took them two at a time. Damn him. She nodded to the coachman, who had to leap out of her way as she almost tumbled to the road and hurried toward the green-painted front door of Eloise's salon and her own chambers. Although it galled her to admit it, she'd accepted Gibb was correct in his summing up of her stupidity in using the alleyway, and had since used the front door, with a heartfelt apology to the doorman each time. He responded with a smile and, "It's my job, miss," but Evangeline still felt it was unfair. After all, if

Eloise wasn't out at night, his working day should be over.

"What's the hurry?" Gibb grabbed her elbow. "You almost came a cropper and tumbled down the carriage steps. A broken arm wouldn't help your act now, would it?"

"What do you care?" Evangeline sniffed and felt moisture at the corners of her eyes. She would not cry. Crying was for innocents and did no one any good. Red eyes and a headache were not helpful. "Oh, go back to your isolation, my lord," she said in exasperation. "Enjoy your misery and let me enjoy mine." Those were not the words she had meant to utter. Strange how the truth came out when you didn't think about what you were about to say. She rapped on the door and heard the locks being drawn.

"Misery is a cold bedfellow," Gibb said in an undertone. "And lonely. Perhaps I've wallowed long enough."

Evangeline turned to look at him. Really look at him. His usual lackluster eyes sparkled and for once there were no frown lines or signs of weariness on his face. "Perhaps?" she queried.

In the light of the lantern over the door she watched him redden.

"Yes, I know I have, but it is a hard habit to break. Misery loves misery. May I come in?" he asked as the door opened. "And atone for my sins?"

She had seconds to make her mind up. "Be my guest."

* * * *

"If I am to put my cards on the table," Gibb said, the best part of an hour later, after a hearty and enjoyable meal, "so must you."

"I?" Evangeline opened her eyes wide. "Whatever do you mean?"

To him her look of polite astonishment was unreal. "You," he confirmed. "For although my agenda is simple—I neither want nor need to be in charge of another person's hopes, dreams and destiny—yours, I think, is more complicated."

"What makes you think that?" she asked him warily. "I just need to make a living."

"By knife-throwing?"

"If necessary, yes," she said in an agreeable manner. However, her look of innocence was *too* innocent, Gibb decided.

"What is wrong with that?" she asked him. "It earns me an honest penny."

"But afterward?" he persisted. "When the season is over. You will tour the country estates? Live in rat-infested attics and be at the beck and call of everyone and anyone? Be prey to the passing whims and fancies of the ton? Ladies and so-called gentlemen?"

"No doubt I will. If I'm asked." She sounded puzzled. "It seems my act causes a lot of interest. Even so, I feel you exaggerate and you are scaremongering. I would be under the protection of the mistress of the house, and rats shouldn't be able to climb all those stairs to the attic."

Gibb shook his head. "The two-legged male sort would. As for the mistress of the house? Lord, woman, have you learned nothing? Become a mistress of the lord of the house more like. Evangeline, I know these people. Oh, I admit, not everyone is like that, true, but

Chapter Five

Gibb inhaled as he touched his lips to Evangeline's. Her scent surrounded him, teased every sense and tightened every sinew and muscle in his body. It would be oh so easy to sink into her and let himself be overwhelmed. She was everything he thought a woman should be. Without any deliberation whatsoever, he intensified the kiss and blocked any other notion out except there and then. Evangeline sighed and the noise reverberated through him. Gibb realized he'd growled in response, and deep inside him something almost forgotten stirred. He ran his hands over her back and down to the soft, rounded globes of her bottom, holding her in place, insisting she felt his body's response to her.

To his delight Evangeline let her tongue mesh with his. Her lips softened and she sank into their kiss. His senses whirled as he deepened the caress, and almost dream-like swayed with her in his arms.

It was… *'Gibb, Gibb, why are you not with me?'* Violently, he pushed Evangeline back and held her shoulders as he trembled uncontrollably.

"Oh god." The words tore from him in anguish. "Why now, oh, why? It's over. No more." A sob escaped him as he saw Evangeline's wide-eyed and hurt expression. "Not you, Evangeline, not you. Oh, bloody hell, never you."

"Hush." She kissed his cheek and rubbed his back like a mother comforting a child. "If not me, who then?"

He shuddered and it was her turn to embrace him and hold him close. "Tell me, Gibb, share your terrors with me. Let me help."

"Will it never go away?" he asked in despair. His forehead was clammy and beads of sweat dotted his skin. "Will I never stop hearing her? Am I to be tortured forever for not being what she wanted? I told her what I was, she said it was fine. She said she wanted no more than I did. She lied and I couldn't change. Why should I? I told her what I am. Told her, and she accepted it or so she said. She lied."

"Who, Gibb?"

He took a deep breath and looked into Evangeline's eyes. He wondered what she saw as she hugged him closer.

"H…Hester. My late wife."

Did she see a shell of a man? A man who could not save his wife from killing herself? Someone not worthy of her attention? He hoped not, but he couldn't blame her if that were the case. It was true.

"Ah." There was a wealth of understanding in her voice. She held him tight as if to transfer her warmth and vitality to him.

"You know," he said flatly. "What happened."

"No more than that she died, and since then you have turned inward and refused to contemplate remarriage," Evangeline said. "I have neither asked nor been told any more."

"I killed her." He waited for her to pull back or shudder. She did neither. A featherlight kiss touched his forehead.

"No, you did not," Evangeline said in a firm voice. "Stop thinking that. She died in a boating accident, even I know that, *and* that you were not there."

"I as good as killed her. Hester wanted more of me than I could give. She needed attention and adoration and I had neither for her. I was told she took my boat out in a temper. My steward explained to her there was a storm coming and it wouldn't be safe to put to sea and she told him to mind his own business. That if I couldn't be bothered to pay her attention she would take something of mine I did care about. I…" He cleared his throat. "I believe she was going to leave me and go to Ireland. Where…oh, where she might have had a lover. She left, and I never saw her again. Even her body didn't turn up for weeks and then…then she was recognizable only by the rings she wore. It was all my fault, I should never have married her."

"You can't say that," Evangeline said fiercely. "She was the one who tried to change your agreement."

"I know, but, but…"

"No buts." She put her hand over his mouth again. "You made your intentions clear. She accepted them. She is the one to blame."

"I try to tell myself that," Gibb said, weary to the depth of his soul. "It is easier said than done."

"Of course it is. It's human nature to feel you have failed. That you haven't given someone what they need. But did she give you what you needed?"

He shrugged. How could he admit such a thing? It would not be the conduct of a gentleman.

Evangeline nodded. "I take that as evidently not. My advice to you is for you to try harder. But, I also advise you to beware. You know the grand dames of the ton think it's time you remarry and beget an heir," Evangeline said. "And they intend to harass you until you agree."

"Of course, they take every opportunity available to them to inform me of my alleged duty. And I suspect some would not be averse to aiding one of their protégées into a situation where a betrothal is inevitable. It will not happen. Forewarned is forearmed."

It was no wonder he fled to his country estate whenever he could and left when he had to. This extended stay, due to Evangeline, must be like manna from heaven to them. "They can harass as much as they like. I have ignored them, and will continue to do so."

"Do they not know of your anguish?" Evangeline demanded in a tone that made him yearn to see her on form with certain older members of the ton. "Misplaced torment, I must say, for as unpleasant as it is to speak ill of the dead, your late wife sounds selfish and spoiled."

Gibb laughed hollowly. Evangeline had summed Hester up to perfection. "Yes, she was, but to them it matters not, and nor do my feelings about it all. To them it is over. To me it never, ever will be. Not just because I failed her, but also because no one seems to accept what is said. Why do people think they can change others?" he asked, bitter as he remembered some of the more unpleasant instances where he had been harangued. "Can one not be accepted for what they are, not what you can make them? Remarry? It's not going to happen. Even if a potential wife swears on the Bible she will marry for convenience and expect no more, I *can*not and *will* not believe them. Someone else can sort out the succession for it won't be me." He was silent for several seconds, and rested his head on her shoulder. Evangeline didn't speak but carried on rubbing his back in a circular, rhythmic motion. Eventually he looked up at her.

"Do you still want to be friends?" he asked dryly. "Dare you risk it?"

"Don't be daft." The British expression sounded strange in her French accent. It seemed with him she had no need to hide behind a false one. "Of course I do and I dare," she said. "We, my lord, will confuse all and sundry with our relationship."

"Do you think it will spare me matchmaking mamas?"

"If not I will throw my knives at them," Evangeline said in such a matter-of-fact way he smiled. "Slowly and with great precision," she added, and grinned. "I am excellent at that."

Gibb laughed wholeheartedly. "I like the sound of it. Evangeline, I am sure you will be good for me."

"Of course I will. I am French."

* * * *

Several weeks later Evangeline sat in front of her bedroom mirror and examined her face with care eyes…two of a deep midnight blue. Brows, a neat semi-arc. Hair, a mass of curls and black as a raven's wing. It had a mind of its own. Nose, what her *maman* called *retroussé* and she called button. Mouth…too wide maybe, but in her job that was nothing to worry about. Complexion. Not like her compatriots' olive tones, but milky. What one swain called Celtic and she thought insipid.

Therefore, a little rouge was, she supposed, necessary for her extravaganzas, but not for a ride in the park with Gibb.

A ride in the park. How nice that sounded, even if it was at the unfashionable time of seven in the morning. Evangeline smoothed down her deep-red twill habit and pondered on how her life had changed over the preceding weeks. Gibb and she spent a fair amount of time together without being in each other's pockets, and were discovering facets of their personalities Evangeline suspected neither of them had known they had. So far no one had commented to her on their association so she suspected it was probably the same with Gibb, but assumed it was a matter of time.

Gibb would, he assured her, inform anyone who was so crass as to prod him that his life was his own and of no interest to anyone else. She hoped she could do the same if she were approached. If either of them thought their answer would satisfy their questioners they didn't say. It was one occasion, Evangeline decided, that it was not worth sharing her doubts.

The sound of footsteps on her stairs drew her to her feet. Giving Gibb a key had been, she reminded herself, a good thing. This way he could use the now on-his-decree-forbidden-to-her rear entrance and make his way upstairs unchallenged. She had mentioned it to

Eloise, who had stared at her through narrowed eyes. Then just as Evangeline was about to scream, nodded.

"On your head."

"Oh yes."

Gibb tapped on her door and she opened it. The swift kiss was as pleasant as it was unexpected. "You smell of summer," he said as she pulled on her gloves. "It is refreshing."

"Rose water," Evangeline said, and wished she could stop her pulse speeding up whenever he was close. If he noticed, not only would she be mortified, he would no doubt also renege on their agreement on the assumption she had. "Just a few drops of rose water, nothing more."

"Whatever, it is a breath of sweetness. Much nicer than the overwhelming scent Miss Jessop seems to think necessary." Gibb grimaced. "I was introduced to her at Lady Wilton's last night and it nigh on overpowered me."

Evangeline quashed the niggle of jealousy that flooded into her—she had no right to feel so—and laughed. "Perhaps that was her intention."

"What?" Gibb closed the door behind them and locked it before he pocketed the key. "What intention?"

"To overpower you."

"I bloody well hope not," Gibb protested. "I swear they are getting bolder. I had no intention of attending any bloody soirees but Stanley Wilton corralled me outside White's and begged me attend, to, as he put it, give him support. As Stanley is one of the few people who never pester me to become my old self once more, or offer to introduce me to a woman, I thought it the least I could do. How wrong I was. The twittering simpletons were all over me like a flock of predatory birds. Not a nice experience. The fact that it was worse for Stanley kept my mouth shut and my annoyance in check. Even so, I was home before midnight, so that must tell you something. Horrendous. If it weren't for you, I'd be miles away by now. Are you sure you don't fancy a sojourn in Scotland?"

"Quite sure," Evangeline said as she squashed the thought that it would be very nice, if only she didn't have secrets to fathom out. "And please, don't feel you have to stay here on my account."

"I won't." He patted her glove-clad hand. "You should know by now I do what I want, not what is expected."

She sniggered. If he thought that, who was she to point out the discrepancies in his idea? "That's me put in my place. In all seriousness, I do appreciate all you do, but I don't want it to, how do you say, have it rebound on you."

Honey, her horse, which after a great degree of argument she had agreed to let Gibb purchase from the stables she had belonged to and keep for her, whickered her welcome as Gibb helped Evangeline to mount and settle herself. It had taken a lot of persuasion on Gibb's behalf for Evangeline to give in with grace and offer her thanks. To be beholden to him, or anyone, was very difficult for someone so independent.

However, each time she rode, she gave thanks once again.

Evangeline held the reins in a loose grip, until Gibb joined her and the groom stepped back. The youthful groom would meet them at the stables later.

"It won't rebound, I promise," Gibb said. "So which way? To the lake or to the paths first?"

"The lake," Evangeline answered. "Before it gets busy. Then we can be more decorous if need be and stick to the paths."

"So be it."

They let the horses make the pace as they moved on in companionable silence. Overhead a skein of geese flew low to settle on the lake with a great deal of noise and fluttering of wings. Evangeline looked at them as they began to glide elegantly across the surface of the lake, creating ripples on the otherwise still surface of the water. "It must be good to be able to roam at will," she said. "To know if this place becomes too hot or too quiet, you can move on without any ties or worries."

"Except for being shot and ending up as someone's dinner," Gibb said.

Evangeline rolled her eyes. "Oh, trust you. Now all my illusions are spoiled. I will never look at geese again without thinking of fruit sauce."

"Sorry," he said and sounded not the least bit repentant. "Did you never eat goose in France?"

"It was out of our orbit. We managed on fish, if we had caught them, eggs when the hens were laying, chicken when they stopped and of course vegetables. I always thought geese so majestic and so free and now you tell me their ending is for our stomachs. One more misapprehension solved." She laughed. "Not true of course, but it is a good thought, eh?"

Gibb inclined his head. "Indubitably. But, my dear, this is life as we know it. One person's freedom is the other person's prison. Freedom is but an illusion for everyone and everything."

"You are a cynic," Evangeline observed as a moorhen squawked and swam through the reeds.

Gibb nodded in agreement. "Now, let us talk of nicer things."

"Such as?"

"Ah, now you have me. You decide."

"My extravaganza next week at Vauxhall? Will you be there?"

"Of course." He sounded amazed she even needed to ask.

Evangeline wondered why. After all, nothing was certain.

"I have bespoken a box," Gibb continued. "Where we will take supper."

"We will?" She was surprised by his assertion. "Won't people talk?"

"Perhaps," he said with indifference. "But as they are talking already, I see no reason why we should not enjoy a good supper after your act. As long as you do not pick me for your victim."

Evangeline sniggered as she shook her head. She might not want to be the center of attraction in any way except on stage, but gossip was inevitable. "I wouldn't dare single you out for that. I prefer someone more aware of themselves and not in a good way."

"Someone whose ego you can deflate a little?" Gibb suggested and she laughed. "That's an idea," he continued. "Can I give you a list, do you think? It would be a long one, though, and difficult to decide who should head it."

"No need, I have one up here." She tapped her head. "I just have to look at some people and know they will suit." They angled down a side track and the horses picked up their pace into a decorous canter, which still left Evangeline able to speak and know Gibb could hear and respond if he wished. "And some I steer clear of."

"Have you ever hit anyone by mistake?" Gibb asked as the horses lengthened their strides a little. "Even a nick?"

"Not ever by mistake, although I have purported to have done so," Evangeline admitted with a wry smile. "I will name no names but say retribution was oh so satisfying. The *couchon* had tried to interfere with the young daughter of someone I admire, who is a friend. I did nothing more than graze his staff and slice his leg. Before he said anything to me the father of the girl threatened to do a better job. I believe the bastard went to the Indies and stayed there."

"Best place," Gibb said stonily. "For if anyone of honor found out his fate would have been worse. Much worse."

"Says the man who professes not to care about others."

"I seem to have forced that attitude into the background at times. That would have been one of them." They had circled the track around the lake and began to walk their horses back toward Bruton Street. "When I see injustice done, I feel beholden to try and reverse it. But that is not personal, it is on behalf of my sex or standing. I sometimes am ashamed I am a man and a peer."

"Women can also behave as bad," Evangeline remarked. "It is a sad state of affairs that most people do not believe it to be so. Me? I know so. As I work I see things that people do not realize. To them I am part of the furniture."

"What do you do if you see injustice?" Gibb asked with interest. "Apart from throwing a knife at whoever is the cause of it."

She laughed bleakly. "Make sure someone in authority finds out. Often it is a young gentleman's mama who receives the news. There is no one better to put the fear of God into a young imbecile."

"Then I commend you." The park was getting busier with traders and milkmaids. Gibb sighed. "I expect we need to get back."

"I suppose so. I enjoy our outings." Evangeline slotted Honey in behind Gibb's horse and made sure she presented a picture of subservience. Gibb turned around in the saddle.

"What on earth are you doing? You look, not to put too fine a point to it, constipated."

"I what?" Evangeline was so startled she let her hands drop the reins, and it was only due to Honey's good nature that she didn't career into a pie seller and make him spill his tray of pastries. "No, don't say it again. I'm not, I am practicing to be your inferior."

"You…" Gibb did allow his horse to break into a trot and swore as he brought him back into a walk. "Why?" he asked, as they turned into the road that led to the mews behind his house, where the horses were stabled.

"I thought it might help, and make life easier for you."

"Not a chance. It will make people think I've become feeble-minded. Now come on and ride alongside me."

* * * *

Over a month later, Gibb looked back over the previous weeks. Had he been in London for so long? He'd achieved a lot, been frustrated in many things, and to his amazement found a friend in Evangeline.

And, Gibb allowed, made an enemy in Denby Crowe, who could hardly bear to spend time in the same room as Gibb. He'd asked diffidently if he could stay around while his younger sister came to the capital for a few weeks, prior to her debut the following season. Gibb could hardly have refused that, but it made him uneasy. On several occasions he'd thought himself watched, as the hairs on the back of his neck had lifted and his scalp had prickled.

His sojourn in the capital lengthened, with no noticeable end in sight, and, most annoying to him, many hostesses rushed to engage Gibb to come to whatever entertainment they had arranged. It was a fine juggling act to accept as few invitations as possible without offending anyone. If he had his way he would ignore them all, but for various reasons did not. One had always supported him, another was a friend of his late parents. A third's husband had been his compatriot at Eton. And so it went on.

Perforce, at some he encountered Denby. To Gibb's knowledge, Crowe had never been high on any hostess's list of preferred guests, and that, Gibb surmised, was to Crowe another reason to dislike Gibb. As he could do nothing about any of it he took care to watch his own back.

A few days later, early in the evening and deep in thought, Gibb tied his cravat and shuddered at the idea of the hours ahead. It was a pity his friends and acquaintances took the fact he was still in town as a sign he needed to be entertained, and the dowagers and pushy mamas as an indication he was ready to remarry. He required neither and would be a lot happier staying at home. However, some things couldn't be passed over. The entertainment of that evening was one of them. One of the few people who hadn't hounded him after Hester had died was her brother Henry. He'd known what his sister was like, commiserated with Gibb, said he was there if Gibb needed him and let Gibb do as he wished without any comment. Tonight was to be the first ball held by Henry and his new bride. They had married in Norfolk and Gibb had made his apologies as, he'd explained, he was needed elsewhere. An excuse he'd made real. Henry might be forgiving, but his siblings were less so and the last thing Gibb had wanted was to ruin the day.

It was therefore important that he show his face at the ball where, he was reasonably certain, the niceties would be preserved. Henry's bride was what Gibb thought of as sweet, innocent and without an original idea of her own. Someone he would steer clear of if he thought she had any interest in him. However, even though he had no more than a passing acquaintance with the lady, it was obvious she worshiped her husband. Her eyes followed him and he had been informed — in total secrecy — by no less than three of his peers that the lady referred to Henry for his opinion about everything. From whether her choice of hat was suitable to what to eat for dinner or their activity each evening. She seemed to suit Henry, who told Gibb it was gratifying to be deferred to in such a manner, and that he enjoyed the feeling that his wife needed him. Gibb thought that without a doubt she was what Henry, a gentle soul, required. It would not suit him, however.

An image of Evangeline came unwanted to mind. Evangeline, cheeks rosy with temper, as she had looked when she'd confronted Crowe. Evangeline laughing in the moonlight, her eyes sparkling and her scent surrounding him as she walked barefoot across his lawn at midnight. Evangeline talking, a chicken leg between her fingers waving around as she made her point about something with enthusiasm. Evangeline, knives in hand, throwing them at him as he stood in his ballroom in front of a makeshift wall. Evangeline as she guided him in her art and cheered as he hit a pillowcase stuffed with straw roughly where she'd indicated. Her feistiness, her determination and yes, her independence. Everything about her called to Gibb.

But still he hesitated in demonstrating how he felt. How did he know if his feelings of contentment would last? Would she still be as independent if he revealed his feelings? Did he even know what they were? What did he want?

Gibb put on his signet, adjusted his cravat and picked up his snuffbox. Somewhat of an affectation as he didn't take snuff, and it was of plain tortoiseshell, not over-decorated as many were. Plus he had neither a secret compartment nor any risqué paintings on it. Such a difference from those of many of his acquaintance, or from the large, ornate ram's horn mull full of snuff on his dining table in Scotland. That, filled with 'his sort', was used a great deal by fellow lairds. This portable pocket one, he supposed, was just something he used as a prop. It often helped to ease awkwardness if, or should that be when men hesitated about how to deal with him. He would open it one-handed and propose the gentleman in question try 'his sort'. He didn't mention it was a generic mix from Fribourg & Treyer in Haymarket, with the addition of a hint of whisky from the distillery on his estate in Scotland. The ladies he just complimented on their dress, perfume or jewelry. Very few took snuff and those who did were considered beyond the pale.

"Don't wait up," he said to his valet. "I doubt I'll stop late at Sir Henry's, but I might drop into Watier's afterward." Evangeline was spending the evening with Eloise, making her costume for her booking at Vauxhall. They were, she had told Gibb, deciding on sequins and slippers. *'And of course I need to make sure I can move without catching my knives in chiffon,"* she'd said *with a laugh. "For how galling that would be, if I cut my dress in half instead of my victim's, er, willing partner's handkerchief.'* Gibb thought victim was a better choice of title than partner, willing or otherwise, but kept quiet about it.

With Evangeline happy at home sewing on sequins and ribbons, Gibb entered his carriage and admitted he'd rather be spending the evening with her. Not dependent on each other, he told himself firmly. Just two people who enjoyed each other's company. He had not many evenings before been invited to take supper with Evangeline and Eloise and enjoyed every second of both ladies' company.

This evening, he arrived at Henry's townhouse within minutes and wondered why on earth he'd called for his carriage when he could have walked the distance almost as fast. The quirks and vagaries of the ton astonished and annoyed him in equal measure. He told his coachman he wouldn't be needed anymore that evening, he'd walk or arrange for a hackney, and thought, not for the first time, how he wished he could leave London.

With Evangeline?

That notion had him rocking on his heels. Did he want that? Whether he did or not, an hour later he wished it was her company he was enjoying, not Henry's and his bride's, however welcoming they were. Balls were not his idea of entertainment. In fact, he would admit that this one was rapidly becoming one of the worst evenings of his sojourn in town. As he had expected, Hester and Henry's sisters were distant and scarcely polite and one too many debs had made sheep's eyes at him.

"So, my lord, is this not the most exciting evening imaginable?" Lady Penelope, or was it Prudence or Prunella Sunley — he had no idea which sister it was, to him they were interchangeable — fluttered her lashes at him and tittered.

Tittering, for god's sake. Does she know how idiotic she appears? Does she care?

Whichever Sunley chit it was leaned in toward him — much too close for a so-called innocent debutante — and Gibb gagged as an unpleasant amount of a strong scent hit him with the power of a horse and carriage. "I do love to waltz." She looked up at him expectantly.

Gibb, who had told Henry in no uncertain terms that he was stopping for an hour, no longer, and had no intentions of dancing *or* squiring any young lady, looked at her without expression. "Really?" he said in a scarcely polite tone. "I see young Cedric Popplewell coming over, and I suggest you look to him for a partner. "

"Oh, I must say," she spluttered, reddened and glared at him.

"Must you? I wouldn't bother if I were you," he said, unrepentant at how rude he was. Gibb bowed as the young lady glowered. He smiled grimly and turned on his heel. That was it. His duty was over and he could leave in the knowledge he'd done as he said and showed his face. He made his brisk farewells to the newly married couple, let Henry extract a promise to meet him at Tattersall's the following day, and left the ballroom before he could be accosted by anyone else.

As he reached the front door and accepted his cloak and cane, a fellow peer and someone who was more than an acquaintance but not a close friend approached him.

"Ho, Gibb, you off to Watier's?"

Gibb inclined his head. "Just so."

"Then I'll come with you, if I may?" Anthony Tarporly asked. "I'm heading that way myself. I've had enough of the ball. There wasn't even a decent card game. What made you show your face?"

"Henry is my late wife's brother," Gibb said, rueing the stiff note in his voice. He forced himself to relax. "I promised Henry I'd take a look in and toast him and Mary."

He watched the other man assimilate his words. And those unsaid, along the lines of, 'Unlike her parents, Henry never blamed me for Hester's death. I blamed me, though.'

"Ah yes, a lovely couple," Anthony said in a sickly voice after a second. "Almost it makes me think about putting my head in the parson's noose. Almost. What about you?"

"Me?" Gibb stood back to let Anthony precede him down the shallow flight of steps to the pavement. "As I've intimated ad nauseam, I've done it once and once was enough."

"Ah. Pity. Are you sure?" Anthony stared at him earnestly as they made their way down the street, their footsteps echoing hollowly on the cobbles. "Because if you do need to beget an heir, I could have a solution.

The thing is, I did wonder if, now that you're back in circulation, and getting bothered, you'd find your way to perhaps offer for Margaret, m'sister. The pater says she's nigh on the shelf and needs to wed and soon. She's had a season already, plus this one, and not taken, and would make someone a suitable, biddable wife. I thought maybe…" He raised one eyebrow and let his voice trail off. "You need an heir and all that, and she'd not bother you to change your ways or… Oh blazes."

"You thought?" Gibb said in a voice icy enough to freeze water as he resisted the urge to throttle Anthony. "Did you not hear a word I said? You thought that I would be willing to tie myself to someone half my age? Someone who is no doubt needy and would not be satisfied to plow her own furrow within the precepts of a marriage I, I mind you, dictated. A child. Whatever you say, you *know* the way a woman, even a female, half woman, half child's mind works. Want, need… Good god, have you learned nothing about me?" he burst out as his ire began to force every other emotion out of the way to let itself be known. "My first wife died because I could not give her the attention she wanted, and you, you think to inflict that on me again. To say nothing of how it would affect your sister." He threw his hands in the air in disgust. "Some brother you are."

Tarporly's mouth dropped open as he stared at Gibb. As it might, Gibb thought unrepentant, as every last annoyance and irritation came to the fore.

"Is this all your own idea or did your parents put you up to it?" Gibb demanded. "I doubt it came from your sister, who on the one occasion I recollect I ever noticed her looked as if she was about to burst into tears and almost ran in the other direction." He paused, swallowed and reined his temper in with difficulty.

Tarporly looked at him warily, as if trying to decide whether to run or stand his ground. Sensibly, he kept his mouth shut.

"Does that mean you have told her she should look in my direction?" Gibb demanded. "For if so, be thankful dueling is frowned upon."

Tarporly shifted from one foot to the other. "Oh, come on, Gibb," he said, placatory. "It was a suggestion, nothing more. I thought it would prevent you having to trawl the debs."

"Anthony, to save yourself further embarrassment, listen to me. I have no intention of trawling anywhere," Gibb said, his anger gone. What was the point in continuing to lose his temper with someone who had no idea why Gibb was so irate? "Or remarrying. Where did you get the idea I would?"

"Mama. She says the tabbies are saying you need to and it's best to do it now. So as Margaret is single and ready to wed, the obvious conclusion was suggest her to you." He shrugged. "Nothing ventured and all that."

"And does your sister know you are talking to me like this?" Gibb asked in a voice that could crack glass.

"Lord no." Tarporly looked at Gibb in horror. "She would be mortified. A private person is m'sister. Never has a word to say for herself. Drives Mama mad. I mean, there's such a thing as too shy and retiring."

Almost, Gibb felt sorry for the poor woman. Not sorry enough to offer for her, though. "Anthony, take it from me, we wouldn't suit. No one would. And please, if you value our friendship, pass this about. Gibb Alford is not going to marry. Not today, not tomorrow, not next year, not ever."

"Oh, I thought…" Once more Tarporly's voice trailed off as the carriage rattled over cobbles and slowed to a halt.

"Don't think," Gibb advised him. "It is obvious it addles your brain. How about sorting your own nuptials out? There are plenty of young ladies out there who would jump at the chance of being a bride."

"If you won't marry Margaret, I suppose I'll have to set my cap at someone," Anthony said gloomily. "There are heavy hints that I could do worse than Lady Lucinda Best. She's got a fortune and only brays like a donkey when she's excited."

It was no wonder Gibb lost heavily at cards.

Or woke up the following morning with the headache from hell.

Chapter Six

The note Gibb received was terse and to the point. "I have been given information I think we need to do something about. I am home all week." It was signed with a simple 'E'. He studied it for several minutes and wondered.

Wondering got you nowhere he decided as he ran through his must-go-to engagements for the following days—and nights—in his mind and penned a swift reply.

Another letter had rearranged a lot of his plans. He'd been waiting to buy Cresswell House, the childhood home of Lady Millicent Cresswell, his late and beloved godmother, for years. But what a time to be told the owners were ready to sell.

Three months earlier the Dowager Lady Mendip, his godmother's late son's wife, had at last agreed it was time to move in with her daughter—much, Gibb surmised, to the annoyance of that lady's husband—and as no one wanted Cresswell House she'd given

Gibb first refusal. At an inflated price, of course, but between them, he and his man of business had managed to get it at a price they'd accepted. Slightly more than he wanted to pay but a considerable amount less than Lady Mendip wanted to sell at.

However, with a lot of humming and hawing and crocodile tears on Lady Mendip's part, a deal had at last been struck. Now, though, he had to go down to the house, and look it over to see what he wanted done. Nevertheless, he didn't want to leave Evangeline without his protection.

Would she go with him? If he didn't ask he'd never know.

First things first. He'd go to Evangeline after a mandatory showing at Lady Arthur's ball. Along with Henry, Julia Arthur was one of the few people who had stood by him through all his earlier troubles and had been kind enough not to say 'I told you' so when Hester had disregarded all the warnings he had given her and died for her defiance.

Now with Anne, her youngest daughter betrothed, she had no more offspring to, as she so elegantly put it, send off into the big bad world without a cushion to fall back on. Julia had laughingly told Gibb he could come drink to the happy couple and escape with his honor and reputation intact.

* * * *

"The reputation you cultivate with such assiduousness," she said with a chortle and a rap of his knuckles with her fan. "But you know, my dear Gibb, it does not put the chits off. If anything it encourages them. Each desires to be the one who tames the tortured duke."

He snorted. "Mutton-headed halfwits. They'd be better off sorting out their own lives and leaving me to arrange mine."

"Take it from me, that's what they think they are doing," Julia said. "Marriage, and thus saving you. I promise you can disappear before supper if you desire, and therefore you need not be overmuch bothered by them. Nevertheless, I do want to see you, and as an old friend, I could say if you hadn't attended I would feel slighted." She smiled to soften her words, but Gibb heard the steel and intention behind them.

"My dear Julia, you are the one person who I can say with all honesty I truly love." He kissed her cheek and she guffawed

"Ridiculous boy."

"Not at all. Leave Bertie and run away with me."

As Lady Arthur was a compatriot of his late parents, she took his declaration in the spirit it was meant, and he watched in amusement as she guffawed out loud and tapped his shoulder, this time with enough force to rock him. "Ha, I wonder if Bertie would even notice?" she asked with glee.

"Oh, believe me, he would." The Arthurs' was one marriage that had more than doing their duty to hold them together. "And as I don't want to find myself facing him in the park at dawn, I rescind my offer. I'll go and congratulate the happy couple and make a swift getaway. Already I feel hundreds of pairs of eyes boring into my back." It was true. He had a very uncomfortable itch that ran up and down his spine. "It is not a comfortable experience."

"Not hundreds, dear. There aren't even half that many people here. We kept it to a select few. But it's your own fault, you know," Julia said, unperturbed by his scowl. "You have stayed around for so long, people think you have had a change of heart."

"I haven't," he said. "Nor will I."

Julia chuckled. "I wish you luck in trying to persuade the debs and their mamas of that."

He nodded and sighed as he left her side and went toward the happy couple. Although Anne Arthur was a dozen years younger than him, Gibb had always had a soft spot for her. A quiet girl, albeit with a wicked sense of humor, she was the perfect match for the young Earl of Sonning. David Sonning worshiped her and she him. Although it made Gibb slightly nauseated to see so much blatant affection on display, he could own up to a slight bewilderment as to how anyone got into that state.

"So we wanted that knife-thrower to come and entertain us," Anne said as Gibb stood by the happy couple. "Evangeline someone. But we couldn't find a way to get in touch with her. Mama said we should have asked you," she finished. She raised one eyebrow in a speculative manner. "Is she right?"

Gibb shrugged. "I know her," he said with a nonchalance he didn't feel. "But I have no influence on what she does or who she entertains."

"Pity," David said. "If you ever do, remember us."

The incident unnerved Gibb. If his and Evangeline's names were being linked together he'd need to keep an even more careful watch that it was not detrimental to Evangeline and her livelihood. Although she had never mentioned why she had to work, and he hadn't pursued the question, it was evident Evangeline needed to and wanted to. He was not going to harm that.

As he pondered the knotty question, and sought to find an answer that would satisfy everyone, Gibb hunted down the room set aside for gentlemen to relieve themselves. Lady Arthur had flat out refused to allow anyone to water her beloved plants, and told them to use the commode like right-minded people. Gibb did the necessary, and wandered into the small room next door to give himself a few moments to regroup before he braved the ballroom and left.

The room was unfurnished, and Gibb assumed that was why the door wasn't locked. It was not somewhere anybody would need to enter. Unless, of course, you were someone like him, who needed a respite from the crowds. Gibb headed toward the velvet drapes that partially covered the window and noticed with pleasure it was open to allow fresh air into the room. He stood behind the curtains for a second to enable the night-scented flowers outside to invade his senses. At this time of year, when the spring flowers were at their best, it was a heady perfume. Farther north, his daffodils would have just about flowered. Here they had been superseded by other blooms, and a strong sense of homesickness made his head light.

So light he didn't realize the room had been invaded until he heard someone speak.

A female—and she didn't speak to him, but to someone with her.

"Tarnation, I know he came in here, and it is my best chance," the unknown female said. "If we are found here alone he'll have to marry me. You'd leave and I could cry—"

"Rape? Never, for no one would believe that of him. Besides it is unethical," someone else said. "I can't believe you would stoop so low."

"Who cares about things like that? Can you imagine," the first female sighed dramatically. "To be the one who wins the dangerous and tortured duke's hand?"

"You're playing a dangerous game, Cornelia."

Cornelia? Cornelia? The only Cornelia he knew off was Denby Crowe's sister. The one Crowe has asked if he could stay in town to escort for a few weeks. What was she up to? Without alerting the occupants of the room to his presence, Gibb climbed over the windowsill and moved behind a convenient tub filled with a nice bushy syringa, its pink flowers providing even more cover for him. He was lucky it was a still night, albeit cloudy, and he could hear the occupants of the room with ease.

"It is no game," Cornelia said. "I need to wed and as he has refused you then it is up to me to throw my cap at him."

"I didn't offer myself to him, Anthony my idiotic brother did, and I still think you are playing with fire. Anyway, he is not here. Time to go." It must be Tarporly's sibling who spoke.

"He was here and he could not have left," Cornelia said in a stubborn tone. "We would have noticed."

Oh, couldn't I? Lucky for me you are wrong.

"Then stay by yourself, that is what you want anyway. Don't involve me in your games anymore, Cornelia. I thought you wanted to speak to him about leaving me alone. To champion me, you said, not to compromise him."

"Lord, you are naïve. You'll be the old maid and I will be a duchess," Cornelia said. The spite in her tone was easy for Gibb to hear. It would almost be worth appearing to give her a piece of his mind. Almost but not quite. To be unnoticed would give him the upper hand.

"I think the response to that is in your dreams and not your reality." There was the sound of the door closing with a definite thud.

Gibb waited. It seemed Margaret Tarporly wanted him no more than he wanted her and this chit, just out, was all set to be allegedly compromised to get him to the altar. Presumably to repair her family's fortunes.

Not in his lifetime. Gibb backed along the terrace and headed for the kitchens. He'd go inside that way and out of the front door post-haste. With a bit of luck the chef would understand and he'd be able to snaffle a couple of the man's famous pork-and-apple patties as he exited.

* * * *

The resounding clang of her doorbell woke Evangeline out of a light doze. Her head had spun from all the worrying thoughts that filled it, and she had kicked off her shoes and sat down to rest her eyes. That, she realized as she squinted at the clock on her way to the door, had been over two hours earlier. The time surprised her. Judging by his usual appearances after he'd attended whatever he needed to, she had expected Gibb a good hour before and it was perhaps a good thing she'd dozed. Otherwise she might have been in bed.

She rushed downstairs in her stockinged feet and pulled back the lock before the thought that Gibb usually let himself in hit her. Once she saw him, that thought fled her mind.

Gibb stood there with one arm on the doorjamb, the other on his cheek. He looked weary, and a slight tic showed at the corner of his eyes. Eyes that once more were dull and lifeless. "You should check who is here, I could have been anyone. I forgot my key."

Was this what stopping in the capital on her behalf did to him? Evangeline's heart sank as she watched his eyes light up briefly — all too briefly — as he looked at her and leaned in to kiss her cheek. His lips were cold and his skin clammy. The weather was neither hot nor cold but a pleasant and warm temperature with little breeze. What on earth was wrong with him?

"*Salut, cieux*, what's wrong?" She stood back to let him enter and relocked the door behind him. He smiled as they climbed the stairs side by side, although it didn't reach his eyes.

"Now? Nothing. Before, everything. I need your company and a drink in that order."

The total exhaustion in his tone was something she had never heard before and it worried her more than she thought possible.

"Then you shall have my company."

"Lord, you are too good for me." He sighed as they entered her sitting room. "God, this is all such a mess. We need to talk, but first, can I make one more request?"

She raised one eyebrow, a trick she had learned from him.

He gave her a tired smile. "A dram, please."

"That is an easy request to solve." Evangeline nudged him away from her until the backs of his knees hit the daybed and he toppled into the mounds of billowing pillows. "Stay," she commanded. "I'll get your dram." He'd sent her several bottles a few days earlier. "A double with half water?"

Gibb yawned behind his hand and did his best to turn it into a cough. "That sounds perfect."

"I won't be a moment." Evangeline left the room. She would wager he'd be asleep by the time she returned and she was right. He'd turned his head to one side and rested his cheek on his hand. In repose he looked boyish, with all his cares wiped away. His face was clear of frown lines and his mouth relaxed into a half smile. Evangeline put the glass of spirit and carafe of water down on the sideboard. Gibb didn't stir as she tucked a tartan rug around him and moved to sit in a fireside chair.

Stealthily, Evangeline toed off her slippers, tucked her feet up under her and picked up her book. Then left it unread in her lap as she watched her friend sleep. If she could do nothing else for him she could give him this.

The clock ticked and a coal slipped in the grate, but Gibb slept on. As the fire died down, a sneaky breeze swirled around the edge of the window frame and under the door. Rain began to patter on the windowpanes and branches of the oak tree outside tapped in time to the watery splatters. Gibb blinked, stretched and gazed at her owlishly.

"Hell, I fell asleep. How rude, why didn't you shake me?"

"You did," she confirmed. "And I did not. Why should I shake you? You must have needed it."

He nodded and his mouth twisted into a wry grimace. "How contorted I was. It's a wonder I wasn't rig welted. Stuck," he elaborated. "I suppose anger takes it out of you. How long was I asleep?"

"Not long." Evangeline made up the fire and waited until the flames leapt around the coals once more. "But evidently long enough. Let me get you your dram."

* * * *

"You have news?" Gibb said a short while later as they sat side by side on the daybed with a table full of food and drink in front of them. "We never got round to speaking about it."

Evangeline wriggled until her bottom was in a more comfortable position and tore a chunk of bread off the loaf she'd baked earlier that day. Bread making soothed her and after hearing what Eloise had had to tell her she'd needed soothing. She chewed with care as she selected her words.

"It is known you have a box at Vauxhall next week," she said once she had finished eating. "And there is a lot of conjecture over which one it is."

"I could hardly keep it a secret I suppose," he said. "It doesn't matter. Anyhow, I have things to do before then."

"You do?

He nodded. "I need to go and check over my latest acquisition. I've been waiting to buy Cresswell House for years. It was my late godmother's. Now at last it will be mine. I owe it to Godmama to restore it to its original glory." Gibb paused as he went over everything he was committed to in the next few weeks.

"I need to go and see what needs doing. This will be a brief visit—there and back in one long day. But later I will spend time on the estate and meet with everyone needed to bring it back to what it was in its heyday." He looked at her, considering. "Would you like to come?"

"Come?"

"With me to Cresswell for the day. It would mean leaving at first light and getting back at dusk." He kept his face impassive. Or so he hoped. It mattered not what she decided.

If I believe that I am a worse idiot than Denby Crowe.

Evangeline considered him for what seemed like hours. "When?" she asked him as the silence between them spun out and he was about ready to tell her to forget it, it had been a bad idea.

"Tomorrow or the next day? I want to have a first look before I start work there in earnest."

"Hmmm." She tilted her head and stared into the distance. "What time do we set off?"

* * * *

"So, do you have any more news?" Gibb asked her as he tooled his phaeton out of the city and along the reasonable road toward St. Albans. The gray light of dawn could be seen in the eastern sky, and the lamps were being extinguished one by one

A black cat chased a large rat across the road ahead of them and Evangeline shuddered. "Rats. I have never liked them. Neither the rodent nor the human kind."

"Not many do, except, I suspect, the cats," Gibb said. "We have perhaps a three-hour drive, so settle in."

"And entertain you?"

He chuckled. "Why not?"

"Because what I have heard is perhaps not entertaining but perturbing." Her voice was somber.

"And I do not believe it is all tittle-tattle, as you say. There is truth in it."

"Nevertheless I need to know and I need feeding. There is a basket at your feet with our breakfast in it."

"Of course." She cleared her throat and handed him some cheese and took a chunk for herself. Once she had swallowed and washed it down with some wine she cleared her throat. "So. Your attendance at Vauxhall is now the center of gossip. Are you prepared?"

Gibb popped the crumbly Cheshire cheese into his mouth. "Hmmph?"

"I think."

He nodded his agreement, and in spite of her reawakened worries Evangeline laughed. "It is also known you do not intend to invite anyone, or," she amended conscientiously, "you have not yet invited anyone to share it."

"I've invited you," Gibb said, as he was once again able to speak without spitting cheese crumbs all over everywhere. He navigated around an accommodation coach and increased speed once more. "That cheese is good. Please pass the wine." He drank from the bottle. "My apologies for being uncouth, but this is easiest. Any more cheese? You were saying?"

"That I am to be your guest is not known, to many, if any, nor do I want it to be," Evangeline replied as she passed another chunk of Cheshire to Gibb. "The consensus is you have rented the box and intend not to share, or to have a woman with you whom no one as yet is aware of. For reasons not undisclosed. The majority of those talking about it are swayed toward the first."

"Correct in one way, I suppose."

"Eloise had two young ladies in her salon today, and as she went out of the room to collect some ribbons she overheard their very interesting conversation."

Gibb toyed with a slice of apple she passed to him. "Go on," he said, aware his voice was flat as he held his temper in check. "About me?

She nodded. "It seems so, although you were not referred to by name. The fact is Eloise knows I am to appear. Since I shared my story of the night we met, she keeps her ears open even more than usual. I told her you were going to watch over me, therefore she shamelessly, as she puts it, eavesdropped."

"And was it worth her while?" Gibb asked and crunched his apple slice.

"You can be the judge of that, although forewarned is forearmed. The gist is that one of the females, for I hesitate to call them ladies, was going to secret herself in your box when it was empty and the other would arrange for her to be found with you in a compromising position. If another female was to be present they would find a way of enticing her away for long enough to enact their plan."

"The young lady in question wouldn't be Cornelia Crowe, would it?" Gibb asked. Only the white lines around his mouth gave his temper away.

"Why, yes," Evangeline said in amazement. "How did you know?"

"She has already tried once," Gibb replied. "Last night, and it was by pure chance I was able to thwart her. It seems she has more than one trick up her sleeve."

Evangeline sat aghast as Gibb told her of his evening. Where were the so-called rules of good behavior people said existed in the ton? Was this the etiquette that was extolled? "The *coquine*. Hussy," she explained at his blank look. "Why you? Apart from the lure of the unattainable."

"Money," Gibb said with indifference, as he let the reins out a little and the carriage moved in a steady way up a short, steep hill. "Whenever is it not?"

"Ah, yours, I presume?"

He shrugged. "I expect anyone would do but I am regarded as an easy target. The Crowes are strapped for cash. They imagine me as their savior. Someone to be used to rescue them from whatever mess they have got themselves into. I won't be," he said in an adamant tone.

"Hmm." Evangeline tapped her teeth with her nail and did her best not to notice how Gibb watched the action out of the corner of his eye. "They do not know you very well, do they." It was not a question. "So what shall we do?"

"We?"

"Of course we," she said. She had no patience for prevarication. "Unless you tell me otherwise, we are in this together, are we not? For if I was not here neither would you be. No." She put her finger over his mouth—a favorite occupation of hers, she thought. "You would have left London by now if it were not for me. Own up."

"I would still want to vote next week," Gibb pointed out. "In town and at their mercy."

"Yes, but you would have gone away and come back just for that. So I got you into this situation, *n'est-ce pas vrai?*"

"Not necessarily," he argued. "It could have happened at any time."

"Hmm." She wasn't convinced, but there was no point in continuing to argue. "Whatever, we now fight together, yes?"

He smiled. "Oh yes, so let us plot and decide what we should do."

"I have an idea," Evangeline said.

Gibb laughed, kissed her nose, and she wrinkled it.

"Watch the road," she said in alarm. "We want to get there in one piece. So, are you pleased I have a thought on what we need to do? Have I surprised you? Are you flabbergasted?"

Where on earth did that come from? By the look on his face he was as taken aback as she was by her question. Then he shook his head in apparent bemusement.

"I shouldn't be," he said with a grin. "You always do."

* * * *

It was amazing how much better he felt about life with someone to discuss events with. Someone who had no qualms about asserting herself and not always deferring to him. But also someone who showed him that he could have a female friend without emotional ties. That was a pleasant surprise even if he did have a predisposition to wonder when, not if, it would change.

She had asked if she could practice on him, but intimated it mattered not if he said no. That of course made him determined to say yes. Why? He had no idea.

The day at Cresswell passed in perfect harmony. They discussed what to do with the house and how the home farm should be run. Who was best as housekeeper, who would be perfect for the grounds. Three hours later, just before they left to return to town,

Gibb waited, jacket off, cuffs tucked up inside his sleeves and doing as he was told. Evangeline twirled her stilettos and threw four of them one after another at him as he stood in front of a backboard tacked to the peeling plastered wall that still graced the untidy shabby ballroom of Cresswell House. They'd ignored the cobwebs and spiders and decided it was the perfect place for Evangeline to rehearse.

"I wonder just why people think I need saving," he said as he pondered while Evangeline practiced her act on him. "What part of me shows something that is not true?"

He was so used to it that he didn't flinch when one knife missed his ear by a scant inch. No doubt she'd intended it to. Gibb was under no illusion that Evangeline couldn't have pinned his ear — or any other part of him — to the backboard if she had desired.

"I still think you need a strong man outside the box," she said. "Lift your left arm up straight into the air." He did so and another knife struck the wall and quivered as it dug in up to the hilt.

"No, it will make it all the harder for her to get in," Gibb said. Without thinking, he moved his arm to scratch a sudden itch on his nose.

"Do not do that," Evangeline said sharply. "Or this will happen."

Gibb stopped mid-movement. A whirling glittering *something* spun toward him and pinned his shirt sleeve to the wall, just above the elbow. His heart missed a beat. "Ah, sorry, I forgot. I trust you." He blinked as he assimilated his assertion. "I do, and that is not usual."

Evangeline nodded. "I'm glad you trust me but, my dear Gibb, complacency is not good. In anything. You relaxed and dropped your guard. That is dangerous."

He smiled. It was just like her to cut to the chase. "True. I will be aware from now on."

"Not just here but at all times," she said with mock severity. "You are a challenge so many people seem to feel the need to overcome. So a strong and armed man?"

He shook his head. "No. We need to catch her in the act. This will be one time too many."

"Then let me threaten her with a stiletto." Evangeline plucked four of the five stilettos out of the backboard, left him pinned in place and looked at him seriously. "It might help." She began to juggle the blades she held in a circle. "I would threaten with one at first."

"You are more bloodthirsty than I realized." All at once, he understood he relished that. "Do not change."

She nodded and smirked. "*Bien sûr*, I am French."

Gibb inclined his head an inch. "True and I will not forget it. Sweet Evangeline, I thank you for offering, but what if it made things worse? I do not want any of this to reflect in a negative way on you. Threatening a young lady of the ton is not the way to make friends and influence people."

"Such a shame," she said mournfully as she caught the four stilettos in one hand, found a cloth and began to wipe them down. "I have not threatened anyone for an age."

"Be thankful, for it is frowned upon. That is the way of our world. Do you need to practice more?"

She shook her head. "Not today, thank you. You make a good partner. Maybe I should pull you out of the audience?"

She tilted her head to one side and put her finger over her mouth in a parody of surprise as Gibb handed the knife to her with a bow. Judging by Evangeline's wide-eyed expression her words surprised her as much as they did him. "But give me warning so I can practice the 'why me, oh lord, is this safe, what am I doing', expression," he said with a grin.

"Somehow I do not see you ever achieving that," Evangeline retorted. "Therefore, maybe one day I will just spring it on you. For now, I'm happy with my act although I wish somehow I could have a wheel to pin my target to, one that spins," she said almost to herself. "It would be interesting and very exciting."

"I don't see why you can't," Gibb said." I'll ask a wheelwright to see what he can come up with. What do you intend to do with it? And your victim?"

Her eyes twinkled. "Victim, ha. All my subjects volunteer or are, shall we say, volunteered." She gestured a hand up someone's back. "All I do is spin him and throw my knives around him as he spins."

"Dangerous woman."

"Very," she said and grinned. "Unless you know what you are doing. I always do."

"Of course you do." Gibb held out his arm to her. It was an automatic courtesy these days, and he reveled in the fact she accepted it as such. "Come on then, let's go back to London and on the morrow seek out Flood."

"Flood?

"The wheelwright I use in London."

* * * *

What on earth could go wrong?
Nothing surely? Or so Gibb told himself as he got ready for Vauxhall a few days later. Therefore, why the uneasy feeling and that itch of apprehension that slithered up his spine and lodged in his scalp? Why the

tentacles of unease that sent goosebumps over his skin, and the lump that lodged in his stomach and encouraged spiders to crawl around? There was no answer.

He and Evangeline had plotted and planned and gone over so many possible scenarios it was a wonder they weren't dizzy. In the end they had sorted out what they thought was their best form of attack and defense. To that end, Gibb had sought out Henry and Mary and, to his utter amazement—and no doubt theirs—asked them for help.

Evangeline had prodded him into action. "Gibb, we cannot do it all ourselves. There will be a lot of the evening when the box is empty or you are alone. That is not a good scenario."

"Or you would be alone," Gibb had replied. "If I stayed in the box. I won't do that."

"Yes, or I would be," she'd agreed with a quirk of her lips. "Therefore, we need someone to aid us. You know who you could ask, so be brave and do so. It is not a weakness to admit you need help, but a strength."

Gibb had recognized the truth in her words and sought out Henry. To Gibb's pleasure, Henry had jumped at the chance with an eagerness that had surprised Gibb. Mary had also been just as enthusiastic

'You've had a hellish time, Gibb, and whether this is altruism, friendship or just spiking someone's guns, I'm all for it,' Henry had said. He thumped one fist into the other to emphasis his remark. 'Some of those chits are far too forward, and as for their parents...' He had shuddered. 'Even after I offered for Mary and our betrothal was known, they still did their best to get me in their clutches. We will do anything you want.'

'*It means also helping the young lady whose services you wanted for your ball,*' Gibb had said. He and Evangeline had discussed it and agreed that information needed to be shared. She had also said she would perform for them, but Gibb in his wisdom had held that information back. He'd wanted help given willingly and not for a favor.

He'd gotten it.

'*Dare I ask what she has or hasn't done to need help?*' Mary had asked. Up until then she had contented herself with the occasional nod of agreement. "Or if you would rather not tell me…"

Gibb had considered for a brief second. If he had to ask for help he had to be open. It went against everything he knew but… '*May I bring her to meet you?*'

Mary had nodded and looked at her husband. '*If Henry agrees?*'

'*Of course. When?*'

Gibb had considered. '*Tonight? In an hour or so?*'

'*Perfect. We'll look forward to it,*' Henry had said.

* * * *

"I can't," Evangeline said without even thinking about her words, as butterflies danced in her stomach. "I thought you would use servants to help. Lord Henry and Lady Mary Lawrence are of the ton."

"So am I," Gibb pointed out.

"That is different," she said with impatience. "And you know it."

"Why?" Gibb asked with interest in his voice. "I don't know it, or even understand it." He paused and ran his finger around the rim of a nearby empty vase. "Unless you are going to point out in a sanctimonious voice that I'm a duke or some such nonsense."

Drat the man. "You are," Evangeline said. "Also, I am French, therefore I never have such a voice." Why could he not merely agree?

"And your point is?"

"It just is different," Evangeline said, stubborn as ever. "They are aristocracy. I am a mere knife-thrower."

"That's as may be but the rest is rubbish, my dear, especially the 'mere'. You are not a *mere* anything. What you are is craven."

"I am not," she said with indignation. How dare he say such a thing? She was just being cautious, wasn't she? "I offered to demonstrate for them. I am not of their standing."

"Pusillanimous."

"Pu…" Evangeline glared then began to giggle. Only he would come up with such a word to describe her attack of the nerves. "You do not pull your punches, do you? Pusillanimous indeed."

"I thought you would prefer that to lily-livered or chicken-hearted," Gibb said, and sobered. "I am serious, Evangeline. You need to come and meet them. If nothing else, to say thank you for their immediate and unquestioning support of both of us. There was no hesitation. I asked and they said yes even before I explained what we needed. Come to think of it, I still haven't told them that yet. We can do so together." He paused. "And nor did I offer your services as an entertainer. They agreed without any strings."

Put like that she accepted she had no option. "What do I wear?" she asked as she began to panic. Up until now, the sole connection she'd had with the ton was

Gibb, or as the entertainment. This was something new and frankly scary.

Stop being so pathetic. "Where are we to meet them?"

"I best not say go as you are," Gibb drawled with a grin as he looked at her bare feet and lack of stays. "Nothing fancy, they are at home tonight and Mary has promised us a late supper."

"Gibb Alford, you have just eaten."

"Evangeline… Hold on, what is your other name…?"

She had wondered when he would get to that. "I never use it."

"So be it." He sounded disappointed.

"It's not that I don't trust you, it's just… Mama called me Evangeline Coeur, and herself Madame Coeur. But somehow…" She hesitated. "I often wondered if it was our name," she finished in a rush. "But instead something chosen to hide Mama's identity. She often seemed surprised when she was addressed so. I suppose I will never know." But maybe, she thought uneasily, she might. Now that she was in England.

"Evangeline Heart sounds fine," Gibb said. "We will use it if we need. I may have eaten but intrigue and conspiracy make me hungry. Now go and change. Put on that pretty red dress with the golden leaves in it. It suits you."

His visit had been unexpected and she had, as ever, removed her footwear, changed into a comfortable but somewhat shabby gown and discarded her stays. Eloise had left not half an hour earlier, after they had discussed the last few changes to the Vauxhall costume. The knock on the door had made her heart jump until common sense had reasserted itself. The one person who could get into the garden via the alley, apart from her and Eloise, was Gibb. No one else had a key. Even so, she asked who was there before she unbolted the entrance.

And the upshot was she was now dressed in a smart red day dress covered in golden leaves, with her stays back on and ready to go out with Gibb. It was lucky Meggie, her maid, hadn't gone to sleep. The last thing she'd wanted to do was ask Gibb to pull the laces tight.

"I confess to being nervous," she said as they sat side by side in Gibb's carriage. "I do not know how to behave in such illustrious company. Unless I am throwing knives at them."

Gibb laughed. "Don't do that. Just think of them in their nursery, or nightclothes. No different from anyone else."

Lord above, now she had an imaginary picture of Gibb in *his* nightclothes.

Chapter Seven

Gibb scanned the area around his booth and nodded his assent to the hovering lackey. It was perfect for what he wanted. Not too near any other boxes, with shrubbery close to the rear. Ideal for someone to use as a means to enter unnoticed, also for anyone else to use to hide and see what transpired. He glanced at the covered dishes and fruits on a side table, the overlarge — and empty — cupboard set across one corner, and the Chinese screen to hide the servants' entrance. Calculated that unless someone stood close by and peered through the window the occupants of the box would be out of immediate view, and smiled at the anxious manservant who waited with patience in the doorway.

"Excellent, thank you. If anyone asks you, I am not sharing my box this evening. Understand?"

His voice held a hint of menace and the servant swallowed, his Adam's apple bobbed nervously and he bowed. "Of course, your grace."

Whether or not he meant it, or whether if someone greased his palm he would say otherwise, Gibb didn't know. He could but hope his reputation as someone who preferred not to socialize, *and* as the type of man not to tangle with, had gone before him and made that seem feasible. Perhaps even some of the doubts with regards to how Hester had died – was she pushed to do it? – would work in his favor for once and show him as a definite man not to cross.

It was a double-edged sword. By removing himself from the capital and not commenting on anything that had happened in his marriage, he had left himself open to the tittle-tattle and gossip the ton thrived on. However, it also meant no one knew much about him as he now was. A few hints about how he had always had a hard streak, and that hadn't lessened with the years, helped to foster the myth, as did the fracas with Denby Crowe. As Henry had pointed out to him when they were alone, no one knew how Gibb would behave in any given circumstance or how his mind worked.

'*It is easy to show you as a hard man who takes no prisoners, especially after the poison m'sister spread. Your true friends know it's rubbish and will defend you, but that works because others will think it's friendship that makes them say so. And'* – Henry had grinned wolfishly – '*no one knows we are friends so if I say you are hard it will be believed.'*

Gibb had to hope so. A lot depended on no one approaching him when he left the box to watch Evangeline. Up until her display she had, after a lot of arguments, agreed to Wiggs, an ex-pugilist and now one of Harry's grooms, staying with her. He was to all intents and purposes her new handyman, sick of Gibb's high-handedness. It had taken all of his persuasion to get Evangeline to agree. Only after meeting Wiggs, and Gibb explaining how he would then be able to carry out their plan without worry, did she accept her shadow.

The manservant employed to service the booth left through the door at the rear of the building—the servants' entrance—and Gibb sat in the chair to one side of the window and absently looked outside. The gardens were beginning to fill up. Already an orchestra was playing outside the gothic folly and he could hear the strains of some violins playing a gentle piece. Something that reminded him of summer days and a warm woman.

What? Since when had he felt like that? Since now it seemed. Gibb shifted in his chair and steepled his hands on his stomach and chin. He was uneasy about the evening and wanted everything to go without a hitch. Had they thought their plan through properly? Nothing untoward must happen to Evangeline.

Was it all down to Evangeline's influence or had this change of heart been creeping up on him unnoticed for longer? He examined his thoughts carefully. He still had no inclination to have anyone rely on him. That idea, even in the abstract, brought back the black cloud he had tried so hard to disperse. The intimation that another person might put their life in his hands made him shudder in horror.

But was that not what Evangeline was doing? That insidious notion tensed every muscle in his body. No, he decided, that was different. He had offered to help, no more than that. She was still very much in command of her life. Look at the way she had railed at the thought of Wiggs. He relaxed again. This scenario was different from the one with Hester, he had subconsciously always known that. Evangeline would never ask for more than he was prepared to give. The opposite was more likely.

Gibb sat upright, his heart pounding, as he waited for the voice of Hester begging, pleading, shouting, to invade his mind.

And waited.

It didn't.

He had no idea whether to laugh or cry. Instead he poured a goblet of champagne and toasted the air. Was this the beginning of a new chapter of his life? One where his late wife did not invade? He hoped so. Not that it would change his attitude with regards to relationships, that was fixed, but for other things... He could only pray. Gibb sank back into the chair once more.

A couple he knew walked past without seeing him even though they gave the box a brief glance. It was therefore seen as what it purported to be. Almost unnoticed. The door, which led out into the public area, was to one side, not at the front as most were, and he could tuck his chair into a corner and spy happily.

The rear door opened with the tiniest of squeaks, just enough to warn him someone was about to enter. As it was hidden by the screen he sat up and watched as a handkerchief waved around the edge.

Gibb laughed. "Come in, friend. All is as it should be."

"Phew," Henry said as he and Mary entered and sat in Gibb's hidden corner with him. "This cloak and dagger lark is nowhere as easy as I thought it would be. We had to dodge Gibbons and Fitzgerald along with several ladies. Plus the family Crowe, sans Denby. But here we are safe and sound."

Gibb pulled the lacy curtain across the glassless window and poured more champagne. "As long as we keep our voices low this is the perfect place to meet," he said. "I've checked that you can both stand in the cupboard that on any other occasion would hold all the crockery and cutlery and not be seen. Cornelia will have no reason to open it, for everything will be to hand. I've moved it so she won't think to try and hide behind it, but use the screen instead."

"So we stay here while you go to watch Evangeline," Mary said and sighed as she undid her cloak and let the hood fall across her shoulders. "I so want to see her act."

"You will one day," Evangeline said as she also entered the room from the rear door. "Oh, this is perfect. Before you say anything else, Wiggs is outside, watching for anything untoward or unexpected visitors. I just popped by to say everything is set, and I hope we can stone those Crowes once and for all tonight. There is a good crowd, and I for one do not feel even one iota ashamed of what we are about to do. It is fate," she opined in a pious way, which she spoiled by sniggering. She grinned at Henry and Mary as she remembered their recent meeting.

With her knees knocking and her heart in her mouth, she'd stood quietly as Gibb had introduced them. *'Evangeline, this is—'*

'Henry and Mary,' Henry said before Gibb could decide how to introduce them. *'And we are looking forward to helping you. Mary has confessed Denby was a dashed nuisance to her sister Letty a week or so ago. He's a pest.'*

Evangeline nodded. *'It is not convenable — suitable — for me to call you so, my lord.'*

'*Then the deal is off,*' Henry said cheerfully.

'*Henry, do not tease. Please, Miss…Evangeline,*' Mary said as Gibb watched in amusement. "*I was plain Mary Higginbottom, and my papa is in trade. We are friends here, I hope. I need a friend.*'

'*So do I,*' Gibb said. Evangeline nibbled her lip. '*What do you say?*' Gibb continued. '*It is up to you.*'

Evangeline let her breath out in a *whoosh*. '*Then, thank you, Henry and Mary, I appreciate all you re going to do.*'

'*What about me?*' Gibb said in a mock sorrowful voice. '*Do you appreciate me?*'

Evangeline had patted his cheek, much, he saw, to the amusement of Henry and Mary. '*Always.*'

There was a knock on the rear door and they turned as one to stare in that direction. Gibb walked over and opened it.

Wiggs stood outside with an apologetic look on his face. "It's time Miss Evangeline went to get ready."

Gibb nodded as Evangeline joined him at the door. "Ready?"

"Oh yes, I hope to see you all later. And Mary, pick an evening for a ladies' night. I'll show you how to wield a knife."

"Oh…my…but…" Mary looked at Henry, who shrugged.

"As long as you don't aim it at me."

"Does Mary defer to Henry over everything?" Evangeline asked as Gibb escorted her to the edge of the bushes and stood with her while Wiggs reconnoitred the way ahead. It was important she got to her dressing area unseen. "Does she have no say in matters, or any ideas of her own?"

"It seems to work for them," Gibb said.

"Not for you, though," Evangeline said. Poor Gibb, did he know what he was missing not allowing anyone through his self-imposed barriers? She might not want to be subservient or reliant on others but she was happy to help and be helped. In general. "Nor for me either." She crossed her fingers behind her back. It was almost the truth, and she wasn't prepared to say any more.

"As you say, it is not for me," Gibb agreed. "Theirs is an unusual marriage, and they know I will tell you this. After Hester, my...late wi..." he stumbled over the word, "wife died, her father turned to drink at a rapid pace, oh don't say it, I accept that was not my fault." His voice belied his insistence but Evangeline stayed silent. This confession was enormous and very important.

"The man had always drunk to excess, but now he made no attempt to hide it, and Henry had to marry into money. Mary's papa is in trade but has the money. To their utter amazement, they discovered a mutual liking, I imagine you would say, and the marriage works. Some people shun them, but a marriage such as theirs, of mutual convenience and between the classes, is now more common than you would think."

"As you say." That was one of the stupidest retorts known to man or woman. Evangeline was glad to see her 'minder' return. "Ah, that is Wiggs beckoning. I will see you later." She picked up her skirts of green and brown, chosen for their ability to meld in with the scenery, and followed Wiggs without looking back. Now she had to move her mind from Gibb to her performance.

"A good number ready to watch, miss," Wiggs said as they reached the area curtained off for her. "I'll keep out of sight, but I'll have my eyes peeled."

Evangeline nodded. "Good," she said absently and stiffened as she saw a figure out of the corner of her eye. "Keep a watch on Denby Crowe. I wouldn't put it past him to try something stupid."

Wiggs inclined his head. "His grace said much the same thing, miss. I've got my eye on him, don't you worry. I know him, he's not over liked by his servants, and when we're in the Boar's Head, we talk."

She'd bet they did, and guessed a lot of scurrilous gossip would be mulled over in the tap. "If he looks in any way, shape or form to be about to intervene, stop him, otherwise let him be."

"I'll do that."

The orchestra changed to playing a dramatic piece. Her signature tune. Evangeline checked her knives and stilettos were where she wanted them, took a deep breath and strode into the makeshift arena. The crowd was larger than she had anticipated, and the organizers had roped off a fair-sized space for her to use. Several burly watermen had been hired to make sure no one ventured into her throwing line, or behind the thick wooden wall she used to position people against.

As she bowed very flamboyant and showman-like to the watching crowd, she saw Denby Crowe out of the corner of her eye and wondered uneasily if he was there to try to make trouble, or to ensure Gibb was also there and out of the box. Whichever, she had to trust Wiggs and Gibb and get on with her act.

The knives were honed to perfection and the painted screen she'd flung over the wall bright and eerie, as red bled into orange and purple and the outlines of people and animals could be seen if you looked carefully. This part of her act she could do by rote, throwing her knife so no outline was pierced, chatting to her audience and drawing them in. The applause was loud and long and Evangeline took stock. Maybe the redhaired gentleman over to one side would work as her target?

"Now, Messieurs and Mesdames, I look for a willing helper. Do I have a volunteer, or do I need to press-gang someone?" The laughter was nervous. It seemed, as ever, no one would step forward. "No? No one willing to show their bravery?" Silence then…

"I will." Gibb moved toward her. His expression dared her to argue.

"You, your grace? You are willing to put your" — she raised her eyebrows — "body in my hands." The innuendo was one she used every time, and always raised a laugh. This time was no exception.

Gibb grinned. "Oh yes." That drew even more titters and raucous laughter. He bowed extravagantly, a parody of what a true bow should be, and winked at her. "Any time, but be gentle with me."

"I, *monsieur*, am always gentle. If the situation warrants it." Someone whistled long and loud and she curtsied in the unknown's direction. "Just so. However, now I must explain to my vic…ahem…" She coughed theatrically. "Partner." Evangeline drew Gibb close and spoke to him in rapid French, something she had learned he understood when she had sworn about Denby Crowe. "What are you playing at? Why you? I thought you were going to stand back."

"Crowe is up to something, I know it," Gibb responded in the same tongue. "The rumors are he is going to show you who is boss. Therefore I want to be able to look out at him and the crowd. I have no idea who his cohorts are, if anyone. What better place than from in front of the wall? And, you must admit, I know what to do and will not flinch."

That was true. "In that case, follow my lead, and a little flinch on occasion will add to the atmosphere."

He chuckled. "Noted."

"So, your grace," Evangeline said out loud in the pretty French accent she emphasized on such occasions, "if you would please stand on the marks and do exactly as I tell you."

"That's something new, eh? Gibb Alford doing as a woman tells him," Crowe sneered. "Dictated to instead of dictating. How the mighty have fallen."

Gibb smiled. "You should try it," he advised as Evangeline checked he was where she wanted. "It is a revelation."

"That's told you, Denby. Not under the thumb, eh?" someone shouted. Catcalls echoed around the gardens and Crowe reddened.

Probably not a good thing, Gibb thought as he took his jacket off, tucked his cuffs up and made sure his cravat was tight. He knew Evangeline would pretend it was to save his neck, reduce something for her to fix her eyes on and not have buttons to aim for. He also knew it made no difference whatsoever. Nevertheless, he pretended to listen with care to her instructions, nodded and grimaced where he would be expected to and took up the position she indicated. Then he waited and watched her as she twirled her stiletto into a whirling, gleaming, flickering indistinct shape of silver. The audience, as they stood, seemingly transfixed by the action. Denby Crowe. Wiggs — almost hidden in one corner. All concentrating on Evangeline and him.

"Wave this handkerchief," Evangeline instructed as she handed Gibb a linen square. He did and the stiletto she used to pin it to the wall flew through the air so fast it was a moving blur of color. The audience cheered, and Crowe jeered as Gibb let them see the handkerchief fluttering in the breeze.

"Easy," Crowe shouted and was hushed by several people around him. He scowled but subsided.

"Take off your cravat. I will do my best to miss your throat, your grace. It might make it easier to breathe when you see you are still alive."

He grinned as she winked at him.

Several gentlemen shouted out encouragement, most of it only just the correct side of racy. One or two ladies tut-tutted and one walked away with her nose in the air. Gibb unwound the yard-long strip of linen from around his neck and waved it with a flourish.

"And next?"

"This, your grace." Evangeline pointed at the stirrups of an arc, which rocked from side to side. It was the forerunner of the wheel due in a week or so. "If you stand just so." She indicated two footholds.

With a bow, Gibb did as she asked and scanned the crowd as the implement made him sway and the cravat he held high shifted as if it was caught in a breeze.

Gibb made sure he moved only his eyes, not his head, to keep track of Crowe as the man edged forward to stand halfway down one side. What were his intentions?

For the first part of the rest of the show Crowe remained silent. Then, as Evangeline changed tactics and gave Gibb a flurry of instructions, the man tensed and step forward. Evangeline noticed and her eyes narrowed. Gibb stared and willed her not to react. She gave an imperceptible nod to show she understood, and threw her knife high in the air. "Lift your left arm," she called.

As Gibb obeyed, Crowe made his move. "Hey, Gibb, look out, over here," Crowe called urgently. "Watch out, Alford, move this way."

It took all of Gibb's formidable will not to give in to his instincts and turn toward the voice and react as most people would. However, he steadfastly stared ahead and ignored Crowe as Evangeline's knife headed in his—Gibb's—direction.

"Move, Menteith, move now." The insistent note in Crowe's voice was hard to ignore. If it had been anyone else, or had he not been forewarned something might happen, would he have obeyed? Gibb would like to have thought not but he wondered as he stood, seemingly relaxed, and the knife landed quivering in the wood two inches below his armpit. If he had done as Crowe demanded it would have hit him square in the chest. Presumably what Crowe wanted?

The crowd cheered and clapped. Gibb took his time to turn his head toward where Crowe had stood. It was no surprise to note Crowe was no longer there. He nodded to Evangeline, who had pulled out her knife and stood close by. "Finish the act and we will see what happens next," he said out of the corner of his mouth. "Wiggs will follow him."

Her eyes narrowed as she searched his face, then she gave a tiny nod. "And now for our finale..." Knives flew toward him so fast they appeared to meld into each other. They surrounded him and at the end, and as she demanded he released his cuffs she pinned him to the wall by those. The crowd went wild.

"It was a success," he said as they took a bow together. He waited patiently, his eyes scanning the crowd as Evangeline chatted to all and sundry before she was able to move toward her equipment. It was longer than he thought before they could get leave. As Evangeline packed away her knives, to be put under the safekeeping of Wiggs, Gibb spoke with various friends from the audience and acted as if he had no idea what Crowe had been about. He chose not to acknowledge he had noticed Evangeline secrete a stiletto up her sleeve. As she locked her cases, Wiggs reappeared. Gibb made his farewells and proceeded in a circuitous manner to where Wiggs stood in the shadow of the tress.

"It was a success," he told Wiggs. "I hope it augurs well for the rest of the evening. What have you discovered?"

"Crowe's gone over the river by boat," Wiggs said. "I 'eard 'im tell someone it was all because he thought he saw a hornet attack you, and he were off home. Load of rubbish and I reckon his mate thought so for he said Crowe was an idiot. Didn't go down with his cohorts the way he wanted, I don't think. Anyhow, Crowe scowled and got into a boat. Wants to get out of the way I reckon. What have you done to upset him, your grace?"

"Don't ask," Gibb advised as Evangeline joined them. "Just stay back outside the box and listen in case I call, Wiggs. You too," he said to Evangeline. She pouted and he tapped her cheek. "No sulking. You promised."

"Oh, but it is not fair. I want to hear." Evangeline rolled her eyes. "Men get all the best bits."

"If you stand to one side of the door you will. Hear," he added. "And somehow I think throwing knives is not too shabby a thing to do."

"I'd hear more by the window," Evangeline pointed out. "Nothing to filter the sound. And if something goes wrong, I can throw one of those knives through the aperture. It would be perfect."

"And stand a better chance of being seen by others." Or killing someone. Neither outcome appealed to him. A little of the ice that had encased his heart meted and drifted away forever.

She sighed dramatically. "True. I promise to stick to the plan."

Another chunk of ice joined the first. "Good. Then let's go and put the next part into action."

* * * *

Gibb made sure he lifted the latch on the booth's door with as much noise as possible and scraped his boots as he entered for good measure. Not only to let whoever was inside, if indeed anyone was—apart from Henry and Mary—know that he was there, but also as a warning to Wiggs and Evangeline at the rear of the tiny building. As he had expected, the room seemed empty. The food table was untouched and unless you looked closely you wouldn't know that the carafe of wine had been moved. Not, he thought, by Henry or Mary who were now ensconced in the cupboard, but by whoever he thought was behind the screen.

He whistled nonchalantly and poured himself some wine, taking care not to look toward the screen. So much depended on Cornelia, if it was she, behaving as Eloise had overheard her saying she would. As it was well known once the food was delivered, unless you specifically asked for it, there would be no servants in the immediate area until called, it was a natural assumption Cornelia would act as she had planned.

Gibb lifted the covers from the food and studied it as if it was the most important thing in his life at that moment. He turned his back on the screen and watched the reflections in the large silver epergne he'd placed in a strategic position. He had to hope that Cornelia hadn't wondered why such an incongruous thing was in a booth at Vauxhall, and had guessed she was unaware of the niceties in the booths. When he'd mentioned it to Mary, she'd smiled and agreed with him. *'I'd hazard a guess that Cornelia has never been to Vauxhall in a peer's booth so she'll be none the wiser. It's a good idea, leave it.'*

The reflection of a woman showed briefly in the epergne's shiny surface. Gibb counted to three in his mind, turned and looked the young woman up and down. He'd wager his best bagpipes her parents had no idea she was dressed as she was. Her cheeks were rouged, her hair in a complicated coiffeur and her gown was little short of shocking. It was so low-cut her breasts threatened to spill out of the just decorous neckline.

"Cornelia Crowe, I presume? It's hard to tell in that outfit."

Evangeline strained to hear what was happening inside the room. There were voices, but so muffled she couldn't decipher words or who was speaking. Not even if the speaker was male or female. Next to her Wiggs put his ear to the door and frowned. "The besom is in there. Hold on, miss, and let me see if this door is locked."

"Don't make a noise," Evangeline hissed. "It might squeak."

"Not how I do it." Wiggs opened the door a scant inch. Immediately the voices condensed into a male and a female. "Anyways, I got a mate to grease it so as to be double sure."

She had to commend his forethought.

"So what brings you here, Cornelia?" That was Gibb.

"You have compromised me. You will have to marry me." Evangeline assumed the speaker was Cornelia Crowe. Her voice was high and excited. "We need to go and tell my parents at once."

Evangeline went down on her knees and glanced through a tiny knothole in the door she'd noticed earlier. As she'd hoped, Cornelia had her back to where Evangeline knelt. She held a glass in one hand and waved it around. "You turned Margaret down, and she wouldn't try to do anything else, but I will. The Tarporlys have no spine. The Crowes are different. You upset Denby, and now he is snapping at us all. Papa has lost all our money in the gambling dens, I am here alone with you, so you will have to marry me."

"And rescue your family, I presume," Gibb drawled.

"Exactly," Cornelia said in triumph. "You have enough to do that and still be as rich as Croesus."

"Not quite, but do go on."

"You will marry me and I will be a duchess."

"No." Gibb sounded bored.

"No?" Cornelia said with astonishment. "You have to."

"Wrong, I don't."

"Ha, if you do not I will tell everyone you ruined me."
She stamped her foot. Evangeline rolled her eyes, even
though no one could see her. What next? Drumming
her heels or thumping the table with her fists? Or just
noisy tears?

Through her tiny view hole Evangeline watched Gibb
shrug. "Go ahead, you will not be believed."

"I will, for I will scream and insist you molested me,"
Cornelia announced. Her eyes sparkled with malicious
glee. "What do you say about that?"

"The same as before. Go ahead," Gibb invited. "It will
do no good. I am not one you can blackmail or coerce.
It will be you who comes off worse."

She opened her mouth only to shut it in astonishment
as Henry and Mary appeared, one out of the cupboard,
one from behind it, like two jack-in-the-boxes, and
stood in the middle of the room.

"What do you need help for?" Henry asked.
"Nothing seems amiss."

Cornelia dropped her glass and her face went from
mottled to ashen. "B-but..." she stammered. "He
ruined me. I was alone with him, so he has to marry me.
He has to."

Evangeline sighed. No doubt Cornelia would now
stamp her foot again and pout.

She did.

"Silly girl, of course he hasn't," Henry said in an
aristocratic drawl Evangeline envied. "We were here all
along. Now we can tell the truth—that we saw you try
to blackmail his grace into marrying you, to whit by
lying that you were here with him alone. Or, if we feel
it is worth our while, and you might learn something
from this sorry mess, we can tell everyone you came

with us to say how brave he was with all those knives flying around. The choice, Miss Crowe, is yours."

There was a pregnant silence. Outside someone walked by chattering loudly in a light female voice and was answered by a deep baritone. Gibb took Cornelia's glass from her and filled it. "Miss Crowe, I did nothing to harm your family, and if Denby told you I did, he lied. In fact, I have had little to do with him. He is a good ten years younger than I. The sole time I have actively faced him down was when he tried to intimidate La Belle Evangeline, the knife-thrower. I would have done the same to any man who terrorized a lady. Those are not the actions of a gentleman let alone a peer. He did our sex a disservice that night, and has continued to do so. Does he know you are here?"

Cornelia sniffed, wiped her eyes and shook her head. "But if you don't want Margaret Tarporly, and you don't want me, who do you want?"

"No one."

Evangeline nodded to herself. It was as she'd envisaged. She needed to think hard. Not at that moment, for Cornelia broke into noisy tears.

"Enough." Mary spoke for the first time. "You brought this on yourself, you silly girl. Now be quiet, blow your nose and tell me how you got here, and who knows your whereabouts."

Cornelia shook her head. "No one knows. I crept out and came in a hackney. I used my pin money."

"Good lord, you idiot," Mary burst out. "Do you know what could have happened? Do you? Argh." She flung her hands in the air. "Do you have no sense whatsoever?"

"Mary, enough now." Henry spoke firmly. "She is an idiot, I agree, but I suspect it is up to us to make sure she doesn't add ruination to stupidity. Come, Cornelia, we will take you up with us and hope you can get into your home unnoticed."

Cornelia sniffed. "My maid is waiting to let me in."

"Thank the lord for a grain of sense," Gibb said. "Even if it is miniscule." There was a muttered conversation between Gibb and Henry, before Henry and Mary escorted a still-sniffing Cornelia out.

Gibb waited until the door had closed and their footsteps receded into the distance then walked across to the door that shielded Evangeline and Wiggs. They both looked up at him, Wiggs shamefaced, Evangeline not so.

Evangeline smiled. "Hello. That went in an excellent manner I think."

"You can come out now," Gibb said evenly. "What if you had sneezed?"

"But we didn't. How did you know we were here?"

"I know you," he said, and winked.

Chapter Eight

Dissatisfaction was a hard bedfellow. Gibb threw back the bedcovers in disgust, strode naked into his bathing chamber and thought about what he wanted to accomplish over the next few days. He had to vote in the House the following evening, check that Crowe and his sister had left the capital as he had demanded and also speak to Evangeline. The problem with the last part of his mental list was that he still wasn't sure what he was going to say to her. Did he want to move their friendship forward? Did he want to risk spoiling what they had? At present they spoke freely to each other and neither seemed to have the need to temper what they said.

They embraced when they met and when they parted. He could tell by the way she stood, the way her body reacted, that she was as affected by him as he was her. His body hardened to the point of pain when he held her close.

But to take a step toward intimacy? Was it right? Was it fair? He knew there was no fail-safe method of avoiding an unwanted child other than abstinence, or playing, as he thought Evangeline might say.

Even then it could easily get out of hand. With a mistress, someone world-wise, precautions could be taken, and it could be a way of sating himself if nothing else. However, he was sure, by the way Evangeline had reacted to his erection the first time she'd felt it next to her, she was unspoiled and innocent and wasn't someone prepared to be taken advantage of in such a way.

For the first time in years he felt uncomfortable at using a woman — any woman, not merely Evangeline — just to slake his desires, even if they knew and accepted it.

He had to decide if it was right to ask her to change that state of affairs. Especially when he had no promises he could give her about a future — except there was not one together.

No. I cannot do it.

So he suffered cold baths and frustration. Even though there *were* plenty of women prepared to help him out, in some indefinable way Gibb thought of that as cheating.

He flicked through the four-inch-high stack of invitations on his desk and wrinkled his nose at the perfume-scented ones, the coy ones and the downright blatant ones. By the time he'd sifted those out he was left with a handful of them he might perhaps be interested in.

A card game for the following evening, a request from his solicitor to visit at his earliest convenience, with regards to a house he wished to purchase that might be available at last, and a note from Lady Lisette Tonge, a friend of his late mother's whom he kept in touch with, interested him most. He glanced at his secretary, who stood waiting for instructions.

"That lot can go in the bin." He indicated the large pile. "Tell Dudley I will perhaps pop in, instruct my solicitor that he can set the purchase in motion and I will head to Lady Tonge's after I've eaten. A note to say I will be with her at noon would be appropriate. It is, she always says, a good time to catch her at home and awake."

Evans nodded and made some notations on a tablet. Gibb smiled. "That's it, I think." He waited until Evans had left and leaned back in his chair, deep in thought. Evidently talk had started. Whoever had decided to gossip about them had done it in such a way it was like casting a stone on a pond and discovering how the ripples spread out. Lady Tonge had said little in her note except she needed to speak with him about his activities and interesting information he might want to be apprised of. As she was not one to cry wolf, and always had her thumb on the pulse of ton activities, Gibb would go and see what she had to say.

For the first few days after the Vauxhall episode there had been very little bandied about with regards to the evening, other than that Gibb had seemed to be a very willing victim. Although Evangeline had been reluctant to be seen abroad with him, for she had said in earnest it would do him no good and set them both up for more unwanted speculation, she'd conceded she enjoyed his company and that their time together was not something she wanted to dismiss.

Neither did he, so increased gossip was inevitable. Not that anyone had come out and asked him why he'd offered to be Evangeline's partner. Then people had begun to remember they'd been seen together on other occasions. That Gibb had helped her when Crowe had allegedly, or definitely, depending on who the gossip was, been a little too friendly. Plus, how Crowe had spouted to everyone about the way Gibb could hardly keep his hands off Evangeline who, according to Crowe, nigh on ate Gibb with her eyes. No one had yet questioned Gibb about his version of that, but even so, he felt like a man besieged. He hadn't seen Evangeline for a couple of days—she'd been performing at a special ladies' evening as promised for Mary, he'd been giving a speech in the House. She'd helped Eloise with a rushed order, he'd accompanied Henry to Tatts to buy a horse. Little things that had conspired to keep them apart.

However, ladies there were a plenty. One had even approached him between the aisles of Hatchards bookshop as he had searched for a specific book his housekeeper had wanted. He'd spoken to her so coldly he'd thought for a moment she might faint, before she'd turned on her heels and almost run away.

Gibb had picked up the book and walked toward the assistant, who had watched the interchange with interest, although had neither interfered nor commented. If the volume had not been something he'd needed to purchase, he would have walked out. However, he did his best to treat his staff in a fair and reasonable way. The lady he'd chosen the gift for had grown up on his estate, learned to read and write and was an avid reader of gothic novels. This book was a present for her birthday. Gibb had accepted he was thought as eccentric in the way he treated his staff and he wasn't at all bothered. Happy staff meant a smoothly run estate.

He'd picked up his parcel, nodded and strode away, deep in thought. Tonight he had arranged supper at his home for Evangeline and himself. First, though, he had another long, boring city day to get through. What was he going to do once he'd visited Lisette Tonge?

London was slowly driving him mad.

* * * *

"My dear Gibb, I wanted to see you alone," Lisette Tonge said with a smile. "I hear rumors, and your dear mama would want me to apprise you of them." She spoke in her charming accent as she patted his cheek and accepted the kiss to her hand. "Such a gentleman. Your mama would be proud of that part of you." Her tone intimated, 'but not all'. "Ah, I miss a rake, though. Would you like to practice that?"

"It's not me, I'm afraid. I'll settle for the gentleman instead." Gibb kissed her hand for the second time in as many minutes and ignored the rest. Would she ever get to the point of his visit? "However did Reginald cope with you?"

She grinned. "He knew me, and accepted me for what I am. Something everyone should remember and practice. We are who we are."

"True." Gibb thought of Hester. The anguish hovered but did not settle. Instead a sense of compassion for Hester's unhappiness hit him. And the knowledge that whatever he had done would not have satisfied her. She had not had it in her to be happy.

Five minutes later, Gibb was settled in a chair with a cognac. Somewhat early to be drinking the fiery spirit, but he knew Lady Tonge's habits.

"So," Gibb said with a smile. "You have discussed Lady Arthur's ball, Lady Attley's ball, your grandchildren when they eventually appear, the weather, the price of candles and whether the latest on-dit regarding a perceived slight at Almack's is true. None of which, I believe, is why I am here. Spill, my dear. What is on your mind?"

Lady Tonge smiled and shrugged. "Perhaps nothing. Look, feel free to tell me to mind my own business."

"I would never be so crass," Gibb protested, uneasily aware that on more than one occasion he had done that very thing to others.

"Then, you are a friend of La Belle Evangeline, aren't you?" she said in a rush. "I don't want chapter and verse, a simple yes or no will do."

Trust Lisette to cut to the chase in such a way. "I know her," he said cautiously as he wondered where the questioning was leading. "Why?"

"My dear Gibb, can you never answer a question without another one?" Lisette said with a quirk to her lips. "I also know her, and wish to ask you something. Oh, not personal, but if you do not know her there is no point."

"Yes."

"Yes what?" Lady Tonge asked in a puzzled voice.

"Yes, I can answer a question without asking another one."

"Oh, you." Lisette was silent for several seconds — a record, Gibb thought, for the garrulous Lisette Tonge — then buffed his shoulder and burst out laughing.

Gibb joined in. It sounded somewhat rusty, as if laughter was unknown to him, as it had been until Evangeline, but he thought he was getting better at it.

Eventually Lisette wiped her eyes. "I asked for that."

"I'm afraid so," Gibb said. "And I'm glad we are on good enough terms for us to be so comfortable together."

"Pshaw," She made a noise like a pot boiling. "I've dandled you on my knee, seen you go from petticoats to short coats and as you are now. If we can't be informal, who can? And it is good to have someone I can be myself with. At my age those people get less and less." Her eyes twinkled to show she didn't care how old she was. "So, Evangeline?" she prompted. "Whilst I'm still breathing."

Gibb burst out laughing. "I've not been prevaricating," he pointed out. "Nevertheless, I will say that I am friends with Evangeline. Just platonic friends," he stressed. "Neither of us are looking for more. You know I will not be responsible for another's being."

"You think not?"

"I know not," he said. "So why do you ask? That," he added with a grin, "was a question without being related to a question."

Lisette shook her head in bewilderment. "Oh good, I think out of all that I got is that you are not friends who give each other succor, just friends."

"That's about it."

"Then apart from all the gossip about you both, which I'm sure you have heard, and says you are intimate friends, I swear she reminds me of someone." Lisette sat back in her chair and sipped her drink.

"You do?" That caught his interest. The hints about gossip were, he decided, something to mull over later. After all it was inevitable, whatever either he or Evangeline wanted. "Who?"

"That's just it." Lisette gave a very Gallic shrug. "I don't know. It is so frustrating. We were at Vauxhall and saw your stunt and Crowe's idiocy—I must say you coped with that in a manner that—yes, all right, stick to the point. I'll say it for you. So, La Belle Evangeline. The way she stands, the tilt of her head, I don't know, her silhouette. It reminds me of someone but I've scoured my mind and I cannot for the life of me remember who, nor if it is a male or a female. Does she have relatives here?"

It was Gibb's turn to shrug. "I have no idea. She has never said and we don't...don't invite confidences as such."

"Pity. If I can remember who I will let you know. All that apart, people are talking, Gibb, so beware, both of you. Mud sticks."

* * * *

"I met with Lady Tonge today," Gibb said as he and Evangeline sat side by side, on a comfortable chaise and cradled brandy goblets in their respective hands.

Evangeline hoped he didn't notice the involuntary jerk she gave. "A lovely lady," she said, proud of how her voice didn't waver and she held her drink steady without it slopping over the rim. What was he doing meeting a lady old enough to be his mother?

"You know her?" Gibb asked.

She bit her lip and nodded. "She is also French."

"True. She is also not one to gossip, but gave me some news that she thought we needed to hear."

"Not Lord Crowe again?" Evangeline asked him. "I thought he was in the country."

"He is safely ensconced in Cheshire," Gibb confirmed. "This was more along the lines of the fact she is sure you remind her of someone."

"Really?" Spots danced in front of Evangeline's eyes and she swallowed several times to get rid of the nasty taste in her mouth. Was she going to learn something else she needed to know? Why had Lady Tonge not spoken to her again instead? "Who?"

"Ah, that is the rub, Lisette has no idea. Just someone, she said. Do you have relatives in England? Or the rest of the country? Lisette has never been abroad since she came here as a young bride, so it must be over here."

"Not to my knowledge," Evangeline said, aware she was being economical with the truth. However, after all, she *didn't* know, did she? Evangeline hoped she didn't look as dishonest as she felt. It was strictly true but… She really would have been no good as a spy. One look at her face and the thumbscrews would be out. Not for the first time she wondered if she should take Gibb into her confidence.

No, he does not want involvement. "I wonder who it is."

"So does she. We might find out from her one day."

How to reply? "That would be interesting. I might discover a cousin four times removed or something."

"Would you like that?"

She considered how best to answer. "It is always nice to know you have family, I suppose, but how would they react to me or I to them? Are they prince or pauper? French, English or neither? Would they welcome me or turn me away? Perhaps I am best not knowing."

"You don't think that," Gibb said. "Everyone wants to know who they are."

"I do not know what I think," Evangeline replied. "Except who I am at this moment. Anyway, it is immaterial. She has no idea, nor do I, so I will not spend any more time on the puzzle and move on."

"Then you won't mind if I eat the last piece of cheese," Gibb said with a grin. "After all, it will go stale if we leave it."

She laughed, as he had no doubt intended her to. "You and your cheese." She passed him the plate with two wedges of cheese and an onion on it.

Gibb twitched his nose and stroked imaginary whiskers. "Squeak."

Evangeline's heart missed a beat. In this lighthearted mood, if he asked she would give him anything. She was too fond of him, too involved with him, and something would need to come to a head soon. As an unmarried female, she wasn't totally ignorant of the facts of life, but knowing them and knowing how to act were two very different things. Now that she knew she was illegitimate, the thought of bringing a child up alone was not a pleasant one. She remembered the stigma of his birth status being thrown at a lad in the village they had both lived in. No child should have to go through those taunts if it were at all possible not to. Now she had almost saved enough to give up knife-throwing and set out on her quest to discover why her *maman* had wanted her to come to England and a child was not to be thought of. Even so, if Gibb pressured her to make love, she would be hard-pressed to say no.

"I best go," she said as Gibb waved the brandy at her. "If I have any more I won't want to."

"You could stay," he said in a voice that gave nothing away.

"I could but..." She bit her lip. "Gibb, I like you very much. You are the friend I never had. In all honesty, I do not know if I could cope with more. You, I think, do not want any more emotional entanglement and if we took the next step there would of course be some. So...?"

"So, stay as a friend," he said. "Separate rooms if you desire. Or if you trust me, just to hold and be held. I would do no more unless you asked, I promise."

The silence was overwhelming as he looked at her without speaking. The choice was hers. He always kept his promises.

At long last she sighed. "That sounds perfect. It is an age since I slept in anyone's arms, and that was my *maman*."

"I'm not your *maman*," he pointed out with a smile. "Anything but."

"No, but I trust you as I did her."

"Then come with me." Gibb stood up and held out his hand. Evangeline took it and let him pull her to her feet.

"Show me," she said.

Chapter Nine

Surely she should have felt uncomfortable? Awkward or out of her depth? She didn't. Gibb led her to a large bedchamber where the bed, high-legged with an intricate headboard and footboard, took center stage. The wallpaper was light, pretty and not at all what she expected. The fireplace held a large display of rushes, and as Gibb lit the lamp Evangeline was able to admire the patchwork quilt on the bed.

"You do not sleep here," she said as Gibb turned to her. It did not seem possible that this was the duke's quarters. Was she not good enough to go in there with him?

"I do. The ducal chamber holds memories I don't want to think of. This was my room as a young man, and I had it redecorated for me after" — he cleared his throat — "after Hester died. It is no secret what our life together was like toward the end. She would storm into my room to rant and rail. I hated it and that chamber.

This is a happy room. I want to be happy in it with you."

"Then you will be," Evangeline said with certainty. The dynamics of the situation hit her. She had no nightrail, no gown and needed the facilities. "Ah…" She would wager her cheeks were as red as the velvet curtains that draped the windows.

Gibb looked puzzled then his eyes twinkled. "Oh yes. Through that door. Meanwhile, I will find you something to wear."

She prayed that whatever he came up with, it wouldn't be something that had belonged to his wife.

Evangeline rushed through her ablutions. It was unnerving to know Gibb was in the next room as she used the twig brush he had found for her to scrub her teeth with, with a smile at her astonishment.

"I admit it is a conceit of mine, to have an unused toothbrush at hand. I have them made for me a dozen at a time," he'd said before he indicated towels. It was an intimacy she'd never thought she would know and one she didn't know how to think about. Was this what it was like to share a house with a man? To share a room? If it was, didn't it make one uncomfortable?

Deep in thought, Evangeline finger-combed her hair and twisted it into a loose plait Sadly, she had no ribbon to hold it in place and she had no intention of going to bed with a head full of hairpins. Gibb would have to run the risk of a mouthful of hair.

That brought up another thought. What *were* they going to do?

I will never find out skulking in here. En avant. She took a deep breath and jumped as there was a sharp knock on the door.

"Evangeline?"

It was Gibb. Who else would it be? she thought as she stifled a nervous giggle. The man in the moon?

"If I open the door an inch I can pass a shirt through for you to wear," he said gruffly. "It will also swallow you up, but I thought it best in the circumstances."

"Oh yes, thank you." Her voice was as unnatural as his had been. It was ridiculous. They were friends for goodness' sake. "I don't want to shiver," she said in a normal tone. "Or make you cold." She stood to one side as the door opened and a garment was held out.

"I would squeal like a stuck pig if you put your cold feet on me," Gibb said with a laugh. "And retaliate. So here you are. One shirt, to wear to save your blushes and me cold feet."

It was indeed a shirt. Evangeline looked at it, realized how she was dressed and groaned.

Stays. The dratted torture item of clothing she despised. There was no way she could unlace them herself, and no way she was going to sleep in them. She gave an impatient huff and stared at the now-closed door. There was nothing for it. Evangeline took a deep breath, opened the door to the bedchamber and stepped into the room.

The empty-of-any-other-human-being room.

She let her breath out in an amused hiss. There she was, all churned up, emotions on high alert and embarrassment ready to take over as she asked Gibb for help, and he wasn't there.

What now? She wandered around the room and took her first long, unencumbered glance around. When she'd entered with Gibb she'd had impressions, but nothing concrete. His presence and the sense that something out of her orbit was about to happen had seen to that. Those first impressions, though, to her relief, had been correct. This room was beautiful.

I could be happy here. Not that she would get the chance. This was something out of the ordinary. A chance to receive comfort and give it back. *No strings, no ties, no emotional connection.* It was getting ever harder.

"Evangeline?" Gibb had once more crept up on her unnoticed. For a tall man he was very quiet as he moved. She noticed that now he wore a banyan striped in shades of blue, and his feet were bare. She glanced at his face, not allowing herself to look elsewhere. "What's wrong?"

"Stays," she said, brief and to the point, and hoped her embarrassment didn't show. "I need help."

"Of course, I should have thought of it," Gibb said gravely. Either he didn't see her chagrin, or was gentleman enough to ignore it. "If you perhaps take your gown down to your waist and ah, cover your front with a towel?"

"Thank you." She dashed into the next room to do as he asked and returned with a large sheet of linen held over her bosom.

"Turn around."

She complied then, *oh my,* his hands stroked her skin as he began to fumble with the laces. Why did they always go into knots when you didn't want them to?

His breath was warm on her neck as he bent his head and his fingers deftly began to undo the knots. He muttered something under his breath as he moved closer and Evangeline stopped breathing.

Something was hard up against her spine. Something virile and male. Gibb laughed.

"I can't make it go away, but I promise I will not let it do what it wants to. Ah, almost done." His matter-of-fact attitude helped Evangeline. She was mature enough to accept that sometimes close proximity could make people over-aware of each other. After all, her pulse was jumping and her muscles tight.

"There," Gibb said in satisfaction. "You should be able to step out of them now. One of the knots is too tight for me to move but this should do."

Her stays slid down and she stepped out of them. Now what? How to get into the shirt he gave her without baring her all. Maybe she should have said she would sleep in her shift? But then... *Oh shut up.* She moved from one foot to the other. "Er..."

Gibb snorted. "I promise to turn my back until you do whatever you have to do. I suggest you then get under the covers before you tell me it is all right to turn around."

That she could do. But never, she thought, in the history of mankind, had anyone pulled off their undergarments, struggled into a man's shirt and scrambled under the blankets as fast. She was panting when she told Gibb he could turn around. He did so slowly, looked at her and stood stock-still, like one of the statues in the park.

"You," he said in the voice of a man at the end of his tether, "appear as if you belong there."

Evangeline pushed an errant strand of hair behind her ear. Her plait hadn't stood up to all her frantic undressing and redressing without unravelling. "And?"

He shook his head. "I don't know."

If he didn't, she as sure as eggs were eggs didn't either. "Get into bed?" she suggested. "And we can relax."

"If you think that, you are very naïve, my dear," Gibb said as he pulled back the covers on the empty side of the bed. "But I hope we can be comfortable." He stretched out against the pillows and with a grin tugged his shirt down and pulled her into his side. "Now then." He put his arm around her and pressed her head to his banyan-covered chest. "Is that not comfortable?

His heart beat unsteadily under her cheek, comforting, shouting in some indefinable way 'security'. His arm circled her with warmth and slowly she relaxed.

"It is for me but…" She left her question unsaid. Was this a step too far? It felt intimate to her, but how did that affect Gibb? Was it going to mean he looked at her with annoyance, or told her he didn't want to stay friends? Lord, life was complicated.

Gibb tightened his arm and pressed a soft kiss to her hair before he laughed ruefully. "I can cope. Now go to sleep."

He turned the lamp to low and began to stroke her back in those rhythmic circles she had once used on him. Much to her surprise, she slid into sleep.

* * * *

In the dim light that filtered around the shutters Gibb moved his head, looked at the sleeping woman in his arms and willed his erection to subside. The lamp had long gone out and the room was lit by that glimpse of the eerie predawn sky. Someone, or both of them, had moved around enough during the night hours to bunch her borrowed nightwear around her waist and his own garment even higher. At some point he had inserted one long leg between her slender ones and now she was half over him, her soft contours molded to him, her long black tresses a cloak over his chest. Her breath disturbed the hairs on his neck and her arms were as tight around him as his were around her.

It was oh so beautiful. How difficult it was not to move and do what he craved. Especially when his staff was hard and his senses so aware of her. Would it be so bad? To fill her, take her, slake his thirst, his neediness, and make her his? His? Perhaps that was going too far. His for now maybe, but sadly, even that was not going to happen.

Still fast asleep, Evangeline scrunched up her nose and muttered something unintelligible. She shifted a little and took hold of some of his chest hair. A sweet, unbearable pain. Gibb began to move.

"No...n..." She muttered as her hold tightened and her other arm pressed even closer to him. Gibb watched and saw the exact moment Evangeline woke up, took in her surroundings and her present position and blushed. A blush he would love to trace and see where it covered.

"My apologies," he said, and did his best to ignore his erratic pulse and the soft, half-awake expression on her face. "We both seemed to know what was needed and took it." It was half true. He thought it better he didn't add that he had refrained from taking *everything* he desired.

Evangeline blinked and looked up at him skeptically. "And that is it?"

He shrugged and dropped a kiss on her nose. "Found out. No, not really. If we had done that, for my part we would be naked and I would be deep inside you."

If possible her blush deepened and she swallowed hard. "I would love that," she said and dropped her head back to rest on his chest. Did she speak wistfully? "But…"

"*But*," he agreed with a heavy heart and a dry mouth. "But maybe I can let you discover a little of what a man and woman can do? Without going too far. The choice, my dear, is yours." Gibb held his breath, conscious that he had made the biggest step ever in his post-Hester life.

He counted to thirteen before she nodded, and didn't reply. Would it be lucky or unlucky thirteen? Gibb opened his mouth to say not to worry, he understood that it was too much to ask. Evangeline put her fingers over his lips.

"Always you are impatient," she said solemnly. "This is a big decision for me and not to be rushed."

He nodded and stayed silent. Evangeline played with the hairs on his chest and wriggled as his erection did its best to be involved in her decision-making process. It was hell not to move his staff to a place where he might be able to tempt her to let him show her extra delights of the flesh, but Gibb held himself rigid. He would not seduce her into intimacy. *More intimacy,* he amended in his mind. After all, if semi-naked in each other's arms was not intimate, what was?

That thought made his heart miss a beat. He did not want intimacy. That led to dependence and heartache. But… Evangeline lifted her head and stared at his eyes.

"I think," she said, "I would like that."

New aches in places she'd never even known existed, Evangeline mused as she made her careful way down the internal stairs to Eloise's quarters the following evening. Gibb was attending Parliament for a debate and she and Eloise were about to have supper together. It was perhaps a good thing, she reflected, for Gibb and her to spend time apart. It would be all too easy to read more into their friendship than there perhaps was, and a little distance might clarify it for her. For Gibb, she had no idea and did not intend to press him for his thoughts on the subject.

She'd made a hearty cassoulet as her contribution to her and Eloise's supper, and was sure Eloise would have some of their favorite cheese and wine. It was the sort of evening they both enjoyed and never seemed to get often enough. Evangeline was aware that she spent a lot of time with Gibb, and hoped it didn't mean she had neglected Eloise. She vowed to ask her as soon as possible if it were the case.

She asked the question as soon as they were settled.

"Neglected me? Where on earth did you get that idea?" Eloise seemed surprised at the query as she began to pour them each a glass of deep red wine. She stopped when the glasses were only half full and held the decanter in the air. "I think, considering what busy lives we lead, we meet a lot. Now disabuse yourself of such stupidity and tell me how Vauxhall went. I'm agog to hear your version of events. My salon has been awash with twittering women and their versions, of which no two were the same. If I believed half of them you had a dancing bear, a naked man, three small people who threw knives at you and Denby Crowe being his usual obnoxious self."

Evangeline stared and shook her head to clear it. She blew hair out of her eyes and blinked. "Vaux... Ah, yes, Vauxhall, I forgot we have not had a chance to converse in any great depth since then." Had it been only four nights ago? It seemed like weeks, not days. "Take it from me the one grain of truth is Crowe, and apart from him it went as I hoped. It was, as you intimated, the place that Crowe, the imbecile, thought to interfere." She shuddered as she told Eloise the story and remembered what could have happened if Gibb had not held his nerve. "It was to his grace's fast thinking and disposition he didn't manage to do so. Instead it was he — Crowe — who was seen to be in the wrong. His sister also tried to entrap Gibb, in the manner you said she would. Thanks to your advance notice she was also thwarted."

"The besoms." Eloise appeared outraged. "What is the ton coming to?"

Evangeline laughed at Eloise's outraged expression and assumed the question was rhetorical. However, she chose to impart her thoughts on it. "As far as I know nothing is different from ages ago. All is fair in war and the ton. The upshot is that I believe Crowe and his sister are now out of the city and in shame. I wish I could say I am sorry, but it would be a lie." She recounted all else that had happened at the gardens. "Now I hope I can move on with my quest." She didn't mention Gibb or their recent togetherness. It was all too new to share. Plus, Evangeline was uneasily aware Gibb hadn't yet come to terms with how he considered this new stage. Perhaps she hadn't either.

"Be careful," Eloise warned her as she set the table. "Crowe will have friends who would back him up, and I swear the tabbies would do nothing to help you."

Evangeline nodded—it was something she was very aware of. "Of course not, but they would aid Gibb I trust?"

"Only if it were in their interest," Eloise said. "It's the system they live by. Now let's eat."

"This English society is so rigid and strange," Evangeline said as they sat down and she eyed their repast with hunger. "And stupid."

"At least they don't behead aristos without a good reason." Eloise poured some more wine into their goblets. "*A votre santé.*"

"*Et tu.* Hmm. Madame Guillotine. That's true." Evangeline rolled her eyes, speared a piece of meat and ate it without tasting it. "But there are other ways of crucifying someone. I would not wish that on Gibb, he's been through it once already. He's a gentleman, and, although I dare not tell him, he matters to me."

Eloise nodded. "Then take care, for the talk has started."

Evangeline knew and it worried her. Gibb might say it didn't matter but she understood differently. "I'm ready for this," she said, changing the subject abruptly. "It was simmering all day, so the gravy is perfect."

Eloise nodded. "And me. So now we eat, talk of something different and enjoy our wine. Where is your next engagement?"

* * * *

"I need it to swing all around in one sweep." Evangeline stood in Flood's—the wheelwright's— workshop and looked at the contraption in front of her. "And continue to do so as I work. I need to be able to trust the momentum and know it will decrease speed at a rate I can work with."

Gibb stood next to her and swung the overlarge wheel around in a lazy arc. "Won't it?" he asked. He gave it one thrust and watched as it went round and round. "There."

"That is all very well, but what about when I have someone on it? A man of oh…" Evangeline tilted her head and looked from him to the wheelwright and back again. "Around six foot tall and medium build."

Flood, a short rotund man, put his hands in the air. "Not me, I'd get dizzy. Anyhows, I'm too short and enjoyed too many of my Martha's dinners to be of any use. I reckons it's got to be you, your grace."

Gibb laughed. "Now why did I know you would say that? So, what do I need to do?" he asked Evangeline. He'd had an idea he would be inveigled into something like this when he'd collected Evangeline and accompanied her to see what Flood had come up with. To that end he had dressed in clothes that allowed for ease of movement. Comfortable knit pantaloons and a coat his valet would prefer to accidently-on-purpose lose. He discarded his jacket, tucked his cuffs up his sleeves and grinned as she chuckled.

"I'm well-trained, as you see," he said to Flood who stood, arms folded, and leaned on a sawhorse, watching the interplay with interest. "I do as I am bidden."

Evangeline rolled her eyes. "I'll remember that. Right, if you put your feet in the block on the swinging arc, take hold of the handgrips and hold on. Do you want tying down as my real vict…helper will?"

Gibb shook his head as Flood guffawed. "This will do. Now what?"

"Pray you will not vomit."

It was lucky he was never seasick, and held his own in a gale for the rocking motion — which rapidly changed to a whirl that blurred his surroundings — not unlike the movement of a ship at the mercy of the wind and waves. He closed his eyes and almost imagined he felt the wind and spray on him as he spun. Faintly he could hear Evangeline mutter as the wheel slowed and he rocked to a halt. Was she plotting how to throw her knives? No doubt that would come next, with him coerced into helping. The idea held no fears.

"Enough?" he asked as he rocked back and forth.

"Something needs to be altered," she muttered. "I do not for one moment think it is enough overall." He could tell by her expression she was trying to work something out.

"What? Oh, yes, sorry," Evangeline said, and held the wheel steady as he opened his eyes and blew his hair out of his eyes. "For now indeed. That was very useful."

Gibb got off and retrieved his jacket from Flood. "What next? Always have someone my size on it? Preferable, I think, someone who does not get nauseous."

She laughed. "Something like that." With an elegant movement that swished her skirts, she turned to Flood and shook his hand heartily. "Mr. Flood, you have done me proud. Thank you. It will work perfectly."

Flood blushed. "Made a nice change, it did, and it's good to have a customer who knows what they want."

"Then send your bill as soon as you can and I will settle it," Evangeline requested as she collected her reticule in preparation for leaving.

Flood looked at Gibb.

"What?" Evangeline asked, a suspicious expression on her face. "Oh, no," she said emphatically. "My act, my prop, my bill. Is that understood?"

Gibb sighed. She was a wilful lady. "Can I not give you this?"

She shook her head. "Thank you, no. I pay my way."

A flash of hurt hit him like one of her stilettos had struck him. Why was she so independent? It was a little thing he chose to do for her. What was the reason why she was so chary of any help? Look at the problems he had in getting her to accept the horse, for example. "It is nothing in the grand scheme of things, Evangeline." He did his best to explain his reasons to her. "A small present, that is all. Why not accept in in the manner it is given? In friendship."

"I need to know I can cope," she said. "I don't have the English words to explain," she said. "I have a fear I become reliant on anyone."

"You wouldn't," Gibb said emphatically as Flood looked on in interest. "I wanted to give you a present. I thought this more appropriate than rubies."

"Why? Oh, not rubies, but a present?" she asked, wide-eyed.

Gibb lashed a swift glance at Flood, who stood up. "I'm off to sort out a carrier for you, your grace."

Gibb waited until the other man was out of earshot. "For being my no-ties, no-dependency friend. You restored my faith in the female sex."

* * * *

"Opera dancers a touch too pricey for you, your grace? Got to downsize to a mere knife-thrower, have you? Mind you, for a body like hers I'd compromise my standards. Tell me." The bosky peer, a contemporary of Denby Crowe, swayed on his feet and leered at Gibb. His eyes were wild, his dress unkempt and his Hessians needed a good clean. Even here in the garden of one of the scions of the ton's London home, where a little dirt from the soil paths could be overlooked, he stood out for all the wrong reasons.

"Does she threaten to cut your staff off if it doesn't perform to her satisfaction?" Lord Allinson laughed and hiccoughed. "What's it worth, eh? Not to be a laughing stock. After all, a knife-thrower and a frog. Does she do everything in French? Must add an edge to it all. Thrust and parry and..." Allinson obviously saw the expression on Gibb's face, for his words faltered to a halt.

Gibb stared at him, uncaring of how the man broke out into a sweat and droplets slid down his shiny, ashen face. If the man saw menace and retribution when he looked at Gibb so be it. Ire, when icy, was a force to be reckoned with, and Gibb knew just how cold his anger was. No red-hot swift fury, but a rage that built slowly, inexorably stronger with each passing second. He counted to ten in his mind, relieved that no one else had been close enough to hear the exchange.

"Duelling may not be in fashion, but I would be happy to change that scenario for you," he said in a voice devoid of any emotion. "If you choose not to rescind your words and your character assassination." He could have expanded on his statement, but judged the menace greater if he did not.

The man in front of him sobered faster than Gibb thought possible and swallowed several times. Gibb watched Allinson's Adam's apple bob three times before he was able to speak.

"I, I, ah, apologize, your grace," he said rapidly. "My words were out of order."

"And?"

That one word made his lordship go even paler, if that was possible, and fiddle with his cuffs. His nails, Gibb saw to his disgust, were black with grime and badly bitten. Down on his luck and after a quick injection of cash perhaps?

"I take them back. They were spoken in a state of inebriation. It was not my intention to…to…" Allinson stuttered to a halt. "Ah, to suggest anything untoward." He swayed again and shut his eyes. "Please excuse me."

Gibb was not naturally a cruel man. He nodded. "I suggest you watch how much you imbibe in future." He didn't bother to add the warning he was sure would be expected with regards to himself and-or Evangeline. It was, he thought, a given. A sudden thought hit him as Allinson turned to leave. "Wait."

The man stopped dead in his tracks and looked up at Gibb in misery. "Your grace?"

"Who put you up to this?" Gibb asked. Allinson's expression became wary, a sure sign, Gibb thought, that it wasn't drunken bravado that had made Allinson behave as he had. More likely he'd had to get drunk to speak as he had. Gibb searched his mind for any more information he had about the man and his circumstances. Pitiful little. He was a good ten or twelve years younger, the son of a man who, if Gibb remembered rightly, had lost their fortune on the cards before he'd left for the continent, leaving his son to cope with the resulting mess. "Allinson, I know you wouldn't have done this without some reason. What is it?"

Allinson sighed and ran his hand through his hair. "Mama's mantua maker's bill and my sister's come out. I was asked to, to…"

"Annoy me?" Gibb said evenly. "At the risk of your own health."

Allinson nodded wearily. "To put it as mild as possible, that's about it. Hell, I know it was stupid to agree, but I'm in dire straits. I can *not* get it into my mama's head that we are unable to go on as we are. Cutbacks need to be made. If we retreated to the country I could perhaps salvage something from this mess, but she won't listen. To her, to keep face is the most important thing in the world. To me it is to keep a roof over our heads and food on the table, make sure the younger ones will have a life ahead of them without scandal and penury. Not to pay for dresses to be worn once, hats that are ugly and a ball for people who will still mock us." He shrugged. "That is it in a nutshell. The less-than-noble house of Allinson is broke. The coffers are empty."

"And Denby Crowe knew this and used it to his advantage?"

Allinson inclined his head. "He said if I was able to needle you into showing yourself up, he would pay me three thousand pounds."

Gibb whistled. "He is determined to ruin me, it seems. He will not succeed." He thought fast. "Scotch as many rumors about me and-or La Belle Evangeline as you can. Tell your parent you leave, all of you, for Cumbria at the end of the season, and if any more money is spent on fripperies you will lose your home. Do this and I will engage to pay those bills for you."

Allinson went red, white and red again and gulped. "Why?"

It was Gibb's turn to shrug. "Altruism, perhaps? Plus, I have a great distaste for people who try to benefit by using others' misery. I will undertake to purchase your townhouse from you, with the proviso you may use it during the season to enable your sister to make a good match. Does she have a dowry?"

Allinson nodded. "One that cannot be touched, I saw to that as soon as I could."

"Then do we have a deal?" Gibb held out his hand. Allison stared at it as if he had never seen a hand before then slowly shook it. "Good." Gibb smiled. "Come to see me in the morning and we will sort everything out. Not too early, I intend to watch the knife-throwing exhibition. Not as the assistant this time."

"Your grace, I…" Allinson sighed. "Thank you. You do have a heart and compassion, never let it be said that you do not. I will go and sort my mama out." He inclined his head and walked away.

Gibb stared at him as if he'd been struck. He did not want to have emotions.

This was wrong.

"I will not let my emotions become involved," he said out loud to himself and the sky. "I am just acting the gentleman. I will *not* let myself get involved in that way, ever again. I neither need nor want it." If he said it out loud it would be true?

* * * *

"I'm so pleased you were able to come and perform," Lady Arthur said, excitement in her tone. "Anne was beside herself when I told her. So often we poor women get to see nothing of interest, or if we do it is a small part. The fact you agreed to perform all of your show is perfect. I almost made this a ladies-only event and then I thought, no." She held her hand up in an arresting manner. "After all, it will do our so-called lords and masters good to see we are not shy, shrinking violets to be shielded from anything of…interest, shall I say. Oh yes, they are in for an unwelcome shock." She must have seen Evangeline's expression because she laughed. "I am a fervent follower of Mary Wollstonecraft. She has very good ideas on what women deserve and we do not get."

Evangeline nodded — she also agreed with a lot of that lady's ideas. "Then I better go and get ready to show the men what we women are capable of, eh?"

"And don't forget I'm your victim," Lady Arthur called after her. "I'm looking forward to it."

A lovely woman, Evangeline mused as she trod down the steps of the terrace and onto the path, dimly lit by sconces. She would make a good victim. They had gone over what was needed and Lady Arthur professed she was ready, willing and able, and Evangeline had no reason to doubt her.

As she rounded the last bend before the manicured lawns and her stage, Evangeline heard voices and slowed to detour around whoever it was. The last thing she needed was to be drawn into yet more conversations laced with sly innuendo with regards to her and Gibb.

Ahead she could see two men who blocked her way. Evangeline swore under her breath and stood behind a clump of bushes. Then if the men moved, she could use the most direct way toward the stage.

One voice came back to her clearly. Gibb! She didn't pretend not to eavesdrop, but stood where she was. Apart from him and a rustling in the undergrowth where she presumed a small creature was going about its nightly business, she could have been alone in the garden.

"I will not let my emotions become involved," she heard him say. As no one replied, she assumed whoever else had been there had left and he was talking to himself. Her heart went out to him. Did he not realize he already had let himself do so?

"I will *not* let myself get involved in that way, ever again. I neither need, nor want it."

Evangeline knew what it was like to be hurt, it had happened many times in her life. But never before had it hit her in such a visceral, gut-wrenching manner that she bent double with her arms wrapped round her waist. With a hastily bitten-back sob, she froze, unable to move or breathe. *Oh lord, what have I done?* What she now wanted to do was run and hide. To take her sorrow and wrap it around her like a cloak and sequester herself until that sharp, hell-like pain went away.

And she couldn't. She had a show to put on.

How will I cope? What if he watches, how do I pretend? With infinite care she drew upright and forced herself to take deep, calming and regular breaths. Cope she would, and her pride would allow no one to know what pain she was in. Deliberately she pinched her cheeks in such a way that they would once more have color, and walked along the dusty track to her stage. If she was said to perform an act, then act she would. Even if her heart had shattered into tiny pieces. For whatever she had thought, hearing Gibb speak so emphatically had made her understand she had given her heart to him. Now, knowing how he felt, she had to cope as best she could then move on.

* * * *

It was a small miracle that the show was perhaps the best she had ever given. Julia Arthur was brilliant, Evangeline thought, as hand in hand they took bow after bow. That lady had done everything as she had been asked, never flinched, and even stood firm when Evangeline had rocked the arc.

"I could use you all the time, my lady," she said as, after great applause and cheers, they left the stage and made their way behind the curtains. "You are a star and gave each and every member of our audience the perfect show." After the success of the evening, there was no formality between them. Julia had decreed it would be so, and for once Evangeline was happy to agree. She needed something good in her life, even though said life would never be the same again. "You made my act, and I think gave several ladies palpitations when you appeared in those britches. Thank you."

Lady Arthur giggled like a young girl as she looked down at her buckskin-clad legs. "My house, my rules, and to be honest I did tell Bertie what I was going to do. He laughed until I thought he was going into apoplexy and told me to go ahead and damn those who thought I should do otherwise. Therefore it is I who should be thanking you. This has been one of the best nights of my life," Julia declared. "If Bertie loses all his money on the 'Change I know where to come." She took Evangeline's chin in her hands. "At the risk of being told to mind my own business, why the bruised look and sad eyes?"

Evangeline bit back a sob, scowled and shook her head. She couldn't share her despair or break confidences. "It's nothing."

"Nothing does not make you look as if you have lost everything you deem of value," Julia said, as shrewd as ever. "Take that expression off your face, it would sour milk. For once I won't nag, but I will tell you this. Two things. First, do not give up on Gibb Alford, he is the most human he has been since that awful Hester episode. And second, you remind me of someone, and when I bloody remember who it is I will tell you. And I'm always here if you need a friend or a shoulder to cry on."

"That's three things," Evangeline said with a wobble in her voice. *Someone else who thinks I remind them of someone?* Her heart pounded. Perhaps she *was* getting to the end of her search.

"So? I never said I could count," Julia said unrepentantly. "Now, let's go and find some food and a large brandy. We both need it."

That was truer than she knew.

* * * *

The letter was damning. Cresswell was in need of urgent and immediate attention. Pugh had warned him it wasn't in the best condition, and when he and Evangeline had made their brief visit he'd had to agree. Even on that flying visit, he'd discovered the chimneys on one gable were crumbling, a new front door was a necessity and if he wanted a chef there a new range would need to be installed as a matter of urgency. Plus, he'd had to discover which staff would stay and who needed pensioning off.

Now there was nothing for it. He would have to go back again, and stay for a few days. Not just to see those he wished to do the jobs but to find staff to ensure those jobs were carried out successfully. And talk to the housekeeper and see if she could engage new servants for the house where necessary, and oversee them.

Why had he never realized how much needed doing? *Because I have always had other people to do it for me. I'm spoiled.*

However, he didn't want to leave Evangeline, and to have her by his side would be preferable to worrying. Would she go with him? If he didn't ask he'd never know. *It matters not if she refuses, it is a mere thought she might like to get out of the capital for a few days, nothing else.* Gibb went over his next few appointments in his mind. If she could work with him, they should be able to have four or five days at Cresswell. Long enough to discover what sort of state it was in. Long enough to become closer friends? He shut that line of thought off abruptly. Closer was not what he wanted, was it?

Disgruntled, uncharacteristically out of sorts, he found his hat and left the house. A few hours in Jackson's salon might help him to get into a better frame of mind.

* * * *

It did. Several close friends were there, Henry being one of them, and Gibb enjoyed the banter, the boxing and the bruise Henry inflicted on him. Who was most surprised was a close-run thing. By the time several of them made their way to White's — he never favored one club above another as a lot of his peers did — Gibb had lost his introspective mood, and when he reached home he was once more on an even keel. He'd see Evangeline later and put his proposal to her.

If his staff were surprised to see him dining at home, they were too well-trained to show it. The meal was tasty and full of flavor but something was lacking. Halfway through his postprandial port he realized what it was.

Company.

How pathetic. He was lonely. When was the last time he had admitted to that state of affairs? He had no idea. Gibb contemplated his port and sighed. What was happening to him? This attitude was alien to him. Made him uncomfortable, and wary. If he wanted someone with him, what next?

Neediness? Never. He wouldn't visit Evangeline that evening. After all, it was not a firm engagement, only if he was in the area. Therefore he would not be. Nor would he invite her to Cresswell. There was no need.

He stared into the fire and counted the ticks of the mantel clock. After eighty he tossed off the port and left the house to head to Evangeline.

* * * *

"That's enough." Evangeline slapped her hands on each of his chair arms and glared at Gibb. He looked somewhat amazed at her sudden outburst and she didn't care. Enough was enough.

"Whatever black dog is riding you, lose it now or go home," she said. "You have been nothing but morose since you got here. Almost as if you were coerced. And that, I assure you, was not the case. Now either treat me as the friend you say I am and share what is wrong, or go and sort it out. Either way, you are not going to continue to sit there as you are at the moment. If you looked at some mother's milk you would curdle it."

He gave a short, humorless laugh. "That's a fine description. I thank you."

"For goodness' sake." Could she get away with plain speaking? Why not, Evangeline decided. Something had to be said, and straight talk was no doubt the best way to get through to him. "I implore you to listen to yourself. You came in, gave me the most perfunctory embrace ever known to man or woman. Sat in the chair, and played with that goblet. I swear the contents will be giddy along with me as I watched you fidget. Then you answered everything I said with a grunt or a monosyllabic reply and look as if you'd rather be anywhere else but here. If that is the case, just go."

She straightened up and forced herself not to stand arms akimbo.

Gibb sighed. "Was I that bad?"

She shook her head. "Oh no."

"Thank the lord for that."

"Don't get complacent. You were worse. Much worse." The misery in his eyes melted her annoyance. After all, she'd known to be his friend would not be all sweetness and light, so why, on the first occasion since he had opened up to her and spoken about his wife he was in a black mood, was she so annoyed?

Because he seemed to be moving on. Because it is one more sign that he will not let me into his life. Because the time for me to say goodbye is getting ever closer. Because I would like more. And I know I will not get it.

"Gibb, friendship means sharing. I'm not asking for you to fall onto my shoulder and sob all over me, heaven forbid. Or think I can do that to you. But if something is troubling you, why keep it to yourself?

You said you wanted to be my friend. This blow hot and blow cold is wearing, and, not to put too fine a point on it, unhelpful." Would he understand or choose not to do so? It was bad enough to know their future together was limited, but she had reluctantly accepted that she had to bide her time and let him take things at his pace. But this night he seemed to have regressed.

"Do you want to end our friendship?" she asked in an undertone, hoping he didn't agree it was the thing to do. One day it would happen but, pray god, not yet. Butterflies danced inside her and her palms itched. "Is this where you think things are all too much for you?"

"What?" He looked up at her, startled. "Good lord, no. I'm just blue devilled. I have to go to Cresswell and I'd prefer to stay here to keep an eye on you. Crowe may have left, his cronies haven't."

"Cresswell again so soon?" She ignored the comment about Crowe and his cronies. She could and would sort them if necessary.

"If I don't go and start the work that is needed it will crumble and become a ruin with the first frost of winter according to Pugh. I can't let that happen."

"Have you decided if you're going to live there?" The love when he spoke of his godmother made her wonder.

Gibb shook his head before he ran his hands through his hair. One perfect brutus cut was now a mess. "Oh no. Or not often, although I will visit until I decide what to do with it. I just want it restored to how my Godmama loved it."

And he says he cannot and does not have emotional feelings about anything or anyone. Rubbish.

"That seems a good thing to do," Evangeline said. "When do you leave?"

He smiled wryly. "I hope to persuade you that it will be when do *we* leave," Gibb said. "If we could perhaps fit a few days there together. I'd value your input about the house and gardens once more. You seemed to enjoy our day there, and a woman's view is always welcome."

Any woman, or me?

"A French knife-thrower?"

"My friend," Gibb said in a way that brooked no argument. "Who happens to be both French and a knife-thrower."

* * * *

Four days of pleasure was not too much to ask, Evangeline decided on the fourth day at Cresswell, as she swung her bonnet in one hand and held Gibb's with the other. She deserved some.

Here, Gibb was a changed man. Relaxed, in casual country clothes, with his hair bleached at the tips by the strengthening sun, his arms a deep, burnished bronze and his worn Hessians and leather waistcoat, he could be taken for a country squire. He laughed with the workers they met, gave clear and concise directions with regards to how he wanted the estate to be run and, Evangeline thought, made friends with each and every person now in his employ.

They had reserved rooms in the village hostelry, two very elegant chambers, side by side but not connected, and Gibb had introduced her as a friend who was going to help him sort out the house. If anyone thought it meant they had an understanding of the to-be-married variety, no one mentioned it. Instead she was welcomed wholeheartedly. If that in itself seemed strange to Gibb he didn't mention it, and Evangeline wanted nothing to mar their time together so she chose not to comment.

For, even if he didn't realize something momentous was soon to happen, she did. This would be their last time alone. Evangeline had come to the sad but inevitable conclusion they couldn't go on as they were and nor would she ask him to alter his opinion of who he thought he was. If he couldn't come to terms with his changing persona and see himself for who he had become, she wasn't going to do it for him. It was unfortunate, her emotions were involved and she could not change that. So, cowardly or sensibly — she wasn't sure which — she had decided she'd have to draw back.

But not yet. First, she would enjoy these few days.

The picnic basket, packed by the housekeeper and carried by Gibb as they made their way across the field toward the river, was heavy, but he held it as if it weighed no more than a feather. Evangeline knew that was not the case. She'd watch it being packed. A bottle of champagne wrapped in a cold cloth along with two goblets, ham, cheese and fresh-from-the-oven bread. Tiny cakes, some pastries, lots of early fruit from the ageing session houses and several handfuls of nuts completed the repast. How they were expected to eat it all she had no idea.

But then Gibb was a big man with an appetite commensurate with his size. No doubt he would make good inroads into it.

She mentioned it to him and he laughed. "The more I eat, the less there is to carry home. A winning situation, I'd say." His expression was animated, his face carefree and he appeared ten years younger.

What was it about this place that did that? He'd told Evangeline his heart was in Scotland so why now did he seem so happy? She pondered how best to ask him as they reached the riverbank and he spread a blanket over the grass under a willow tree. Its drooping branches created a cool, welcoming haven from the sun.

Evangeline tossed her hat to the ground and sank onto the blanket as her skirts billowed around her. She stretched her arms above her head as Gibb eased out the cork on the champagne with a gentle pop, filled two goblets and leaned them against the picnic basket.

"One for you when you're ready." He made his way to the water's edge and sank the bottle into its cool depths.

He turned and wiped his wet hands on his buckskins before he slipped his jacket off and rolled it into a ball. Once he reached Evangeline he dropped it behind her back. "There you are. *Voilà*, one pillow. Relax and enjoy the peace."

She grinned and kicked her sandals off to wriggle her scandalously bare feet in the lush grass at the bottom of the blanket before she took the proffered glass. "Thank you." She took a sip and savored the fresh tingles it left on her lips and the way it slid down her throat, citrusy and oh so French. "I so love this. It goes with this place." She gestured to their surroundings with her glass. "Oops." The liquid had almost spilled. "Too good to throw away."

Gibb laughed. "True enough." He opened the picnic basket. "Food?"

"Eh?" Evangeline opened her eyes, which she hadn't even realized she had closed. "Not yet." She yawned. "Lud, I am so tired. Why is it the noise of the clock on my landing, the lamplighter, street sweepers and raucous revelers never bothers me in town, but the clock on this landing, the owl in the nearest tree and the fox coughing in the copse keeps me awake here?"

"Different bed?"

She shrugged and sipped some more champagne, embarrassed to show herself as perhaps ungrateful. "It could be, but this bed is as comfortable as mine in town. The pillows are feather, the sheets silk and the room as dark or as light as I want it. Ah, one of life's imponderables I fear." She yawned again. "Sorry."

Gibb plucked the half-full glass from her lax fingers. "Stretch out and relax for a while. We're in no hurry."

"Hmm." Evangeline wriggled until her head rested on his jacket. "I'll just rest my eyes."

Chapter Ten

Back in their favorite spot under the willow tree, Gibb chewed a blade of grass and watched a kingfisher as it swooped down to the water. Its iridescent wings reminded him of the woman sleeping by his side. Quicksilver, bright and fascinating. A woman with secrets, but also open, warm and… And what? A woman made for loving, but not by him.

A woman who reached out to his soul, but he dared not let her in. *Dare not* give anything back. A woman he wanted to care for but… Gibb sighed. And therein was the problem. That tiny word with a big meaning. *But.* He couldn't do it to her. Try to be all she deserved and perhaps be found lacking.

Cowardly, maybe, but better in the long run, no doubt.

What if you were able? a tiny voice niggled him. He ignored it. After all, he knew he wasn't — didn't he?

Beside him Evangeline sighed in her sleep and muttered something he didn't catch. Gibb stretched out his legs until he lay next to her and her soft breath caressed his cheek. How easy it would be to lean over and undo the ribbons at her neck. Lower the dainty sleeves down her arms and slide her dress to her waist. To feast on her luscious breasts once more, and revel in the soft mewls and gasps she would make. To lift her skirts and find that soft feminine place, to tease those curls and…

His staff rose and hardened to the point of pain in anticipation of what could happen.

On arrival at Cresswell, they had talked and decide not to consummate their relationship and complicate it by sex. Loving caresses, hot and heated kisses, had been exchanged on more than one occasion, but Evangeline was adamant she would take no chances on becoming pregnant. Gibb had to commend her, even if it did give him uncomfortable nights, where he stayed awake and thought of ice-cold baths or took himself in hand. At those times he was grateful they occupied different rooms. Here, away from town, it had been both their decision not to put too much temptation in their way.

Apart from themselves, only the elderly housekeeper was around and it would have been oh so easy to give in to temptation without fear of anyone knowing. But… He shrugged as he thought of the happiness of the last few days. It had been for the best.

However, they had to return to town tomorrow, he had to vote, and sex with Evangeline was something he'd thought long and hard about. Maybe if he was careful and withdrew?

Gibb had moved one hand to her shoulder when she opened her eyes and blinked sleepily at him.

"Hello. Was I asleep long?" Her voice was low and her accent definitely French. "It seems my nights awake have caught up with me." She stretched and her thin gown tightened over her breasts, her nipples clearly outlined under the fine material.

He spat out the grass, cleared his throat and dropped his hand onto the blanket between them to shield his reaction. His staff now pushed against his buckskins so hard he wondered how durable they were. "Asleep? Not long."

"Ah."

Why was the silence no longer comfortable? Had she noticed his state of arousal? But why should that affect her so. They had discussed it, she had touched him and he her. They might not have consummated their relationship but nigh on as good as. Just not taken that final step.

"I almost…"

"I wondered…" They spoke over each other.

Gibb nodded. "You first."

She smiled. "I almost asked you what you were thinking. You looked pensive."

He shrugged. "I was about to break our agreement and try to coerce you to take me inside you."

She looked at him, her face expressionless. "To… Ah, you mean to make love. But we agreed it would not be a good idea. That we use those other ways you have shown me to sate ourselves."

"I was about to try and persuade you to have sex," he corrected and ignored the stricken look in her eyes. What was the point in using flowery language and trying to make it into something it wasn't? "However, I decided better of it."

Evangeline smiled, although it didn't reach her eyes. "A good thing," she said with a slight quiver to her voice. "It would complicate things."

He nodded and pulled her into a sitting position. "I have a proposition."

"I thought you changed your mind?"

"No, not sex," he said with a patience he hadn't thought he had. "This is of a different sort." Gibb cleared his throat. "I wondered if you would like to live here."

"Here?" she replied incredulously. "At Cresswell?"

He inclined his head. Where else did she think he meant? Under the damn willow tree? "At Cresswell."

"But why?" Evangeline asked. She seemed bewildered. "What for?"

"Why not? It is simple. I thought you might like to have the opportunity to live away from the capital."

"But my livelihood is in London. How can I live elsewhere?"

"If you lived here you would have no need to work. Everything necessary would be here. So what do you say?"

"Why?" she asked once more. "Explain."

"Why what?" he asked, irritable and out of sorts. At this rate they would be going round in circles ad infinitum. "I told you why."

Evangeline shook her head and curls sprang from their pins and danced around her head. "You told me part of it. What would I be here as? A friend? Your lover... Oh no, I forgot, not a lover. A mistress? Someone to help you scratch your itch?"

"That is unfair and you know it," Gibb said stiffly. "I just thought it might be nice for you to have a bolt hole. Somewhere to relax and not be worried with knives, nuisances or the ton."

"Then, my dear Gibb, perhaps you should have thought about how to phrase your offer before you spoke about it. For that is not at all how it came across."

"My apologies. I've never offered anyone anything like this before. So, what is your answer?"

"I'll let you know when I've thought about it."

Her noncommittal answer was like a red rag to a bull. Inflammatory. "What is there to think about, woman? A simple yes or no will suffice." He forced himself to unclench his hands and relax. "Please."

"Then no." She stood up, shook out her skirts then shivered theatrically. "I should have brought my shawl. Perhaps we ought to make our way back? It's getting cold."

It wasn't, but Gibb was not about to argue. Why were things going so wrong?

* * * *

Two hours later Evangeline wished she had a glass of brandy in her hands, if only to stop them shaking.

"Say that again," Gibb said in a flat, dangerous voice. He'd removed his cravat and loosened his waistcoat in the manner he often did when they relaxed together. "Look me in the eyes and tell me once more what you have just said." He paused and scrutinized her in such a way she wanted to crawl into a hole and stay there. "If you dare."

"I dare, for why should I not?" she said with more composure than she felt. Her heart thudded so hard it was a wonder it wasn't heard in the room. "I think it is time we accepted we need to spend time apart. Not to be involved in any way. You, my lord, have been very kind but—"

"Kind?"

His roar was so loud she flinched. Thank goodness they were not at home. His shout would have brought servants — or Eloise — running thinking he was mortally wounded. To know they had any idea of her and Gibb's true circumstances would be galling in the extreme. They might wonder, but they did not know. Even Eloise had no more than the bare facts.

The grandfather clock in the hall chimed the hour and Evangeline jumped. This was not going as she had envisioned. She had anticipated he would be pleased she no longer needed his attention. How wrong could she be?

"You think I've been kind," he said in such an icy voice she flinched. "I offered you this house, a life without idiots annoying you and no need to earn your living by throwing knives at people and you dismiss it so. Thank you for nothing." Gibb paced across the room and swung around to point at her in accusation. "All this time, summed up thus. *Kind.*" He made it sound as if it were a disease. Perhaps to him it was.

"What else would you call it?" she replied and clenched her hands into fists. This was so much harder than she had anticipated. Nevertheless, it was all for the best. If she could get him to understand and let her cry in peace, she wouldn't have to face the ignominy of telling him how she felt about him, and see him reject her emotions. "I appreciate you offering me this house." *And not putting any conditions on my occupancy.* "You have helped me, given me backing and much more. I have lo…liked every moment. But… I'm sorry, Gibb, I can*not* carry on as we are. As you insisted no emotions could be or would be involved, what else would you have me call it?" She held her breath. Had she misheard him?

He inhaled long and hard. "I am not kind. I dare not do emotions. You know that."

"I know you choose not to," Evangeline replied. "And I also know we cannot carry on as we are. Therefore I decided to say enough is enough. Time for us both to move on. Before we do anything we might regret." *Like taking you inside me and becoming yours in every way possible.*

Gibb rubbed his eyes. "You have it all planned out, don't you? Then there is no more to be said. I'll remove myself from your presence forthwith and…" He shook his head and thumped the bureau with one hard fist. A decanter and three glasses jumped up and tinkled as they rubbed together. He stared at them blankly and Evangeline forced herself not to move.

It has to be done.

"And?" she said, determine to be polite, even though she quaked inside.

"And nothing, except stay at Cresswell for as long as you want. There are rooms furnished comfortably now. You could stay and enjoy them."

Before she had a chance to react Gibb spun on his heel and took the three steps necessary to reach her. She looked up at his dark eyes and winced at the pain she discerned. Her fault?

"Hmm, now I think of it, there *is* one thing more. This." Gibb grabbed her roughly by the shoulders and drew her into a long, hard, tongue-meshing kiss.

Evangeline stood rigid for several seconds then let herself lean into him. If this was goodbye she'd enjoy it and think about later a long time later.

She hardly had time. Gibb pulled back and looked at her with torment uppermost in his expression. "Damn you." He stalked out and slammed the door behind him.

Evangeline listened as his steps faded as he stomped along the corridor and the outer door banged with such force she could swear the building shook.

He didn't need to damn her, she was damned already.

* * * *

"I told you I'd remember who you reminded me of," Julia said as, a week or so later, she passed a porcelain cup so fine you could almost see through it to Evangeline. The scent of bergamot which came from the tea teased Evangeline's senses and made her mouth water. Good tea was not something she treated herself to very often. Good coffee, now, that was another matter. A day couldn't start without coffee. Luckily Eloise thought the same and always had a supply she shared with Evangeline.

"Someone in England?" Evangeline asked and hoped she didn't sound as flustered and apprehensive as she felt. She sipped her tea and hoped the cup wouldn't rattle as she rested it with care in the saucer. Her hands were not only shaking, but also clammy. Surreptitiously she wiped them on her skirts and accepted a tiny, fancy cake of marchpane. "To my knowledge I have no relatives here." She crossed her fingers. After all, it wasn't a total lie. She didn't know. Only hoped and wondered.

Lady Arthur finished her cake and dusted her hands together. "Right, my dear, this is the interesting part.

You know I scratched my head over it all. I mean, I know a lot of people, and Bertie even more. We're not exactly private people, we enjoy a good social life. And Bertie of course has all his political colleagues and card partners, hunt companions and so on. Between us we know most of the ton and its hangers-on. But could I think who it was?" Her eyes twinkled. "More tea?"

"Oh yes, please." Evangeline held out her cup and wondered when the other woman would get to the point. The summons — for it could be called nothing else — to come for tea had been unexpected. After all, not by any stretch of the imagination could they be considered to be equals. However, Evangeline knew she could not and did not want to refuse. So here she was in her best day dress, understated — she hoped — in its elegance, with an uneven pulse and goosebumps, a dry mouth and a hollow stomach, waiting to discover whom she was supposed to resemble.

The journey to Julia's had to Evangeline's mind been unnerving. At every corner she'd looked for a certain dark head, for someone who walked like Gibb. Once she thought she saw him only to look into the face of a stranger. The sense of disappointment had been so deep she'd wondered if she had done the correct thing in sending him away. After all, she dreamed of him, awoke reaching for him, to find herself alone and in bed. She hadn't heard his laugh, hadn't felt his lips pressed to hers, hadn't...

"Now where was I?" Julia asked, and wrenched Evangeline's mind back to the present as she replaced the teapot on its sculpted stand and settled down in her chair. "Ah yes, your almost-double. I say almost because, my dear," she leaned forward in a dramatic fashion, "it is a man." She sat back again. "What do you think of that?"

"A man?" It was difficult, but Evangeline pushed Gibb to the back of her mind. Was this going to be the end of her quest? Or the beginning of another phase? "Do you now remember who?"

"Of course I do, or why else would I have demanded you come today?" Julia asked in a pseudo-patient way. "I'm not so autocratic that I expect someone to drop everything and cede to my every whim immediately." She laughed. "I tend to demand they appear the next day."

Her humor was infectious, and even though she was too churned up to laugh, Evangeline had to smile. "Such forbearance," she said and stopped short. Julia made it all too easy for Evangeline to forget her place. "I'm sorry, that was rude."

"Not at all," Julia said. "Just truthful however you want to think differently. I have decided we are friends, and friends, my dear, do not stand on ceremony with each other."

"I'm a miller's daughter." *Perhaps.*

Julia raised one eyebrow. "My father was an out-and-out rogue who, I believe, was happy to live his days out in the West Indies. Grandpapa was a slave trader and my great grandpapa a pirate so we won't talk about our predecessors. I'm impatient by nature, and I can't stand people who shilly-shally, and I've been guilty of that just now, haven't I? No, don't answer, it's a rhetorical question. So, my dear, have you ever heard of Le Duc d'Astre?"

Evangeline's heart missed a beat and a sense of despair filled her. The name meant nothing. "No. Who is he, an émigré?"

"Now that is the interesting thing. Oh — " She broke off and pushed the plate of cakes in Evangeline's direction. "Do eat up or I'll have to, because if I send them back the chef will sulk, and if you make me have any more Eloise will complain I've put on weight again and she'll have to adjust my new ballgown. Now Iain d'Astre. What do you think of that for a name, eh?"

Evangeline wondered what she was supposed to say? Attractive? Unusual? Horrible? "Er…" She rolled the name around in her mind. French and Scottish. "He is from a family who supports *Le Vieille Alliance*? The Old Alliance," she elaborated as Julia looked at her blankly.

"Ah yes, it seems so. Of course, Bertie said I must not question Iain, which seems somewhat unfair, because how else can we discover if he is a relative of yours? All I know is that his father was French and died during the revolution, and after some time, he — Iain, not his dead father — came to England with his mother. Which," Julia rattled on cheerfully, "is another strange thing. Because Marie, his mother, has sadly passed on now, but she was from Scotland, so why on earth he chose to settle in Rutland is beyond my comprehension. So, what do you think?"

All that with scarcely a breath. How on earth did she do it? Evangeline felt lightheaded just listening to her. "What made you remember?" It was the one thing Evangeline could think to say.

"Because I saw him," Julia said, as if her answer was a foregone conclusion. "And thought immediately he was a masculine version of you. Or should that be you are a feminine version of him? Whichever, you look alike. Same eyes and brows, same nose. Almost, for his is bigger of course. You even quirk your lips in a similar manner, except your eyes are sad. What has happened? Do I need to give Gibb Alford a piece of my mind?"

She looked like a fierce sparrow. Even though she didn't want to, Evangeline smiled. "No, it is not his fault, it is mine. I," she hesitated, "I felt too much, Julia, and he is adamant he feels nothing. Rather than make him undergo the pain of thinking he had let me down, I chose to end our…to be honest I'm not sure what you would call it…friendship…on his part, which could have developed into heartache on mine."

"And it hurts," Julia said shrewdly.

"Oh yes it hurts," Evangeline said as a rush of pain flooded through her. "But it will pass, I'll make it so. Right." She took a deep breath. "Le Duc d'Astre?"

"Your little finger bends in the same place."

She's even noticed my little finger? How odd. The digit in question had a definite kink above the knuckle.

"So strange to see all your characteristics in him and his in you," Julia said. "I was aching to find out more."

"You saw him?" Black spots danced in front of her eyes. Was she going to faint? Please not, it would be so embarrassing and not at all helpful. He was here? He might hold the secrets to her past.

"Most definitely I saw him. That was how I remembered. I say, are you all right? You've gone the most peculiar color." Julia patted her cheek. "Drink some tea." She held the cup up to Evangeline's mouth.

Evangeline took it from her, noted her hands were almost steady again, sipped the lukewarm contents. It was liquid and moistened her tongue, that was all that mattered. "It's warm in here," she said lamely. "I felt overheated for a second. I'm fine now."

"Hmm, I'm not so sure. I'll open the window." Julia strode across the room and suited her actions to her words. "There now, that's better. So you don't know Iain? Or of him?"

Evangeline shook her head.

"What a pity. I'd wager my pin money you're related. Now let's see how we can discover just how." Julia sat back in her chair and looked deep in thought. Then she blinked and clapped her hands. "I have it."

It was as well someone did, Evangeline decided, because she was totally at sea. "As in?" she asked with caution.

"As in how you two can accidentally meet. You always wanted to be my companion, didn't you?"

"I did?"

"Of course you did. Because tomorrow afternoon we are going for a stroll in the park, and oh my what a coincidence we will just happen to be walking past the end of St. James, not up it, so don't worry, we are not going to be scandalous, when Bertie and Ian are off to their club. I know for a fact they're at Tattersall's earlier, and that is another place we can't go to. So subterfuge will be the order of the day. What do you say to that?"

"Do you ever draw breath as you speak?"

Julia roared with laughter. "Not often, no, or I forget my thread. Are you up for it?"

It sounded plausible except for one thing. "No one will believe I'm your companion." Which was a pity, because now the butterflies in her stomach were of the excited variety.

"They will, you know," Julia said. "For some strange reason people accept everything I do or say at face value. You did tell me you have no engagements over the next week or so, didn't you?"

Evangeline nodded. There seemed to be a lull in bookings before they picked up again and she had done nothing to find any more. She'd mentioned it to Julia when that lady had asked her how her occupation was progressing.

"Then that works perfectly. You do want to discover if you and Iain are related, don't you?" Julia asked, in a cajoling manner. "Because I do."

* * * *

The long ride north should have helped Gibb come to terms with Evangeline's frank demand. After all, what else could he do but check he was headed in the correct direction—he was. Make sure his horse didn't overexert himself—it didn't. And think about recent events. That he did a lot of.

The first day, it was late by the time he left the capital. Even so, he made good progress, buoyed up by a sense of grievance he chose not to delve into. He spent the night in a comfortable inn, rested his horse and chose to go on with it the following day, rather than take a chance on one he was unaccustomed to. Then he'd swap to others and arrange for Challenger to be sent back to London.

Sadly, from then on things went downhill fast. A combination of rain, sun and more rain had turned the Great North Road into a quagmire in places. Progress was slow. Boggy roads, horses that should be dog meat and not allowed on any public highway were thrust on him. Therefore instead of coming to terms with what in actuality was a very reasonable request by Evangeline, he brooded. In his mind it became anything but and festered. With the addition of two of his favorite inns regretful but unable to accommodate him, and nights spent in unaired beds with inferior food and drink, his unreasonable mood grew. When he at last crossed the border into his beloved Scotland several long riding days later it had become totally out of proportion. Now he accepted he was more irate than he had been at first. Why, oh why did she want him out of her life? What had he done to deserve such cavalier treatment? He'd tried to help her — *had* helped her — thought they were friends, then this.

What haven't you done? A nasty niggle invaded his brain and lodged there. He did his best to ignore the words that crawled over him like a snake on a mission. *I told her no emotion. No reliance, nothing. Just friends. But what is a friend?* Words and excuses, ideas and resolutions whirled around in his mind until by the time he'd got to within a good day's ride of his beloved castle it was difficult to hold his head up and check his route. Cold winds, rain and sunshine, a late frost and he swore several flakes of snow, gave him all four seasons in half an hour as he let his weary horse climb the steep hill to a comfortable inn he used when he visited Edinburgh. If it was full he'd sleep in the stables.

His luck held. It wasn't and within the hour he slid under the water of a deep and steaming bath and sighed as his weary body relaxed. Had he done the right thing? True, he'd had to come north at some point, but he'd run like a sullen schoolboy thwarted for the first time then compounded everything by sulking.

How childish. He was thoroughly ashamed of himself. After all, Evangeline had merely accomplished something he would have done himself before too long. *Why am I so out of sorts about that?* Gibb soaped his chest, ducked his head under the water and pulled himself into an upright position once more. He shook his head and watched droplets of water bounce off the surface of his bath, over the edge of the tub and onto the carpet.

Why?

Too much introspection made his head hurt. Or was that the sore throat and cough he'd developed? Whichever, Gibb got up from the bath in one fluid motion, toweled himself dry and drank a large dram as he dressed in his kilt — normal attire in his homeland — and adjusted his sporran. Lowlanders might think a sporran an unnecessary item of clothing, or even pretentious, but he chose to think differently. His sporran was old, worn, and held all his immediate needs on his travels, including a pistol.

Not that he thought he'd need it in The Thistle, but old habits died hard. Gibb finished his dram and made his way downstairs to be greeted by McAra, the landlord, and shown to his favorite private parlor.

It was amazing what a good meal could do to an irritable mood. After putting away the best part of a game pie and several slices of rare roast beef and quaffing a large tankard of McAra's best home brew, Gibb felt a lot better and more able to ruminate over the events of the past week or so.

The knife-thrower. Her independence, feistiness and talent.

The matchmaking mamas. Their annoying ways and machinations.

The desperate debs. The same as their mamas.

His friends. Loyal to a fault.

Himself. A pig-headed, ignorant, stupid, couldn't-see-what-was-in-front-of-him-or-in-his-heart idiot.

Evangeline… Here he paused. And what about Evangeline?

Had he missed something vital? If he had, could he admit it? He was too tired to fathom that out. He took himself to his empty bed.

* * * *

Hard manual labor was a wonderful way of ensuring one slept a good eight hours out of every twenty-four, Gibb decided several weeks later. It was a pity it didn't stop all his dreams. Gibb dragged himself up the stone stairs to the laird's chambers in the turret each night and had to force himself not to fall asleep in the bath. He ate without tasting the food, drank his dram without savoring it and dropped into bed as if he'd been felled.

And dreamed. Snatches of how he'd spoken to Evangeline. How he'd stroked her skin, the softness, her curves and hollows there for him to discover. Shown her how a man and a woman could enjoy each other's bodies without risking pregnancy. Reveled in the way she touched him, caressed him and brought him to completion. Heard her soft voice with its enticing accent speaking to him. "My Gibb." And pulled back when he thought she might be getting under his skin.

Then she'd had enough. Could he blame her? That question stayed unanswered.

Three weeks of outdoors work alongside his estate workers followed his arrival north. He shared the midday lunches of his workers, quaffed their ale and added a basket of pies and pastries from the castle kitchen to each meal eaten sitting against the new barn walls. He always remembered another basket to be shared among their families, for although he was a generous employer, treats never went amiss. Putting in the same long hours they did gave Gibb a healthy respect for just how damn lucky he was with his staff. To say nothing of a leaner, harder body and a golden tan. It was unfortunate it didn't give him peace of mind or a decent night's sleep.

Plus, according to McTavish, his longest-serving worker, who, these days was more of a foreman than a grafter, he wore a look no man should ever have. Unless he'd just laid his mother to rest or lost his fortune at cards. Gibb couldn't explain it was neither and felt like both. Instead he tried to laugh it off. McTavish said nothing else until at the end of the third week. On the Friday Gibb decreed the new barn perfect, the hedges as he wanted them and the dry stone walls nigh on finished. There would be, he declared, a *ceilidh* to christen the new building on Saturday night with food and drink provided by the castle.

As his workers thanked him and made their weary ways home, McTavish hung back. Gibb ducked his head in the horse trough, shook it so as much water as possible fell onto the ground, not his sweat-soaked shirt, wiped his face on his neckerchief and picked up his jacket.

"All right, Gregor, spit it out," he said, short of temper and out of sorts. "I've a dram waiting with my name on it. Two drams even." He wanted to sink into a bath with the whisky and do nothing.

"Go and see her and sort yersel oot laddie." The man's normal thick local dialect became almost unintelligible when he was emotional. As then. "Thons nae daein anyone any good like y'are the noo. We need a laird, no a tattieboggle."

"Are you saying I look like a scarecrow?" Gibb asked, amused at the comparison. Indeed, he was wearing his oldest clothes and he could do with a haircut and to trim his beard, but he'd thought he had a better body than one purporting to scare the crows away. "I thought I was fitter than when I arrived."

"Ah, yae are ben the body, but nae in yer soul," the old man said and spat into a nearby ditch. "It's got to be a wimman. Nae'an else could get ye like that. Got ye by the baws has she? Ach weeel, it's aboot time ye forgot thon besom ye were marrit to." He spat on the ground. "Respect fer the deid has tae be earned. She didnae."

Gibb shrugged his jacket on. "No," he said. "She didn't earn anyone's respect, did she? I'm sorry for what you all had to endure at her hands." On the rare occasion she had visited the castle, his late wife had never said or done anything positive to endear herself to the people of the estate — anything but. Gibb couldn't say who was happiest when she no longer visited, him, her or them.

"Ha, we didnae get much o' her. You did. Anyhoo now it's over, eh? Time ta move on."

"I hope so." *If she'll let me after the way I have behaved.*

"Ach, yer nee tae dae sommat or you'll be a lang streak o' misery." McTavish doffed his cap, cackled and ambled off down the track to his croft.

Gibb watched him go and smiled. Trust the old man to say it as he saw it, and do it in such a way as to make Gibb listen. He watched until McTavish disappeared and turned on his heel to make his own way home. There was, he noticed, a purpose to his steps that hadn't been there before. He had plans to finish the work started and also ideas for the work he hoped to accomplish.

Would Evangeline listen to him if he sought her out on his return to London? Could he now put Hester behind him? Dare he trust and love again? Was he prepared to open up his life and his heart to someone else? To share his thoughts, words and needs with that person and be prepared to do the same for them? The questions whirled through his mind. Too much information to sift through in one fell swoop. He needed to be able to think in a rational manner.

And, he realized, go to Devon and lay those demons to rest. But not before he'd seen Evangeline and tried to discover why she'd called it a day.

"Johnson?" he shouted to his factor as he entered the castle and took the stairs three at a time.

Johnson, a gnarled gnome-like man with a dour demeanor and a heart of gold, popped his head out of the room he used for estate business. "Your grace?"

"I'll be heading south at dawn on Sunday after church. There's a *ceilidh* tomorrow night to christen the new barn. I'll be chatting to Mrs. Cruikshank as soon as I'm decent." The cook was a favorite of his, ever since she'd snuck him black bun on a Sabbath. "Can you arrange things for me, please? Especially for Sunday. Bare necessities."

Now all he had to do was enjoy the sort of occasion he'd shunned in recent years and make peace with his soul.

Nothing to it.

Why did he not believe himself?

* * * *

Gibb soon decided that to ride from one end of the country to the other could be no one's idea of pleasure. Especially as he wondered if a very special lady would ever forgive him. The roads still hadn't recovered from winter, the inns in some places were few and far between and the horses in general were not what Gibb was used to. One in particular took exception to every gust of wind, every sheep in a field and every farm worker with a scythe. After three miles of a buck, a kick and an ungainly sidestep every few seconds, Gibb was almost ready to break the habit of a lifetime and use his whip. That he didn't was a testament to his strong will and reluctance to hurt an animal.

Compassion, an inner voice mocked him. *You have compassion*. The thought didn't bring him out in a cold sweat anymore. He was cautiously optimistic he was on the mend. Even so, he changed that animal at the first opportunity.

Some areas were wild and the moors dangerous. He rode with one hand on his pistol and one eye scanning his surroundings for anything untoward. The last thing he wanted was to die before he'd had a chance to make amends with Evangeline.

By the eighth day he swore he would walk barrel-legged forever. It had been a long while since he'd had to exist on a horse and fight for his life in between times. Now his life was no longer in danger but his future happiness was. Tension was not a good companion on horseback. He vowed that once he arrived at his chosen inn, that night, he would spend longer than usual in a bath.

"Alford, you've gone soft," he said to himself as he clattered over a wooden bridge and into a tiny hamlet where the duck pond seemed bigger than the settlement itself. Times were when ten days in the saddle would have seemed nothing. Not anymore. He yearned to walk, to sit in comfort and, he admitted, sort his life out. At least the Scottish estate was running smoothly. The *ceilidh* had been a great success, he hadn't drunk too much ale or whisky and he'd left the castle the following day within ten minutes of when he had intended. However, a ride of over five hundred miles over a mixture of roads and terrain wasn't going to be accomplished in a day or two.

Now, though, he could almost sniff the sea, and with luck he would reach Cove House the following day.

A rotund man ran out to greet him as Gibb clattered into the stable yard of the tiny inn, followed by two ostlers. The first man — the landlord — took a step back when he saw Gibb dismount, and bowed. Not before Gibb saw the welcoming grin on the man's face.

"Your grace, how good to see you back. Your usual suite is ready and waiting for you."

"I hope you haven't moved anyone out for me, Cubbins," Gibb said as he handed his saddlebags over to a waiting manservant. "I'm so weary that as long as I can have a bath, I'd sleep in the stables if need be." He stretched his arms over his head and rotated his shoulders. "I've had a long ride. I want to soak my aches away, have some food and a glass of ale, in that order. No, the bath and the ale together sounds even better."

"Ah, London is a fair distance," Cubbins said as he escorted Gibb indoors and ushered him into a private parlor.

"Scotland is even farther," Gibb said with a laugh. "I've been in the saddle so long I'm amazed I remember how to walk."

The landlord smiled uncertainly, as if he wasn't sure how to respond to such a sally. Gibb shook his head. "I'm jesting, Cubbins. I'm just sick of horseback. A jug of your ale, a bath to relax in and soak away my grime, followed by one of Jessie's meals and I'll be fine."

"I'll get the ale now and my Jessie'll sort the rest." He bustled out and Gibb heard him shouting orders to someone in the back of the inn. Gibb assumed it was the man's wife, Jessie.

Gibb stretched his legs out in front of him, accepted the ale a fresh-faced maid brought in, and sighed. What if he was unable to lay his demons to rest? What then?

Chapter Eleven

"Are you sure this is a good idea?" Evangeline said dubiously to Julia, as arm in arm they strolled through the park. Although she knew her clothing was impeccable, as befitted a young or, she amended in her head, youngish lady who was unmarried, it didn't negate who she was. A French émigré knife-thrower with no known aristocratic or wealthy antecedents or relations to place her status. Even if she was dressed by the best in town.

"I mean, I am a commoner, your reputation will be spoiled and —"

"And nothing," Julia said and tightened her hold on Evangeline's arm as if she could see the younger woman was ready to bolt. "I am an eccentric, evidently. And if you are seen with me, people will think I know something about your background they do not. I love to send them into a tizzy. So many have nothing better to do than gossip, we might tease them and give them something to gossip about. I wager at least five people will pay a call on me in the morning to try and ferret out what we are up to. I will take delight in confusing them. Now, ignore all that. You do want to see Iain, do you not? In a casual accidental way where no one will pay much attention."

"Yes, of course I do, but it all seems, oh, I don't know, underhand and forward." *And what if he ignores me or calls Julia on her behavior?* "Are you sure this is the right tack to take? Could we not, oh, I don't know, meet somewhere else?"

"Where?" Julia asked with a twinkle in her eye. "Almack's? The clubs? My sitting room? None would work as I desire. There would be too many people or too much of a scandal. This way it is apparently by chance."

"Forward and underhand by chance."

Julia tapped Evangeline's cheek. "I will not allow forward, but of course it is underhand. Men are so clueless. Gibb Alford for instance. He couldn't see what was under his nose and took himself off to sulk, silly man. I had to blackmail Bertie with no...ah..." She colored and grinned. "Need I spell it out?"

Evangeline shook her head. Oh, how she missed that closeness she had enjoyed with Gibb until...until she had decided she could go on no longer. Now she almost wished she had given herself to him, learned those last mystical stages and discovered what it was like to wholly belong to a man. But then, if his heart were not engaged it would be a hollow sham.

"Good, so chin up," Julia said. "Take that mournful look from your face and lose the shadows in your eyes. He's not worth it."

"Pardon?" Evangeline said, and winced at the frost in her voice. But what did Julia know about it? She was happily married, comfortable and lacked for nothing.

Julia laughed. "I know you miss Gibb, but he is a mere man. They always need time to come to their senses."

"But what if he never does," Evangeline said in despair. "What then?"

"Then he is not worthy of your pain, my dear." Julia gave her a swift hug. "Now then, I had to amend our plan a little. I realized that to loiter at the end of St. James was not in order and men can never be trusted to be at any one place at an exact time. All they need is for a wager to be entered in the betting book or for someone to stop them and ask their advice on a horse and then that is all out of kilter. The park was better. I know they always come back this way. You see the two gentlemen approaching from the left?"

Evangeline looked and saw whom Julia meant. Two middle-aged men dressed impeccably were skirting the lake and heading in their direction. She nodded. "Who are they?"

"Bertie on our left and Iain d'Astre on our right. Get ready to see what happens next." Julie waved with gay enthusiasm. "Over here."

"Ever the hoyden, my love," Bertie Arthur said as they reached the ladies, and he kissed his wife's cheek before he turned to Evangeline and bowed to her curtsey. "Hello. You must be Julia's friend Evangeline."

He had, Evangeline thought, the most beautiful smile, even if his expression was quizzical as he looked from Evangeline to his wife, then Le Duc d'Astre before he returned his gaze to Evangeline once more

Evangeline nodded. "Evangeline Coeur, my lord."

"Bertie, for if my wife is Julia, I refuse to be my lord, convention be damned," Bertie said emphatically.

"Bertie," Evangeline said dutifully as she looked at the tall, raven-haired man next to Bertie Arthur. He looked as if he had seen a ghost.

"Eve," he said. He gulped and blinked several times. "You must know my Eve?" He was as white as his cravat and held so tightly on to his cane his knuckles were the same color.

Evangeline went hot and cold. "My mama was Eve," she said quietly as her sorrow washed over her at the thought of that gentle woman. "I'm sorry, she died a year ago."

"Ah." He shook his head and took a deep breath. "So you are her sole daughter?"

"Her only child."

The duc swayed, took her hand with his free one and rested her little finger next to his. The shape and angle of them both matched. As Bertie and Julie stood as still as a tableau, d'Astre swept Evangeline's hair back and looked at her earlobes. "Eve said if she had a child she would call her Evangeline. Eve and Iain. To remind her of our all-too-short time together. But I swear she told me she wasn't with child. I would never have left if I had known."

"Perhaps that is why," Evangeline said gently. It could have just been the two of them with no one else around. Bertie and Julia were silent witnesses to the emotional scene.

"Then the terrors and…" He swallowed. "Your ears. Just like Eve, they are not the same. She, God help us… Bertie, get us away from here and to somewhere I can sit down and we can talk." Iain d'Astre sighed and his eyes were suspiciously bright. "Unbelievable as it seems, and I had no idea she existed, but I think I've found my daughter."

* * * *

It hadn't hurt as much as he'd imagined it would, Gibb decided. He walked out of Cove House at a brisk pace, found a horse, and without saddle or bridle cantered toward the cliff top above the private bay where he kept his boat.

As he rode along the narrow windy lanes of Devon, the closer he got to the border of the estate, the worse he felt. Clammy skin. Short of breath. When he saw the sea with its white-capped waves he had to use all his force of will not to faint or fall off his horse.

A sailing boat beating up the channel didn't make things easier. His eyes were drawn to it like a magnet. Was it safe? Would it capsize? What could he do if it did?

It took twenty long minutes before it rounded a headland and went out of sight. His understanding of the tides and currents reassured Gibb all would now be as he desired and he could breathe easier. Even so, his heart still beat erratically and an annoying tic danced at the corner of his eye. Only the knowledge that unless he faced his demons he would never be healed or have a chance of discovering if he and Evangeline stood a chance of a future kept him going.

The first glimpse of a house he hadn't seen in ten years took him by surprise. Hedges had grown higher, trees taller and the front drive was unkempt. As it was used by visitors, and no one else, Gibb reckoned there had been little traffic over the past years, and even if he resolved his issues it wasn't likely to change overmuch.

He wasn't there to socialize, and doubted that would change in the future. This was a slay the dragons, make peace with his soul and move on visit. It had always been more Hester's bolt hole than his.

He turned toward the cliffs.

The wind whipped the hem of his greatcoat up and tossed the branches of the nearby trees around. Leaves fell and lifted up into the air like whirling dervishes, and below him waves crashed across the sand and onto the rocks, sending spray up to where he stood. Was it this sort of day Hester had defied him and sailed to her death? Gibb honestly had no recollection. Every day had seemed like a stormy one when they had been together. There had been no calm, no peace. It was no wonder they'd spent more time apart than together. He'd only been in Devon at her urgent summons.

Gibb stopped walking and stood at the top of the steep steps cut into the cliff side that made their tortuous way down into the bay, heedless of the way the wind threatened to make a sail from his coat and lift him upward.

Had Hester trodden those steps often? Gone out and defied the elements just because he'd forbidden it? He'd spent so little time with her here. His presence had always set up such demands he'd been happier elsewhere. Not that things were much better elsewhere. She had, he now realized, never accepted what she had allegedly agreed to. Never intended to be the sort of wife he wanted. She would never have been satisfied with anything and always would have demanded more.

Gibb stared down at his yacht, recovered and restored by his workers without telling him, and pondered his thoughts. It was a marriage that should not have happened. However, it had, and Hester had died during it.

Not because of him, but because of herself.

At last he believed that. Carefully he made his way down to the beach and trod across it to the vessel. His boots made deep footsteps in the damp sand as he squelched along. Twice he stepped over rivulets that blocked his path. Soon the tide would be on the turn and he'd need to keep an eye on it he could be cut off.

The *Fairwind* appeared just as it had all those years before. Neat and tidy, the trim picked out in blue, the hull wooden and smooth. The sails were furled and it looked…sad, Gibb decided. As if it were waiting for someone or something. Probably not him.

A halloo from somewhere behind him made him whip around and brush his hair out of his eyes. An old man, bow-legged and nimble, scurried after him.

"Oy, see you… Oh, your grace, I didn't realize it was you." He bowed as he reached Gibb and smiled. "I never thought I'd see the day. Now then, young Gibb, aren't you a sight for sore eyes. Back for long?"

Gibb grinned at the man who looked after his craft. He supposed that to a man who must be in his eighties someone of almost forty was young. Worsnop, who was weathered and gnarled, and had the appearance of an ancient pixie, seemed to defy all the odds with regards to a man's lifespan. If he was to be believed he had lived through three shipwrecks — one by a sea monster — several storms with waves as high as the cliffs or more, press-ganging and three wives. He'd told Gibb that he reckoned marriage to his second wife had been the worst out of the lot.

"Not for long, no. I needed to come and…" How did he explain himself? "For closure. To try and understand why."

"There's no understanding that, begging your pardon." Worsnop spoke with the familiarity of an old retainer and didn't pretend not to understand. "Some people are born miserable and can't understand why others are not. Her grace was one of them. I reckon whatever you did would never have been good enough. She were a right termagant, she were. Nowt anyone did was right, and plenty wrong. We reckon she waited until you went to Exeter afore she went out and I'll tell you again everyone warned her not to. But then, she never listened to any of us, acos we were servants."

"Never servants, people who work for the estate," Gibb said emphatically. He hated the way people used the title servant to intimate someone of little or no worth.

"Ah, to you mebbe. Anyroads, I think you're ready to hear this now. She said more than once that if you weren't prepared to do as she wanted she'd make sure you suffered."

Gibb rocked on his heels. Hearing what he'd always suspected confirmed by someone else was balm to his senses. Another layer of ice melted away without him even noticing it. Warsnop had never been one to moderate his words, but neither had he or anyone else been so open before. "I'm glad you told me," Gibb said. "It is time to move on."

"It is that. You going to sell up?" The words were asked prosaically, the expression on the old man's face was anxious. Gibb looked at the boat, the sea and the scenery, the few clouds scudding across the blue sky, and made his mind up.

"No," he said. "No, I'm not. How often I'll get down I don't know but it stays in the Alford family. And you can pass that around."

Worsnop beamed and looked more like a pixie than ever. "I'll do that, your grace. Now, are you wanting her made ready?" He nodded at the boat.

Gibb shook his head. "Not today. I'll just look her over. You go on to the house and put people's minds at rest."

He waited until Worsnop made his way up the steps and disappeared from his sight, gauged the incoming tide and decided he had time to do what he needed. Slowly he climbed aboard the *Fairwind* and stood by the wheel.

This would have been the last thing Hester touched.

Poor, deluded, unhappy Hester, whom he had never been able to help or make happy. For the first time since she died, Gibb sank to his knees and wept for her.

* * * *

After a couple of months, Evangeline decided London was dull. Her papa had asked her not to carry on with her performances and Evangeline had refused. It was too soon, their involvement too new, and whatever he said to the contrary, she needed time to come to terms with the fact that this gentleman was her father. Reluctantly he accepted her insistence, plus the other edict she decreed. Their involvement in any manner or form was not to become general knowledge. Not until she was sure she would accept her place as his daughter. For some reason she wanted to wait.

To see if Gibb returned? That was folly. She had sent him away almost two months before, the season was almost at an end, Parliament was about to rise for the end of the session, then no doubt he'd be back in Scotland.

A nasty sensation of spiders crawling over her increased her misery, but what else could she have done? He wouldn't let himself care and she needed more than lip-service attention. So it was an impasse. Better to have made the break.

By the third week, she'd tentatively agreed to accompany her father to Rutland within the month. By the fifth week they'd settled on the following Thursday, two days after her final booking. She owed it to them both to get to know him, and give him the opportunity to learn all about her. The decision made, somehow life seemed clearer.

Her final evening performance looked to be somewhat boring, she decided as she scanned the couples who stood on Lady Preston's lawns and sipped champagne and chatted. No one seemed over-interested in the announcement that her show would start soon, and she needed a partner. Evangeline scrutinized those who were now drawing nearer and almost groaned aloud. What on earth was Denby Crowe doing here? Gibb had warned him to leave the capital, hadn't he? But Gibb wasn't here, and Crowe must know it. For the first time since Gibb left, Evangeline was apprehensive about the performance ahead. And afterward.

She took a deep breath. With luck, Crowe would watch and not interfere. It seemed luck was not going to be on her side. Crowe smirked as she put out her plea

for an assistant and took several steps in her direction.
"I—"

He got no farther. A disturbance behind him made him look round and Evangeline and several others craned to see who or what it was.

A tall, blond-haired man shouldered his way past several of Crowe's cronies to Crowe's side. "I say, Crowe," he said plaintively. "Not fair. You've had your turn, now it's time to let someone else have a go. Mademoiselle Evangeline..." The wink was so brief that if she hadn't been watching his face she would have missed it. "Let me be your assistant. I would be honored. Lord Henry Lawrence at your service."

Gibb's friend who had been such a help in the past. Evangeline curtsied, as if he was not even a nodding acquaintance. "Thank you, I would appreciate that." She turned to Lord Crowe who stood scowling nearby. "My lord, I think it only right that his lordship has his moment before the knives, don't you?"

What else could Crowe do, other than acquiesce? He stood and stared at them both for a long moment then went back to his friends, folded his arms and showed no inclination to leave.

Evangeline twirled a knife between her thumb and forefinger as she looked at Henry.

He returned her gaze without expression, and smiled. "Be gentle with me, I'm not as brave as some and newly married," he murmured. "I don't want to be unmanned before I have a chance to father my heir. My beloved would never forgive me."

His smile was infectious and Evangeline found herself responding to it with ease. "I'll be careful. I only hit people when I want to. Did Gibb put you up to this?" she asked as they made their way toward where she wanted him to stand. "Is he in town?" Try as she might, the question didn't come out as disinterested as she would have liked.

"He asked me to keep an eye open for Crowe whilst he was away, for we all thought he might try something without Gibb to keep him in check. Gibb wagered the bloody man would be back in town ready to cause trouble once he thought Gibb too far away to intervene. It took longer than any of us — Gibb's friends — thought, but here he is. With regards to Gibb? As far as I know he's not back yet but I expect him next week at the latest. He'll be here for the last sitting of Parliament."

That gave her a few days to decide whether to go to Rutland with her papa or not. Sadly nowhere near long enough, but it would have to do. Now she had to put Gibb and her thoughts out of her mind and concentrate on the here and now.

"I thank you, and let us begin." She took a deep breath, threw three knives up in the air and juggled them as she ran through the show with Henry and explained what she needed from him. To his credit he didn't flinch, not even when she told him just how close the knives would get to his skin, how he needed to stand and how to tuck his cuffs in.

"No going around in circles, though?" he asked with relief. "Gibb told me that was on your agenda. If we did that I might embarrass myself and vomit."

She laughed. "Don't worry, I wouldn't do that with anyone without plenty of practice. We'll just do some nice gentle tricks." She caught all three knives in one hand, ignored the smatter of applause and someone's coarse comment about how she knew how to play with swords, as long as they were tiny. The ribald laughter and how would she cope with a real man was cut off with an *oooft*.

Henry rolled his eyes. "And some of those real men don't know what to do with any kind of sword." He colored as he realized to whom he spoke. "Sorry."

Evangeline patted his hand. "No need, their minds are as small as their…ahem…swords." She pointed to the spot she'd marked out. "Ready?"

Gibb rubbed his knuckles. Perhaps there was a better way to silence Denby Crowe and his cronies, but the thump to Crowe's jaw and the grinding noise that followed were oh so satisfying, as was the punch in the midriff to one of his cohorts. As the rest melted away when they saw Gibb's expression and clenched fists, Crowe rocked on his feet, opened his mouth and rubbed his jaw. The other man Gibb had assaulted backed away. He didn't take his eyes off Gibb, fell over a statue and scrambled to his feet. It was no surprise to Gibb that the man didn't hang around to say or do any more.

Crowe touched his chin gingerly. "You've broken it."

Good lord, the man is bleating.

"I should call you out," Crowe said in a thick voice. "I should."

"Better than your neck, but if you want that breaking I could arrange it. It would save the pistols at dawn scenario."

"You wouldn't…" Crowe blanched and shook his head in negation. "You would."

"Oh, yes," Gibb confirmed. "I seem to remember a promise I made to you not long ago, what would happen if I saw you in the capital again this season," Gibb said menacingly. It was laughable how a tone of voice could affect the man in front of him. Crowe was almost in tears.

"You weren't here," Denby retorted. "And why should I go away? Do you know what it was like at home with my mama and sisters? It was hell. Mama is determined I marry our neighbor's daughter. She has red hair and lisps. On purpose. So as you weren't in town, I came to escape."

His woe-is-me tone almost had *Gibb* in tears. Of laughter.

"Sadly for you, here I am, and if you value your skin you won't be."

"It's not fair. Who gave you the right to... Oh." Denby gulped as Gibb took a step closer to him. "I'm going."

"Now," Gibb said in a tone tinged with menace. "At once," he added in case Crowe had not got the message.

"Now? But it's almost midnight. It isn't safe."

"Your reasoning means nothing to me. You put yourself in this situation. It's to be hoped you don't meet too many footpads," Gibb said with indifference. "Or perhaps that you do. Then society would be rid of you for good. Vermin is always best stamped out."

Crowe opened his mouth and shut it again. "I need to say my farewells," he croaked. "It would be rude not to."

Gibb shook his head. Lord, the man just didn't know what was good for him and when to give up. He looked over Crowe's shoulder and saw Evangeline throw three glittering stilettos in the air. With an insouciance he envied, she caught them and spun around so her hair became a dark cloud round her head and her skirts a shimmering mist of blues and greens. She grinned and laughed, her sheer joy obvious to everyone around them, then, so fast it was a blur, threw the blades toward Henry. They landed, quivering, around his head.

Gibb smiled. She was better than ever. He gave his attention to Crowe once more. "Unless you do them in the next five minutes, you don't. Ah, Mr. Hislop." He turned to the burly man who had approached. "Take him to the city boundary please."

"Eh?" Crowe stared at him wide-eyed and terrified. "You can't."

"You think not?" Gibb shrugged. "Watch me." He nodded to Hislop and stood back as the ex-pugilist lifted Crowe on to his tiptoes as if he weighed no more than a feather and marched him down the garden and away. Then Gibb turned his attention back to the show.

Henry was doing well. It had been a calculated gamble asking him to run interference if necessary and be Evangeline's partner. Mary had laughed and nodded when Henry had, after a swift glance at his wife, agreed. Now, as Evangeline's knife held Henry in place by pinning his cuff, Gibb made his way across the lawn to stand next to Mary.

"He doesn't look too scared," Gibb commented. "Dutch courage?"

"More like sheer terror," Mary said with a laugh. Her composure and assurance had increased with marriage and she looked happy and amused. "You know a move and die sort of thing."

"I have to thank you and say I'm grateful. Crowe was ready to do mischief."

"I saw." Mary glanced at him. "He's a menace. Gibb, tell me if I am out of order, but I believe you care for her. Why not show it?"

He sighed. "It's hard. For so many years I would not allow myself to have emotions. Now? Now I don't know if I dare give in to them. What if she refuses to believe me? Or I can't sustain them? What then?" Damn, did he sound as pathetic as he felt?

Mary smiled at him and daringly squeezed his shoulder. "Tell her how you feel. Do not give up before you even try."

The cheers and applause brought his mind back to the scene in front of them. Henry and Evangeline were taking their bows as the exhibition had ended. After a few minutes Henry took hold of Evangeline's hand and towed her across the lawn toward Gibb and Mary. She seemed to be dragging her heels. Because of him?

"I should be packing my things up. It's not fair to leave one of Lady Hislop's staff to watch over them." Her voice carried clearly over the yards that separated them.

"Five minutes," Henry said. "Mary wants to say hello. And" — he looked to where Gibb stood — "so does he."

Evangeline abruptly stopped moving and rocked on her heels. To his delight, Gibb saw she was wearing her pretty, sparkling sandals. He fantasized about taking them off and...

"Gibb?" she said in disbelief. "You're here?"

He nodded, relieved his erotic thoughts hadn't run away with him. "As you see. In the flesh."

"Why?" she asked. Her attitude showed nothing of her feelings. "I thought you wanted country life." 'And not me,' her tone intimated.

Not a very promising welcome. Nevertheless he plowed on game to the last. "I have things to settle and discuss with certain people."

She nodded. "Ah, I see." Then she turned to Mary. "I return your very brave husband. Many a man has flinched at being part of my act, and he was cool, calm and collected." She ignored Gibb.

That didn't bode well. "Evangeline, we need to talk." If looks had an effect on the weather, the grass would be frost-white.

"Why?"

Oh, hell. A reasonable question in the circumstances, but not one he wanted to answer in company. "I…I can't talk here, may I escort you home?"

Mary nudged him. "Ask nicely," she said under her breath. "A little humility, perhaps?"

It was galling to be reminded of how to behave. Nevertheless, Mary was correct. He needed to open up and give a little. "Please," he added. *How on earth can I project humility?* It was not something he'd thought he had ever needed to do before. "I do have many things to explain."

Evangeline scrutinized him with care. At last, she nodded. "If you say so, I'm ready to listen."

Now all he had to do was fathom out what to say.

* * * *

Less than half an hour later, Evangeline sat in Gibb's carriage and very properly tucked her arms across her middle and made sure her skirts covered her ankles. As good as it was to see him again, and to relish his nearness, her mind told her something was amiss. The clopping of the horses hooves sounded loud in the awkward silence that surrounded them, and spelled out her uncomfortable sensations. *Why is he here? What have I done? What's going on?* A swift glance at Gibb's shuttered face gave her no clues as to why he had sought her out. Eventually, she couldn't stand it anymore. *Better to ask now than worry longer.*

"We are almost home, your grace. Perhaps you might tell me what it is you want to explain, before we arrive." *There, that didn't sound needy or attention-seeking, did it?*

"Gibb. You used to call me Gibb."

She shrugged. "I did."

"And you do not intend to now? Oh hell, it's not easy," Gibb said. Lord, he sounded irritable as he took a deep breath. "Sorry, I'm edgy."

And he thinks I am not? At least he knows what is about to be said. I don't have a clue.

"They say nothing of importance in life is easy." Evangeline glanced out of the window as the carriage turned into Bruton Street and saw the familiar buildings and the nameplates of the businesses housed therein. It was one of those moments when she didn't know whether to laugh or cry. "You have two minutes before we arrive and I'm home. I'm tired and I want to sleep."

Gibb stuck his head out of the window and groaned. *Groaned? Why?*

"Damn, you are correct. That's not long enough. May I come and explain tomorrow?" he asked in an urgent tone as he returned his attention to her. "It's important. Truly, I need more than two minutes. Let me take you for a ride or a walk in the park, or to the theater? We could talk in the interval."

"I don't think so." She sighed. It all sounded so enticing, but she had to guard against future hurt. Once was more than enough, and time spent together doing social things would not help her there. "Come at eleven if you must." The look in his eye warned her he was about to argue. "I have both an afternoon and a supper engagement," she added in a rush. She'd make sure she did by the morrow.

"Can't you break them?" he asked.

If Gibb had sounded more involved than he did, Evangeline might have given in to his request, but his tone intimated otherwise. He might say it was important, but somehow Evangeline doubted their idea of important was the same. "Why should I?"

The coach stopped and Gibb got out to hand her down. He looked somewhat incredulous at her refusal and perhaps, Evangeline pondered as she smiled her thanks and put her hand in his, she glimpsed a little hurt in his eyes? She owned up to the fact that it satisfied her somewhat to see that emotion displayed, however fleeting — she wouldn't be honest if she didn't. Even so, it wasn't enough to change her mind.

"Eleven. I'll warn the doorman." She tried to tug her hand free but Gibb held on.

"Not yet." Without warning, Gibb pulled her closer and anchored her tight against him. His breath was on her cheek for a scant second before his lips crushed hers. His tongue demanded entrance to her mouth and without volition her lips softened and parted to give him entrance.

Her gown crushed between them as she gave in to sweet temptation and clutched Gibb's shoulders then let her hands drift lower until she held the taut globes of his rear in her palms. He laughed deep and low in his throat and mimicked her actions until they were so close together their clothes were no barrier to what she could feel.

His erection.

His attraction to her.

Was it enough?

Somehow, she didn't think so. However, Evangeline decided as Gibb gentled the kiss and coherent thoughts began to form again, a lot would depend on what he shared on the morrow.

"Hell, love, I could take you here against the coach, but as sure as the sun will rise once the moon has set, the watch would go by or the horses bolt and we'd end up on our backs in the gutter."

She shuddered. That would not project the demeanor she wanted. "Not a good idea." Evangeline disentangled herself and shook her sadly crushed skirts out. "Eleven." She bolted for the door.

It opened at her first peremptory rap of the knocker and she was able to thank the man who stood there before she took the stairs two at a time. Sleep was impossible, so perhaps hot milk would help.

It didn't.

* * * *

Several hours later she watched the sun come up over the chimney pots and heard the clock strike the hour, just as she had every sixty minutes since she'd rolled into bed. Six a.m. and no point in staying where she was.

The thought of any more hot milk made her somewhat nauseous, as did the thought of chocolate. Evangeline found some water that had been thoroughly boiled—it never paid to take chances with well-drawn water in the capital—and stood at the window looking out over the semi-quiet streets.

London never slept, she knew that, and the lamplighter, the watch and several cats of various colors indicated that. But the rumble of carriages, the slamming of doors and the raucous cries of the pie sellers were absent. No hackneys plied their trade, no chimney sweep trod the dusty streets and no peeler looked around suspiciously.

Peace.

If only she felt the same, all would be perfect. However, a churning stomach, goosebumps and something nasty crawling up her spine were not conducive to tranquility. All she could hope for was semi-harmony.

By ten she'd eaten some oats, lost them in the chamber pot and refreshed her mouth with yet more water. She hadn't felt like this since the day she had boarded the smelly fishing boat that had carried her to England. Even meeting her father hadn't brought such a drastic result. Evangeline washed her face and hands, pinched her cheeks to add color and took a deep breath. Eloise, who had appeared half an hour earlier, looked at her anxiously.

"I have to go, I have a client due. Are you sure you will be all right?"

Evangeline nodded. "I will be fine. It seems I just needed to get everything out of my system except him." She shrugged. "Maybe also him, we will see."

Chapter Twelve

Gibb elected to walk to Bruton Street, in part so he could rehearse what he wanted to say. Silly to feel as nervous as a virgin about to discover the delights of the flesh, but there it was. He trembled and had such a toad—it was bigger than a frog—in his throat it threatened to choke any words he tried to utter. He'd best lose it soon.

The temptation to peel off and head for his club was almost impossible to ignore. Only a fierce will, and the knowledge that if he didn't turn up at eleven Evangeline could and no doubt would write him off, kept him walking in the correct direction. He greeted a crony absently and watched the man stare at him as if he had lost his mind. Gibb, not the other man. Gibb accepted he was known for his attention to politeness, and awareness—not due to a lack of them. But then, he knew something others did not. He accepted it was too late to rectify his mistake with his friend, except apologize when they next met, but he hoped not too late with Evangeline.

The next hour would define his future.

To his annoyance it didn't start off in the right direction.

The doorman stared at him long and hard before he admitted that 'Mam-sell' was expecting him. Then he'd had to be shown a room to duck into to avoid a crony of his late mama and her obnoxious husband-hunting daughter. The doorman had smirked as he'd hidden Gibb from sight, and Gibb swore he was left in the closet-sized room for longer than necessary. Even so, he thanked the man. For that couple to spy him would be the final straw. Then, if that wasn't enough, before he'd climbed the last flight of stairs, Eloise had cornered him, taken his arm, marched him into her workroom and proceeded to interrogate him. As he had no intention of sharing his thoughts with anyone except Evangeline it was a difficult ten minutes of verbal sparring on his behalf and enough hard-hitting questions on hers to make him squirm. When Eloise let him go, he could see she was unsatisfied and unsettled and he could do nothing to allay her fears.

Somewhat rattled, he knocked softly on Evangeline's door. At least she opened it promptly and stood back to let him enter. Then, uncertain, he hovered.

"Oh, for goodness' sake, sit down." Evangeline waved toward a comfortable chair set near the blazing fire. "You look like death warmed up."

"I feel it." Gibb grinned against his will as he sat in the chair she indicated and crossed his long legs elegantly—or so he hoped. They could look like a tangle of ropes for all he knew at that moment. "Is it any wonder? I gave an acquaintance the cold shoulder by accident, have been scrutinized by your doorman, had to hide like a criminal to avoid the Countess of Marksham and her odious daughter and had the thumbscrew interrogation by Eloise. All before noon." He rolled his eyes. "On top of a fitful night's sleep."

"Poor thing." She patted his shoulder. "Then if I offer you ale?"

"I'll take it," Gibb said. "And pretend it is noon. Truly, I have suffered."

"So you say." She gave him a sympathetic glance.

Did he look as haggard as he felt? *It must be convenient to pour the liquid and keep your hands busy*. He had to force himself not to pick at his nails or twist his fingers together. *How pathetic.*

"Let us hope this will help." She passed him a tankard. "Perhaps if you just say what you want?"

"That is so easy to say and not so much to do." Hadn't he spent most of the night agonizing over how to explain himself? "However, I will try. Promise you will hear me out and let me finish?"

Evangeline looked surprised. "Of course, but why do you think I may not?"

Gibb grimaced. "I don't know. All I understand is this is important and I am not at my most articulate at the moment. It..." He hesitated. It had to be said. "It worries me."

"That something does is obvious. You are unraveling my tablecloth and performing contortions with your ankles. Spit it out and relax." She smiled. "Have a drink. It might help."

Gibb exhaled loud and long. "I think I had better." He swallowed some of the ale. "Thank you. I never thought I would need this for courage."

Now Evangeline looked worried. He watched her every move from under his lowered lashes. Would she understand? He thought her sympathetic and far-seeing, but… He bit his lip and forced himself to wait until she had poured herself some water and sat in a matching chair at right angles to his.

"Tell me what is on your mind, Gibb, before I copy you and I end up with no table covering and so tied in knots I'm there forever."

Now the 'moment' had arrived, Gibb was amazed to find himself ready to speak. Whatever the outcome, now was the time to open up and be honest.

Evangeline waited with as much patience as she could muster while Gibb rearranged his legs, sipped some ale then leaned toward her without warning.

"When you said you didn't want to see me again, I was hurt," he began slowly. "Not surprised, because, after all, who would want to spend time with someone who could make no promises about the following week let alone the next month or year? So I admit I went off in a mood of both anger and woe is me. I went north in a begrudging, 'all is for the best' frame of mind."

She nodded, and wiped one eye. "I told myself you would."

"It didn't last. I promise," Gibb told her. "I toiled alongside my workers, worried their crops might not be as good as they could be and struggled to help build a new barn so what crops they did have lasted the winter. Then arranged for their homes to be warm and watertight and reiterated that missing school was not an option if you live on my land." He laughed. "I was asked if bunking off was not normal. Bunking off is playing truant."

"Ah, and you do not allow it to happen?"

"Not if they expect to be employed later." He shrugged. "I feel that to grow and prosper we need education. A chance to understand and learn. I know many do not agree with me." He quirked his lips. "Think I am too much of an authoritarian. They have a choice. Stay or go."

"Gibb Alford, why on earth do you imagine you have no feelings?" Evangeline left her chair and crouched at his feet to look up into his smoky eyes and search for something to indicate his mood. "They are there all right, believe me."

He nodded. "Something an old retainer said gave me food for thought. He told me that some people are born miserable and can't understand why others are not, and my late wife was one of them. He went on to say he reckoned whatever I did would never have been good enough, and that she had been determined to make my life uncomfortable."

"That is appalling," Evangeline said without thinking. "Why on earth?"

"That is a question I suspect I will never be able to truly answer," Gibb replied. "She accused me of not giving her what she wanted. I don't think even she knew what that was. Lord, this sounds disloyal, but I have to try and explain my marriage to you."

"Oh, my dear, you don't."

He looked startled. "I don't?"

"No, not at all. All you have to explain is why you are here now. What is different from before. Why…" She stopped as she tried to put her scrambled thoughts into order. "What do you intend next?"

From somewhere outside an altercation filtered upward and added to the tension in the room. The semi-silence was not peaceful, anything but. It was charged with something indefinable. A coal in the fire flared, spluttered and died. Evangeline moved to alleviate the pain in her knees due to her crouched position. "Gibb?" she prompted. "Is that too difficult to answer?"

"It depends on you."

"Me? How so?" It was his mindset that had given rise to this situation, was it not? Yes, she had decided enough was enough but in response to his intractability, nothing else. "You are the one who said the way it should be," Evangeline said, proud of her even, non-judgmental tone.

"And you were the one who said no, it was not acceptable," he replied equably, without censoriousness. "Now I'm asking you if we can try again."

Evangeline stood up and surreptitiously did her best to work the pins and needles from her limbs. She needed a clear head as she asked the words that bothered her.

The argument in the street, which had gone silent, started up again. Someone shrieked outside the window and both of them jumped. "This is daft," she said shakily. "Let's try to do this in a sane and sensible manner. What do you want from me?"

"A chance to be your friend again," he said straight away.

"As in how? A friend who you care about to some degree, but aren't prepared to admit it?"

"I do admit I care," Gibb said. "Haven't I just said so?"

"Not in so many words, no. Yes, your actions often do. Look at the way you look after your estates and workers. But words? No, never."

"That's common sense, is it not? Does it need to be put into words?"

"Not necessarily," Evangeline argued. "Plus, there is also compassion shown. However, I digress. That is not us. I'm asking again, what do you want from us, Gibb? In specific, from me."

He studied her. "I don't know."

"Don't know or refuse to know?" she asked, sick at heart. Had anything changed? "There is a difference between them."

"I know that," he said. "And I don't have a proper answer. I think I care, I'm scared to care and I don't know if I dare care more than I do now. Is not the fact that I take care of things that could affect you enough? Is that not the sort of care you desire?"

If he thought that, they had not moved on. She bit her lip. "I wish it were, Gibb, but we both know it isn't. I could not cope on half a loaf. I'm not asking for your undying affection, for you to shield me from all the winds of fate and make sure none touch me. Life isn't like that. But you are, as you ever have been, putting fences up where none need to be."

"I'm being as honest as I can."

"I know you think you are, and believe me I appreciate that." Good lord, she had almost said how she loved him for it. Too much for him to accept, she was sure. "What you say you are able to give me would not be enough, I'd be scared to show my feelings in case they crossed over some invisible line I didn't understand or know about. You would be ever watchful and on edge. Add that to who we are." She got out of her chair, shook her head and stood on tiptoe to lean over him and kiss his cheek. His hands clenched around her waist and tightened briefly before she drew back and he let go of her. "It cannot be." Dare she be open now?

He stood and strode to the window to turn his back on her, and looked out of the panes of glass. Evangeline saw his hands were white as he gripped the sill. She decided not to hold back.

"Gibb, I could so easily love you, and love that isn't returned turns black and evil. I will not put either of us through that. To be with you would be torture. It wouldn't be the tortured duke, it would be the tortured duke's tortured friend."

He turned around and she saw why he had been given that sobriquet.

"Believe me, I would love you if I could," he said in an anguished voice. "I do not know if I have the ability to love anyone. It might not be part of my makeup."

She shook her head. "I doubt that, somehow. You have come a long way since we first met, but you have still shut a major piece of yourself away. Love is beautiful, and like any emotion, be it good or bad, is an integral part of you and can't be compartmentalized. You either let it in or not. And only you can do that." There was nothing else she could say. She took her glass of water, wished it held something stronger and took small sips. Too big a mouthful would choke her.

Gibb was so quiet she wondered what would happen next. Eventually he took a deep breath and exhaled with a long-drawn-out hiss. "I need to think again."

"Then you must do so." And she needed to make her mind up if she was going to let him know why she was going away for a while. Evangeline decided she wouldn't, not unless she had to. Those explanations weren't about to be shared unless he was prepared to be part of her life.

"I'll be away for a while." She put her hand over his mouth before he asked any questions. "I also need to think. Now go and continue to make your peace with yourself."

* * * *

Why, oh, why does nothing ever go according to plan? That knotty question went around in Gibb's mind over and over again as he went through the motions of his everyday life. He went to his club and spent an hour chatting to his cronies about anything and nothing. Passed half the morning at Tattersall's and purchased a new horse to be sent to Scotland, and went a round in Jackson's boxing salon. He proceeded to Manton's and spent a satisfying half-hour cupping wafers. But most of the time, half of his mind was on Evangeline, not what he was doing. Once they passed in the park as he walked through it from one appointment to another and she was arm in arm with Julia Arthur. He inclined his head, they waved, and as he veered in their direction he was hailed by a fellow peer concerned about a speech he had to give. Gibb sent an apologetic smile to Evangeline, who nodded as if to say she understood. Or so he hoped. Even then it was hard. He wanted to be reassured she was well, and to assure *her* he wasn't treating their meeting lightly and was trying to sort himself out more.

He spent one day at Cresswell, and if he chose colors and furnishings he thought she would like he didn't admit it.

If he fancied he heard her laugh and imagined he saw her skirts whisking around a corner, he didn't admit it. But when he picked up a hairpin and put it through his lapel, he admitted one thing

He needed to sort himself out and fast.

Gibb went back to town in a somber mood, spent most of his time ensconced in his study and thought things over as best he could.

On the tenth night he once again eschewed all invitations and sat in his study with a large dram.

He'd done enough agonizing, now it was make his mind up time. Gibb remembered something his first tutor had told him. If in doubt, make lists. One pro and one con. Sad though that might be, in this case it could just help him. He'd second-guessed himself so much he was dizzy. Gibb scrabbled in a drawer and found a writing tablet and a pencil and drew a line from top to bottom down the center of the tablet. Then he nibbled the end of the pencil before wrinkling his brow and spitting into his handkerchief. The pencil's taste was disgusting. It served him right for prevarication. Quickly, before he filled his mouth with the taste of lead again, he began to write.

Con.

What con? Makes me think? Surely that is a good thing? Makes me aware? Ditto. He mentally shrugged. Perhaps a pro list would help him to decide on the cons?

Pro.

Like.

Like a lot.

Doesn't bore me, or asked for more than I have been able to give.

Patient.

Feisty.

No, not a contradiction.

Interesting, articulate and a good listener. A good heart.

Mine.

The last word made him jerk, stab the page and drop his pencil, but not before it slashed a large line across the vellum, scoring into the sheet below. It amused him to see it had put a thick, dark line though the cons part of his cogitations.

Suddenly it all seemed oh so simple. Evangeline was nothing like Hester. The one thing they had in common was their sex. What a fool he was.

He added three words in capitals to his pro list. I love her.

I love her.

He almost jumped up to shout it to the world. I...love...Evangeline Coeur.

Now he had to tell her and hope to hell she believed him.

* * * *

Five days after they had arrived, Evangeline looked around the pleasant bedchamber her papa had chosen for her and kissed his cheek. "This is perfect. You have gone to so much trouble."

He patted her hand and grinned from ear to ear and she swore he appeared ten years younger. When he had asked her diffidently if she minded him introducing her as his daughter, what else could she have said but of course not. His pleasure had been worth it. Plus, if she were truthful, it was lovely to have that sense of belonging once more.

I could have had it with Gibb if he'd wanted, we could have had it. In case he chose to visit, Evangeline had dallied in the capital for over a week, citing things to clear up before she left to her papa. Not that Evangeline thought he believed her, but he had nodded and put their departure back accordingly.

But those days had shown her Gibb wasn't ready to come and talk to her and might never be. She'd left with mixed feelings after exacting promises from Julia and Eloise that they would not divulge her whereabouts.

Now La Belle Evangeline was no more.

In her place was Mademoiselle d'Astre.

"Come back to Rutland." Iain grinned from ear to ear. "As my daughter."

"I've kept you waiting, haven't I?"

"*Ma chère*, it was a labor of love. My daughter at last."

Evangeline leaned back on the elaborate carved dressing table and studied the man in front of her. "Can you swear you are sure I am your daughter?

He nodded. "As sure as I can be without hearing it from your *maman*'s lips. We have the same deformity in our finger. You have my beloved Eve's earlobes. We both have the same blue eyes with the darkness seeping into the blue. The timing fits, your *maman* would not have slept with anyone else, you detest *les tripes* and *noisettes* but adore *les amandes*. What else? We neither can sing in tune, but both can throw and catch a stiletto without looking. Though I own there you have more skill than I. Do you need more proof?"

She shook her head. "No, Papa. It is enough."

He smiled. "Then we will go and drink Armagnac and you will tell me why you are *triste*, eh? Let your papa put it right." He puffed out his cheeks and raised his fists. "Who must I fight? Pray it is with sabers, not pistols. My aim has never been true with a firearm."

She laughed as she was sure he meant her to. "No fighting please, Papa. For it is me who needs sorting out, no one else."

He took her arm and they walked downstairs to the sunny morning room he had designated also as hers, but where every day after lunch they sat for an hour or so and chatted.

"Do you miss him?" Iain asked suddenly.

"Oh yes." She didn't pretend not to know who he meant. "Like an ache inside."

"But still you came?"

Evangeline smiled, although she felt more like crying. "Papa, I would have come whatever happened. I had hoped I could have come with his blessing, but it wasn't to be. You see, I didn't pay any attention when he said he had no heart. That he could not and would not give in to emotion. I'm like every other woman, I suppose. I believe in the power of love. I made the mistake of thinking I would be the one who changed him. I did not and I *could* not bear to wait forever." She sighed. "Maybe that makes me as bad as him." She pleated the skirts of her dress with busy fingers.

"What rubbish is this I am hearing, my dear?" The more flustered Iain got, the more Gallic he became. He ran his hand through his once immaculately styled hair and looked for all the world like an agitated cockerel. "Your words are neither sensible nor applicable. He is the idiot, not you. Pah, I wish I could share a piece of my mind with him. Just let me see him. I will give him what for." He harrumphed.

"Papa, you will not," she said, alarmed at what the outcome of such a meeting could be. "Promise me? It is my problem, not yours."

"I am your papa. It is what parents should do."

"Papa, no. I am a big girl and have to fight my own battles. Your word?" She waited as he waged an argument with himself.

At last he let his breath out in one long *whoosh*. "Everything that bothers you is my business," he grumbled, but she could see his ire abating by the second. "Oh, I agree. With reluctance, mind you."

"Thank you." Evangeline hugged him tight. "But, Papa, when will this feeling end?" she asked him forlornly.

Iain stroked her hair in a rhythmic, gentle motion. "Ah, if I had the answer to that, I would be happy to share it with you. Sadly I do not, my love. I do not know."

Nor did she, more was the pity.

Chapter Thirteen

"Hoy, Menteith." A stick waved imperiously out of a covered carriage as Gibb walked along The Mall. Lisette Tonge stuck her head out of the window. "Gibb Alford. Come over here and get in. I want to talk to you."

Gibb checked he could cross the road without being mowed down by a hackney or an irresponsible young buck and made his way to the carriage. The door was thrown open and all he could see was a gnarled hand beckoning him in. He thought it was a bit like a gothic horror story—the dismembered hand, he decided whimsically—but accepted it was perhaps best not to mention that to the owner of said appendage.

"Get in before we get hit. I have no idea what the world is coming to, eh. Hell on wheels, more like." Lady Tonge tapped on the roof with the tip of her cane to tell the driver to move on. "Now then. What's going on?"

"About?" he asked with caution. He wasn't going to offer up any information she wasn't after. Lisette had the nose of a truffle hound when it came to scenting gossip, and he didn't intend to help her.

"You and young Evangeline, of course. I know all about Harris and that idiotic chit Honoria Compton."

She did? Gibb didn't and he decided he didn't want to. However, he must have looked as surprised as he thought, because she gave a cackle of laughter.

"Ha, you thought I didn't know Evangeline? Of course I do. She would come to read to me. Help me remember my French, and my youth. Ah, the stories I could tell. I remember one young duc who—" She coughed. "Hmm, never mind that. Not that I didn't have a fondness for Tonge of course, but, typical Englishman of his generation, he had no stamina. Not like you youngsters, I dare say. Or so I hear. High jinks and…" She guffawed. "I won't embarrass you."

Gibb grinned. She was incorrigible. "I doubt you could, Lisette."

"Good, so where is Evangeline? Do you have her hidden away somewhere?"

"I have no idea where she is, and she is not hidden away by me. We no longer see each other," Gibb said levelly. "So I'm sorry I cannot help you."

Lisette hit him none too gently on his shoulder. "Idiot, I suppose you spun her some yarn about being heartless or some such rubbish."

He shrugged, feeling like a recalcitrant child. "Ouch." He rubbed his head where a second, harder rap had hit him. This time Lisette had used her cane and it had stung. He glared. "What was that for?"

Lisette didn't look at all repentant. "You deserved it. Ouch indeed. You do have a heart. Otherwise why would you visit an old lady like me if you didn't, eh? Ask yourself that. No, not now."

He shut his mouth before she decided to hit him elsewhere. He didn't trust her not to use her cane lower down on his anatomy. The part of his body he was worried about did its best to shrivel and hide.

"Whatever you say, Gibb, you have a heart." She dropped her cane and patted his knee with one arthritic hand. "Believe me, you do."

Gibb was embarrassed. It was rare for Lisette to speak so seriously. "I agree it beats but not much else."

"Balderdash."

"Not at all."

"Twaddle. Be honest. What is she to you?" The carriage slowed as it turned the corner into the leafy square where Lady Tonge lived. "Hurry up now, I need my nap."

"Evangeline?" Gibb sighed, his heart heavy with the fear his hopes might never be realized. "My life, except I let her go."

Lisette tutted. "Get her back, you fool." She thrust her stick through the window aperture and waggled it around. Obviously her staff knew what that signified because the carriage swayed as someone alighted and the door opened.

"Ha, and how would I do that? 'Tis easier said than done," Gibb said as he bent his head to kiss the old lady's hand.

"Good lord, Gibb, if you can't see her likeness to Iain d'Astre you do not deserve her." She stood on the first step of the flight to her front door. "Use your brain. I assume it still works on occasion."

"Who?" The name rang a bell but for once he couldn't put a face to it. For someone who prided himself on his memory it was annoying to say the least.

"Iain d'Astre. Wake up, Gibb. He might not be in the capital often or sit in the House, but you know him. My age—give or take a decade. Lives in Rutland, had a Scottish mother. His mama was your grandmother's friend. Maisie Lomax as was."

That name meant more to him. "The Maisie she spoke of with fondness? Why didn't I know this?"

"She is the one, and remember your grandmother died when you were at Eton. Why should you know all the ins and outs? Now sort your life in the manner you choose and don't come and visit me until you do." She began to climb the steps using her cane and the footman's arm to help her.

"Hold on," Gibb said urgently. "Where does he live?"

Lisette halted and turned her head. "Rutland. Barnshot Hall. Use the coach to get home, and good luck."

Gibb jumped out of the carriage, followed her and bussed her cheek as he remembered a recent invitation that he'd perused. "I'll walk, it will be faster if I cut through the mews." He needed to hunt out that note from one of d'Astre's neighbors. It requested the pleasure of Gibb's company at a small house party that coming weekend. He had better send his acceptance and work out his strategy.

* * * *

"Louisa Loxton has invited us to supper and an informal country dance on Saturday," Iain remarked as he and Evangeline sat at the breakfast table a few mornings later. "I'd like to accept. It's not above an hour in the coach and it will do you good to see some new faces. Meet new people. Stop you moping."

"I don't mope," Evangeline said indignantly. "Do I?" she asked, no longer certain her protestation was true.

Iain chuckled as he passed the scribed vellum to her. "Not so much now, no. But that apart, it will do you good. Louisa has a couple of sons who are unwed and—"

"Papa, do not start." Evangeline looked up from the invitation she had been studying to notice a curious expression flit over his face. "What have you done?"

"Not a thing except say we both would be delighted. Her chef is second to none with pig's trotters, and as for his way with fish? He excels with fish. Even the apologies they get around here. One day we must head to Norfolk and try—"

"Try not to worm your way out of whatever it is you need to tell me?" she asked as she hid her amusement at his delaying tactics.

Iain did his best to look ashamed and she waggled her finger at him. In their time together Evangeline had begun to understand him and his wily ways. And she loved him for each and every one of them. "That will not sway me. No matchmaking or I stay here. Promise me."

"Cruel child, how else will I dandle my grandchild on my knee?" Iain sighed. "Very well, but I warn you, you will need to do the necessary, as there will be some other younger people there and I believe her sons have invited a few gentlemen down from London for country pursuits. No innuendo intended."

She giggled. If that was all he was hiding she had nothing to fear. She was well-versed in dealing with such people. "I should hope not. How do you know this?"

He shifted from one foot to the other. "Louisa is a friend. An, ah, a special friend." His face was the color of the rosebuds on the bush outside the window.

"Why then have I not met her?" Evangeline demanded.

"Because you needed time to settle in, and when she called yesterday with the invitation you were in the far meadow with your stilettos." Both Iain and she had decided she should keep her skills honed. "You will meet her on Saturday."

"So what do I wear?"

* * * *

Gibb rode up the drive of the home of Charlie Loxton, one of his friends from Oxford, and congratulated himself on his timing. Not so early as to appear overeager — especially as he had not sent his acceptance until very late — nor so late as to appear to be dragging his heels. Afternoon tea would be ready in Charlie's mother's sitting room, with ale and snacks in the library for the men. Charlie had remarked that no women apart from his mother and his married sister Emily would be there until the ball two days hence, so they need not worry about being hunted. As Emily, seven years younger than Gibb or Charlie, had never been anything other than a friend to Gibb, with no amatory interest, he foresaw no difficulties in enjoying a few days of rural life.

He held the reins loose in one hand as he tooled his curricle into the stable yard and Norby, the head groom, came running out. He knew Norby from when

Charlie and he had been scrubby schoolboys and the Loxtons had lived in the wilds of Yorkshire. That was before Charlie's grandfather had passed on and the family had relocated to this more comfortable house several months earlier. It was Gibb's first visit, and he looked forward to sightseeing. Rutland, apart from an annual visit or three to hunt with the Quorn, was not known to him.

"Hello, Norby," He swung down and clapped the groom on the shoulders in a friendly gesture. "Am I the first?"

Norby appeared somewhat puzzled then his face cleared. "Ah, Master Charlie, oh I mean, his lordship and Miss, I mean, Lady Emily arrived yesterday." He looked at Gibb with speculation. "Is that who you mean, your grace?"

Gibb wasn't going to show his ignorance. "Exactly so. Right, I'd better go and make my bow. Thataway?"

Norby nodded. "Straight long the path and around the side of the house. Nobbut a few minutes. I'll sort tha bags out and have a lad bring 'em up to the'ouse." His Yorkshire accent was still strong and Gibb wondered how he liked it farther south. It would have to be different, that was for sure. He walked at a rapid pace down the path Norby had indicated—the directions had been clear and precise—and within two or three minutes Gibb strode under the portico and pulled the bell rope with vigor. A deep clanging inside announced his arrival, as did deep barking and excited yelps. Evidently Charlie's dogs were also in residence.

The door swung open and several dogs rushed out and ran around him in a dizzy circle. The mass of hair and animals reformed into a terrier, three hounds and a spaniel.

Charlie stood beaming on the doorstep. "No curricle? Good god, you didn't walk?" He laughed uproariously and pointed to Gibb's still-gleaming Hessians. "Long way in those boots."

"Stables," Gibb said as they shook hands. "It seemed easier. Norby said he'll arrange for my luggage to be carried indoors."

"Good show. Come and do the necessary to Mama and Emily and we'll go and talk. I'd rather talk first but as you announced yourself not much chance of that. Get down, you moron," he roared.

Gibb understood it was directed at the longhaired, panting spaniel, not at Gibb himself. He bent down and fondled the spaniel's ears. "Something amiss?" he inquired with a sinking heart. Pray God no marriage-hungry debs or their mamas were due to arrive. Loxton Hall wasn't so large that they would be easily avoided.

"I think so, not sure, tell you later, act dumb," Charlie muttered out of the corner of his mouth as a door opened somewhere nearby.

As he had no idea what was going on, Gibb decided that acting dumb wouldn't be too difficult. He smiled and bowed as Louisa Loxton appeared from a room along the corridor and made her way toward them.

"I thought I heard your voice, Gibb. Glad you could come. Very informal, you understand, just a few friends to supper and dancing on Saturday. I'm sure you and Charlie can entertain yourself until then. Dinner at seven, we're not dressing. Do you want feeding?"

Gibb shook his head. "I stopped in Lyddington."

"We'll have ale and snacks, Mama," Charlie said as Gibb chatted about the state of the roads and the rain showers he'd ridden through. "It's all arranged. You can relax and snooze without worrying."

"Odious boy." His mama patted his cheek. "Off you go, and don't forget—informal tonight." She smiled and retraced her steps.

Charlie watched her with a fond smile on his face. "Meddler. Come on." He took hold of Gibb's arm and dragged him to the billiards room. "Phew. A game or ale?"

"Ale and then a game. And what, Charlie Loxton, is that all about?"

Charlie shook his head. "Lord, Gibb. I wish I knew. I've hardly had time to draw breath since we moved. All Mama said was she thought it was time to be neighborly and why not ask you to come down. As far as I know it's a select few to supper and a mere fifty to the dance. Who, though? Now that is the mystery. Emily is convinced Mama has a beau and this is to introduce us to him. If she has, unless she met him in town, he's a fast worker. She's not been here more than a month or two."

"Almost six," Gibb pointed out. "She's no longer in mourning."

"There is that. Ah, no doubt we'll find out the all on Saturday. Do you want to break or shall I?"

"Pardon? Oh, you can."

Charlie had poured the ale and set up the billiards without Gibb noticing. Then he proceeded to trounce him.

"Your mind is on other things," Charlie said. "What's this I hear about a French knife-thrower?"

Gibb groaned. "What did you hear?"

"A liaison?"

"We are friends, that is all. I rescued her from Denby Crowe and his cronies. You know what Crowe is like in his cups. He thought it would be amusing to harass Evangeline. I disabused him of that idea and kept my eye on the lady whenever possible. She is a friend of Julia Arthur."

"Ah, I did wonder. Thought you'd sworn off women."

"Not entirely," Gibb said. *Not one special woman.*

"No, I'd hope not," Charlie said with a wicked grin. "Right then, now that's all sorted do you fancy another game?"

Gibb raised one eyebrow in agreement. "Why not? I need to win my money back."

He didn't and an hour or so later, after a filling dinner with good food, superb wine and excellent company, made his way to the pleasant suite he had been allocated.

It was strange, Gibb mused, how unforthcoming Louisa had been with regards to just who the guests were.

"The vicar, his wife and some close neighbors for supper, and the local gentry families for the dance. We'll manage twenty or so couples, I think. Perfect for the small ballroom," she had said as she'd swept Emily out of the dining room so the men could enjoy their port. "Don't be too long now or Emily and I will feel neglected."

"Fishy, what?" Martin Mayburn, Emily's husband, had said as they sat sprawled around the table, waistcoats and jackets undone and the port decanted in between the three of them. "I'd watch myself if I were you. She's a devious schemer when she wants to be. Thank goodness I'd had my eye on Emily all the time because whether I had or not we'd have been wed, once Louisa set her mind on it."

"Don't," Charlie had groaned and refilled his glass. "I'm too young to be leg shackled."

"You're three months older than me," Gibb pointed out.

"Correct, and I don't see you rushing to the altar again." Martin reddened as he spoke. "My apologies, that was crass."

"Not at all, it is but the truth," Gibb reassured him. "And I am not."

Not yet.

* * * *

The next couple of days passed in pleasant laziness. They bagged a few wood pigeons and caught enough brown trout for the chef to promise to put it on the menu for lunch. Even though he was chomping at the bit to go and see if he could find Evangeline, Gibb was content enough. If Charlie had given him the opportunity to be in the area, the least he could do was spend the requisite amount of time with him.

On Friday afternoon, Charlie went off to, as he said, *really* see a man about a dog. One that had been worrying his small flock of sheep. Gibb decided he'd let Charlie sort that out himself and went for a ride.

The stables were somnolent in the early afternoon heat, with not a soul around. Several horsy heads nodded over their stable doors and his own horse whinnied when it recognized Gibb, but no human came running.

No doubt the grooms taking their afternoon break. Gibb led Challenger out, pleased he'd trained the animal to be ridden with or without tack and also pull a curricle. Gibb eschewed bridle or saddle, flung himself onto the broad back of the animal, walked out of the stable yard and headed down a grassy track, away from the house and in the direction careful questioning had told him was Barnshot Hall.

Not that he expected to see Evangeline. This was just a chance to blow away the cobwebs and look around the area.

Gibb crossed a lane and into a wider track, known to all and sundry as a ride, encouraged his horse into a canter and sat back to enjoy himself.

* * * *

"Go for a ride, child, and get some color into your cheeks." Iain stared at Evangeline until she squirmed. "I want you to look your best tomorrow night. I'm so looking forward to showing my beautiful daughter off."

"I'm fine," she said automatically.

"Pah, if that is fine, never let me see you not fine. Off you go. Ride toward the river, you like it there." He made shooing motions with his hand. "Now, I need a nap."

Evangeline laughed. He never napped. She guessed he wanted to smoke a filthy cheroot and read the papers recently arrived from London. "Yes, Papa." In fact, it sounded perfect. Within half an hour she had changed, saddled Honey, who after a lot of deliberation and haggling with the London stables Evangeline had decided should relocate with her, and ridden off in the direction of the river. It was a pleasant canter, along lanes and bridleways, and she loved it. Iain had taken her there on their first day and she'd told him that he could do nothing better.

'*Except build you a house here*?' he'd said with a chuckle. '*When you marry.*'

'*Or when you just get fed up of me, when I don't.*'

'*Never.*'

The river came into view and Evangeline understood how well Iain knew her. He was correct. She did need to get away from everything and just enjoy the fresh air. Honey was in the same frame of mind. The horse's stride lengthened and soon they were cantering across the water meadow to a tiny beach she'd decided was her own private spot. That it had a willow tree near it was not, *not*, she thought anything that had swayed her mind. However, it *was* a pleasant thing to have as she sat under its branches and dipped her bare feet in the water.

As usual there was no one in sight. She looked at the passing water, saw how clear it was and that there were no ripples to mar the surface, and made her mind up. How long since she had been able to swim? Longer than she could remember. Her riding habit was easily discarded and as she'd chosen not to wear stays on such a warm day, she soon stood just in her shift. Dare she strip? Why not? She reasoned, if she didn't want to go home without any underwear on and carrying a dripping shift, she had no option. And she'd see someone coming in good time to dress.

Evangeline decided not to out-think herself anymore. With one swift movement she slipped her shift over her head, folded it on top of her habit and slid into the cool depths of the river. And laughed out loud. It was glorious. The water was silky smooth and so clear she could see tiny fish swimming under her. A brown trout came so close she wondered what her papa would say if she caught it and took it home for supper. He no doubt would be pleased and insist that Armand, the chef, cook it as Evangeline directed.

In that case... Perhaps not, not yet. The chef was still coming to terms with two people asking for the food of his homeland and insisting on discovering how he intended to cook it.

The chef was lucky Iain was easygoing, for he would no doubt have given notice if Iain had insisted on 'Mama's way' of cooking everything and lost a comfortable and not too arduous way of earning his living. Evangeline just praised the man, and bit her lip on any thoughts she might have about how he cooked trotters.

She waved the trout on its way, and dived down into the depths to pick a pebble up and bring it to the surface. Her hair streamed over her shoulders, water droplets clung from its length, her eyebrows and lashes. Evangeline laughed for the sheer joy of it. Life would get better, she would make sure of that. If she didn't have a future with Gibb, so be it. She would spend her time alone. She jumped up, using the buoyancy of the water to lift herself high, and took a deep breath. Sank down to her knees, let the water cover her once more and opened her eyes to the underwater delight.

Lack of air forced her to the surface. She spluttered and took in great big gulps of fresh, clean air. Opened her eyes and screamed.

On the riverbank, silhouetted by the sun, was a large, naked male poised to dive in to where she had just surfaced. She took a hasty step backward, slipped on a pebble and fell back onto her bottom with a yelp.

Even as she swept her wet hair out of her eyes, she noticed the man move so swiftly it was a case of now you see him now you don't. He dived cleanly into the river, surfaced next to her and lifted her up before she went underwater once more.

"Are you all right?"

"Good lord."

Evangeline lifted her head, remembered her nakedness and crossed her arms over her breasts before she wriggled free of his embrace and retreated behind a clump of reeds. She couldn't believe her ears. She might not be able to see him in high definition as she squinted in the direction of the sun, but she would recognize that voice anywhere. "Gibb?"

He shook his head to shift some of the water that streamed from it. "The very same," he confirmed. "*Are you all right? What are you doing?*"

"Playing go fish," she said with a giggle as she named a popular children's game. "What do you think?"

He laughed. "Minx. Waiting for me?"

"Now how could I be doing that? I had no idea you were here." She ran her fingers around his lips and he nibbled the end of one very wet digit. "Why are you?" she asked, breathless and wondering. *Why is he here?*

"To find you." He put his hands on either cheek and kissed her in a haze-inducing spine-tingling caress with so much heat it was a wonder, Evangeline decided hazily, that the water didn't boil. "And now I have."

She melted... Sighed and hugged him tight. "And now what?"

"We get out of the water and talk. I tell you how much I love you, want you and miss you. You believe me. I add that I want to make love with you, not just for now but forever. You believe me. How I have a special license for our nuptials and the moment you say you will, we can change it to I do. I hope."

"You do?"

He laughed. "No. You say 'I do', not 'you do'."

She giggled. "Can I add this? I will, I do, I want to. Plus I do need to get out of the river. I'm turning wrinkly. A wrinkly bride would not be a good thing."

"So, my dearest Evangeline, you'll marry me, just like that? No recriminations?" He stood up and swung her into his arms to stride to the riverbank. He dropped Evangeline gently onto his jacket and swung out after her. "No towels."

"No need for either. I love you. We will dry soon enough," she said with a giggle. "Then—"

"Then what? When will we dry?"

"No, when will we wed?"

That, my dearest, is up to you."

"As soon as my papa knows? For now I have found him, I do not want to lose him. Oh, Gibb, I have so much to share with you."

"And I with you, and we have a lifetime to do so."

First, though…"

"First?" he asked, not without a little trepidation. What was she about to ask?

Evangeline took a deep breath. "Can we take that next step? Take things out of order a little…no, not a little, a lot, and make love now. Here?"

"Are you sure?"

She nodded. "Oh yes."

"Then it will be my pleasure."

He didn't think he'd ever initiated a virgin. This was more than that, though. This was Evangeline, his one and only love. It had to be perfect. He wanted it to be a moment out of time. He found his buckskins and made a pillow from them. Evangeline stretched out on her back, closed her eyes and held her arms out. "Mine."

"Yours," he confirmed. He knelt between her outstretched legs and bent his mouth to suck a rose red nipple, used one hand to part her soft folds and slide a long finger into her oh so ready and welcoming depths.

Evangeline moaned deep in her throat and put her ankles around his waist. He moved his hand with reluctance and lifted his head. Gibb looked down at her as his staff stroked her labia and she opened her eyes wide.

"Please." She wriggled to try to draw him nearer.

"Stop it, love. I want to make it perfect."

"It will be if you make love to me now. I wish *le petit mort*. I want to feel you deep in me." Her ankles dug into him, urging him closer.

Gibb gave in to the inevitable. Slow and savoring would be for later. Faster was what he needed for now. "So be it." He hesitated, moved forward and stopped as she glared.

"All of it." He nodded and drove into her. Hard. Drank her involuntary sob with sorrow, smothered it with his kiss and waited, deep inside her, until she relaxed and sighed. "Now I am truly yours."

"You are," he confirmed. "Forever."

"So you become mine also. Please show me how."

"It will be my pleasure." Gibb began to move, adjusting his speed and pressure until she matched him.

As she tipped over the edge he followed her.

It was glorious. His harsh cries mingled with her soft mewls and sobs of pleasure. "It has never been like this, ever."

"That is all I need to hear, *mon cher*. Except for one thing?"

"Which is?"

"What now?"

* * * *

All too soon, Gibb found himself dressing for dinner on Saturday. For some uncountable reason he had butterflies in his stomach. Louisa still hadn't mentioned any names, and when Gibb had run her to ground one evening and asked bluntly if she knew Iain d'Astre she said vaguely the name was familiar and changed the subject. If it wasn't bad manners and not good ton to question the servants he would have. Instead he dressed to kill, made sure nothing in his dress or deportment could be faulted and plotted his departure.

Perhaps, he mused, it was just as well.

As he descended the stairs the doorbell rang and Fisher, Louisa's major-domo, went to open it, with Louisa hot on his heels. She looked both flustered and anxious, not at all like her normal bubbly self.

The next person Gibb saw was Evangeline.

From his vantage point, and as yet unnoticed, Gibb observed Evangeline's bemusement as she watched the man beside her kiss Louisa's hand then her cheek.

"*Ma belle*, as beautiful as ever," the man said to Louisa in an elegant French accent. "May I present my daughter, Evangeline?"

Gibb grinned inwardly, went to move and make his presence felt, and his hand slipped on the bannister. He took an involuntary step forward, missed the next tread and stumbled to save his balance.

The noise in the quiet hall was like a herd of elephants on the rampage.

Evangeline looked up as she thought the twisting wooden staircase was about to fall down.

Instead she thought she might. She had to be hallucinating. That couldn't be Gibb almost tumbling down the stairs, could it? Gibb, as elegant as ever but seeming dazed and as if he could not believe his eyes. Good lord, had their lovemaking worn him out that much? She schooled her expression to one of vague indifference.

Evangeline shot a sideways glance at her papa and Louisa Loxton. They looked complacent and expectant. "You set this up," she hissed as her heartbeat performed an energetic quickstep. "For god's sake, why?"

"To knock some sense into the two of you," Louisa said crisply. "And it was my idea. Your papa did not want to deny me the chance to see you both happy. Plus, he desired to know his beloved daughter was settled."

Before she had a chance to respond to Louisa, which judging by her state of mind was no doubt a good thing, Gibb reached the bottom step, trod across the hall and bowed to her papa. "Le Duc d'Astre, I presume."

Her papa blanched at the frosty, punctilious tone. "Ah yes, your grace. I trust you are fit."

"Do you?" Gibb mused. "I wonder." He turned to the two women. "Lady Louisa, Lady Evangeline, I presume?"

Louisa laughed as Gibb oh so correctly kissed her proffered hand. "Do not take that tone with me, Gibb Alford. You know who we are."

"Oh yes I do." He dropped her hand and took hold of Evangeline's fingers. However, instead of kissing them as he had Louisa's, he tugged Evangeline toward him until she was unbalanced. "A lady by any other name."

The unexpected movement made her jump and as he turned on his heel she was propelled after him, almost running to keep up. Her dancing slippers slid over the polished floor as she tried to slow him down. "Gibb, are you sure this is the right way to do it?"

"Oh yes, look at their faces," he murmured.

Evangeline glanced at Louisa and Iain in turn and stifled a snigger in his chest.

"Next stage." He and Evangeline purposefully across the entrance hall. "Excuse us, we have unfinished business," he called over his shoulder. Evangeline looked around and saw Louisa and her papa lean against each other and grin. *Definitely special friends.*

"Gibb Alford, what on earth are you doing?" she gasped. "Argh." He lifted her into his arms as they reached the staircase. "Put me down." She tried to drum her heels on his legs and he stopped her using one arm to hold her legs tight against him. "If I could reach my stiletto I'd... What *are* you doing?" Her voice rose as did her excitement. "I swear I'm about to laugh out loud. Hurry for the love of god and hide my face." Was she overdoing the indignation? But then she had to be seen to protest. Especially as her papa had informed her on the way over that they were to stop the night. Now she wondered where she would sleep. Or, she thought wistfully and hopefully, with whom. She didn't think Gibb would be willing to let them sleep apart. Or she hoped not, but that behavior wouldn't be acceptable, would it? Did she care? *I should but by the look on my papa's face he sees my future sorted and this — whatever this is — is part of it.* She would follow Gibb's lead.

"Abducting you," Gibb said out loud without missing a step. "You can attack me with your stiletto later if you still want to. If you've forgotten it, I have one handy you can use instead. Excuse us, Charlie, you're in the way."

A puffing Charlie clattered down three stairs and stood stock-still. "Sorry." He obediently moved to one side. Evangeline glared at him as Charlie grinned, raised one eyebrow and asked them…

"Do we hold dinner?"

* * * *

Evangeline bounced, as Gibb dropped her without ceremony onto a large, ornate four-poster bed with barley sugar columns and a carved tester from which hung deep velvet curtains. Her skirts billowed around her as she glanced up at the canopy and chuckled at the painted cherubs portrayed there. Each wore very little clothing and had a salacious expression. There seemed to be a lot of cherubs in bedrooms.

The click as Gibb shot the lock on the door made her move her gaze to where Gibb stood.

"I daren't risk us being disturbed until we have everything as we desire," he explained. "Do you mind?"

"Mind?" she asked stupidly. Her brain was addled. "Oh no, I don't mind."

"Good, one moment." He disappeared into an adjoining room and reappeared seconds later. "All entrances bar the window secured. And if anyone thinks to climb three stories up the ivy, let them. It doesn't look that sturdy to me."

"Perhaps not," Evangeline said, distracted by his intent and loving expression. She recollected his previous words. "I, er, wasn't chuckling at you locking the door, but at the fat and somewhat lascivious-looking cherubs on the canopy. I agree with you over security. If we want to speak in private, with no prying eyes, I'll stuff the lock with my handkerchief."

Gibb laughed. "Those cherubs are somewhat startling at the first view, eh? Save your handkerchief, I've left the key in the keyhole. That should do it. So why the gasp of shock earlier? Apart from me playing barbarian. For which I thank you for not foiling. I know you could have if you really desired to. I thought the best way to get you alone would be to take them by surprise and hope you would go along with it to see what would happen. One reason why I didn't go into too many details yesterday."

Evangeline nodded as tiny shivers and tingles danced on her spine and dried her mouth. "No doubt it was best, for my wits were scrambled and I might have protested in reaction, not in want or need." She could only pray he understood. "Am I making sense? I suspect not. Put it down to my amazement when I noticed this canopy." She gestured upward, to where so many naked nymphs and cherubs cavorted over the material, there was a scant few inches of basic material to be seen. They were chased by satyrs under an impossible blue sky and in one corner a coy milkmaid—*a milkmaid, for heaven's sake*—peeped around a multi-branched tree. Several apples were scattered around a half-naked man, presumably Adam, and the whole thing screamed 'decadence'. "I'm not sure what the theme is. Especially over such a large bed."

The mattress bounced as Gibb sat next to her — fortunately not too close — and looked to where she pointed.

"I did wonder why on earth I'd been put in here," he said with a laugh. "It has always been out of bounds before. I decided there is a moral somewhere and I'm not privy to what it is. By the smarmy grin on the footman's face when he ushered me in, I suspect there is some nefarious reason for this room being allocated to me. Unless my ears deceived me, I think he muttered what a rush it had been to get it ready. There are ten or so bedrooms I could have been quartered in."

"Not unless it's the most innocuous," Evangeline pointed out, proud of her prosaic tone. It was hard to remain composed when what she wanted to do was grab a handful of shirt and plaster him to her and damn the consequences.

He chuckled. "It isn't, I checked. All the rest are beautifully appointed and plainly dressed. This is the one that is, shall we say, risqué. I did hear it was where the last occupier and his wife had their liaisons. They were, according to Charlie, somewhat unusual for their time and were in love and faithful, so chose to meet up here for fun and games together."

She looked up at one particular satyr who had a lecherous expression on his painted face and was reaching out to catch a coy nymph. The nymph, Evangeline decided, wasn't trying too hard to distance herself.

"I like the sound of that." She didn't look at Gibb while she spoke. Why had he brought her here and mentioned that? "Did they live happy ever after?"

He put his hands to either side of her head and turned her so she looked straight at him.

"Oh yes. Like we will. Now, do we go and put them out of their wonderings? I'll formally ask for your hand in marriage, and let them think their ploys were successful. Let tonight be our betrothal ball. Unless you want a big event?"

She shuddered. "No thank you. I'd like it as small as possible. And our marriage similar. Just those who are important to us."

"Then I must say this again, so you are sure of me." It was perhaps the most important moment of his life. Gibb closed his eyes for a second, swallowed, then looked at Evangeline's face, before he pulled her into his arms and settled them both on the pillows. It felt right. She belonged there.

"Although we pre-empted it, your papa and Louisa gave me the opportunity to explain to you something I chose to ignore. So I'm going to say it again. I love you. That is not how I think I should feel but how I *have* to feel. I know that yours is the body I want to wake up next to every morning," he said in a soft undertone. "You are the one I want to share my life with." Once he started to speak, Gibb realized it got easier every time. Easier to share his thoughts with the one person who mattered above all else. "I fought it, oh how I fought it. I didn't want to love you."

Evangeline stiffened. "You don't need to say it all again. I believe you and love you."

"I thank you for that, but we were somewhat rushed yesterday." They'd scrambled into their clothes without the chance to talk very much. "I have to tell you how much I was scared," he said frankly. "Scared and running. After all, I'd never been in love, didn't like how it made me feel. Reliant on someone. I'd had it the other way around and look how it ended. To me it was something I never wanted to endure again. To be responsible for someone else's happiness and wellbeing. So in my muddled mind, if I couldn't do that, neither could I give that responsibility to anyone else."

"But that's just it, you didn't have to give it. It's up to that person how they feel and respond." Evangeline lifted her head and stared at him. "I don't ask you to let me love you. I do it regardless. You don't have to accept it or reciprocate because love, if it isn't given freely and without ties, is not love at all."

"Thank goodness our love is given for free and without coercion then." It was the easiest thing he had ever said.

Showing Evangeline what he meant by his words was the most enjoyable.

"Shall we confound them all by going downstairs now?" Gibb asked as he reluctantly took his hand off Evangeline's breast and rearranged the neckline of her gown. "As much as I want to make you mine again, I'd rather do it at our leisure, lingering over every inch of you. Letting us discover our preferences together. Not in a hurry and waiting for someone to rap on the door. Yesterday was a moment I'll never forget but we did rather rush things. I want a long, slow lovemaking next."

"I would also like that," Evangeline said. "After all, you need to speak to Papa and then there is a dance to go to."

He'd forgotten the dance. "You will have to guide me through our betrothal waltz. I've forgotten how."

"It's like making love, you'll soon remember."

"Of course I will. With you. Shall we go together? Do things our way?" he asked and smiled at the wicked glint in her eyes.

"Oh yes. And let me be with you when you speak to Papa?"

Gibb mock-sighed and flicked the end of her nose. "I am betrothed to a bossy woman."

"Not at all, how horrid." Evangeline wrinkled said nose. "To your equal."

He grinned and nodded. "That sounds better. To my love, my lover and my equal."

* * * *

It had been oh so easy, Gibb thought as a day later he walked out of the tiny local church with his bride on his arm. Iain had chuckled at the way they had outwitted him. He had given his blessing immediately they sought him out and Gibb asked for his daughter's hand in marriage.

Iain had slapped him on the back so hard Gibb had rocked. *'If you promise to treat her right.'*

'Papa, enough,' Evangeline had said with reproach which she spoiled with a giggle. *'He will. Remember, I am the knife-thrower in the family.'*

'Of course I will, knife-thrower notwithstanding. She is my reason for being,' Gibb had replied sincerely. *'I love her with every fiber of my soul.'*

'That's what I need to hear.' Ian had shaken his head in mock sorrow. *'Lost a daughter already.'*

'*Gained a son,*' Evangeline had said. '*Think of grandchildren.*'

'*Ah yes.*' Iain had brightened as Gibb laughed. '*I daresay you want the wedding soon, eh?*'

'*Tomorrow,*' Gibb had said. '*I have the license if you can get the venue.*'

'*Now that is the easy part. The vicar is here.*'

The Reverend Mortisham, once he had verified the license was all in order, had agreed to perform the ceremony. Charlie was roped in as best man and missives dispatched post–haste to London to inform their close friends they were needed. Eloise had protested but been overruled. She, Evangeline had said, was mother of the bride and bride's supporter all rolled into one.

Evangeline nudged Gibb as they exited the church and began the walk back to the hall. "Do you see how Eloise and Charlie are staring at each other?"

Gibb looked. "She is surely several years older than him?"

"So?" Evangeline said with one eyebrow raised almost to her hairline. "You are several years older than me."

He had no answer to that. "Then we best enjoy our wedding breakfast before I'm too old and infirm to dance with you."

She leaned in to whisper in his ear. "And whilst you are still active enough to make love all night?"

He chuckled. "Minx. I'll show you how active I am."

He did.

Eve Marie Alford was born nine months later. She had her mama's hair, her papa's smile and her mother's and grandmother's earlobes. To say nothing of a crooked finger. Her eyes, her papa was wont to say, were peculiarly her own.

About the Author

A multi-published author of erotic romance, Raven lives in Scotland, along with her husband and their two cats—their children having flown the nest—surrounded by beautiful scenery, which inspires a lot of the settings in her books.

She is used to sharing her life with the occasional deer, red squirrel, and lost tourist, to say nothing of the scourge of Scotland—the midge. As once she is writing she is oblivious to everything else, her lovely long-suffering husband is learning to love the dust bunnies, work the Aga, and be on stand-by with a glass of wine.

Raven loves to hear from readers. You can find her contact information, website details and author profile page at http://www.totallybound.com.

Home of Erotic Romance